# Nursing Myself Back

## A Tryst of Fate Series Novel—Book 3

### KARA LIANE

**Disclaimer:** This book is intended for an adult audience. This work of fiction contains strong language and explicit sexual scenes, with mature content, that may not be appropriate for anyone under the age of eighteen.

Also By Kara Liane

\*\*\*

*Playing Heart to Get—A Tryst of Fate Series Novel—Book 1*

*Every Heart Inch—A Tryst of Fate Series—Novella 1*

*A Force of Nature—A Tryst of Fate Series Novel—Book 2*

*Heart to Follow—A Tryst of Fate Series—Novella 2*

\*\*\*

# Dedication

To my family, friends, and faithful readers. My thanks are many and infinite. But this one is especially dedicated to my husband for taking a chance on a gal like me all those years ago. I love a good romance, and I believe Matthew and I are incredibly fortunate to have one—he's my everything!

# Table of Contents

*Watching the Fire*

"Catching every sparkle that comes with watching the fire,
I can't think of anything that could ever take me higher
reflections bouncing off the embers onto me,
the fire lets me see things, the way I want to see.
So quiet and solemn, the night that runs forever,
the solitude I'm finding, I'm wishing it forever
and when the fire is just about to die,
I'll throw another log on, so I can sit just awhile."

—Dain Carlton Mergenthaler

# Prologue

*Caleb*

July 24, 1998

*Pfft!* Life is tough these days being a dorky fourteen-year-old like I am. Well, actually I'm fourteen and a half because my birthday is in September; and that *half* shit means something to us kids. Besides being a dork, I hate that I'm smart. I also hate that I'm rich; I'll get to explaining that one later. I hate that I don't look like the other guys my age. They seem to be getting bigger and more dude-like, and I'm...well, I'm *me*. Glasses, skinny, acne, and no muscle definition to save my life!

No girls will talk to me. I guess I wouldn't bother with me either if I were in their shoes when I have competition that looks better. I hope it changes when I get older. I hope when I get older I'll be somebody. I hope I'll have tons of girls to choose from and ones who will like me back. I guess I don't like the girls at my school anyway. They're too shallow. If any do seem to talk to me, it's usually because of my parents' bank account, or because they need help with homework.

Finding genuine people is difficult. I want to be with a girl who gives me something deep and meaningful. I want a girl who appreciates things like I do and has the same interests. I guess I'm the sensitive, romantic type. The *sweet one,* as they say, which is the kiss of death for guys because once you're labeled, well, you're stuck with it. Girls like assholes. I can't be like that. I respect women too much. My grandma calls me an *old soul.*

My one and only friend at the moment, Nick, has practically grown up overnight. He didn't ditch me like some of my other friends did. None of us were really a tight-knit group to begin with, but we were cafeteria tablemates and would at least eat lunch together at school. Once school ended, though, they all seemed to bulk up—I stayed the same. When I ran into them here and there over the last few weeks, it was like they didn't even see me.

I knew right then that this coming school year would be total shit. But that's when I also swore I'd have an incredible circle of friends when I got older, and they would be more like brothers than anything. I had a brother once, but I was too young at the time to be able to remember him now. His name was Christopher. He apparently died from SIDS as an infant, and my parents were never really the same. After that, Dad threw himself into his IT work as computers took off, and Mom pretty much medicated herself into oblivion. She functions, but just barely.

That's why I have to get good grades, so I can get the hell out of here. Like I said, I hate being smart because it isn't cool—eventually it will work to my advantage. And yeah, my family may have money, but I want to work my way up. I've seen what money does to families, and I'm willing to work for things in life. I don't ask for much, but I'm praying that by some miracle—before school starts in five and a half weeks—I'll be blessed by the *muscle gods*.

I'm currently sitting on the curb outside our nearby *Wawa* convenience store, waiting for Nick to finish up his conversation with Jenny Stevens—the most popular soon-to-be sophomore girl. *Wawa* is our hang-out spot; they're everywhere in Bucks County, Pennsylvania, where we live—I'm from Yardley, more specifically.

I roll my eyes at the way she's throwing herself at him. From my vantage point at the curb, I can clearly see them through the glass windows. I'm making up the dialogue to their conversation in my head. I imagine it's ridiculous in nature, and I'm pretending they're some cheesy couple in a low-budget, D-list actor movie.

I get bored with theater time between Nick and Jenny after a few minutes, and start kicking pebbles with my Nike sneakers to pass the time. As I kick the fifth rock, a shadow falls upon me. I look up, squinting against the blaring rays of the sun.

The figure moves in a little closer, successfully blocking the overpowering light. I can finally make out what is above me. *What* is not the proper word, as it is a *who*. And the *who* is a goddess. She's a woman who looks to be in her late thirties, early forties, I'm guessing; that would make her about my mom's age.

This woman is beautiful. She's wearing a white cotton sundress with sandals displaying her pink toenail polish and an ankle bracelet showing off her nude legs even more. Her hair is long and blonde. Her face is perfection with sparkling blue eyes and full pouty lips that remind me of that hot Cameron Diaz actress. Ya know, the one all the guys are talking about this summer from *There's Something About Mary*. I haven't seen the movie because my parents would never, ever, agree to it. But apparently there's this scene involving hair gel and some dude's spunk. *Whatever.*

Anyway, back to this woman above me. I think I'm falling in love at this moment. She smiles at me in the next second.

*And, yup. I. Fall. In. Love.*

Or as in love as a fourteen-and-a-half-year-old's brain will allow. I don't think her smile is flirty or inappropriate—even if I wished it were the case. Because, duh, I'm a kid, and she's not, and she's hot! It's more like a motherly thing, the way she's smiling. And I can't help it that I'm crushing hard. Hormones in teenage boys are the worst thing because there's not a damn thing we can do about it. Well, I should speak for myself because I'm sure plenty of the other guys get action—I don't. I can take care of it myself, but that's something I'm only willing to do once my mom passes out for the night and my dad leaves for work in the early hours of the morning to commute to the city.

At this very moment, though, well, I can't do anything about my boyish fantasies. I have no game. Even if she were smiling at me like *that,* it doesn't matter. I'm stupefied and mystified by this being. It's like seeing a unicorn. You hear stories that they exist, but you've never seen one, so you're automatically a non-believer. I've never laid eyes upon a woman like this and certainly not ever one who gave me the time of day. Yet here she is! Damn, I'm a believer!

"Hey there, handsome," the unicorn speaks.

No response from me as my mouth is hanging wide open, and I stare blankly. A fly may land in there if I don't close my trap.

She laughs and goes on to say, "Have you seen my daughter, Jenny? I'm assuming you go to school with her. You look about her age. She was supposed to run inside for just a minute, but that was like ten minutes ago. I'm tired of waiting in the car. It's so hot out here."

She begins fanning herself for emphasis. Every damn thing this woman is doing puts me under some kind of a freakish spell. I couldn't even tell you my name if you asked me. I think it starts with a "C," but that's about all I can manage. The sweat that had beaded at my hairline while sitting out here for the last fifteen minutes is now pouring down my face thanks to certain hormones raging like I've been set on fire.

Before she can ask me anything further, and before I can finally manage to say anything, I hear footsteps behind me. Then a girl begins talking. I catch the tail end of what she's saying as I snap back to reality and realize it's Jenny speaking.

"…we got to talking, and I lost track of time. Sorry, Mom," Jenny says to the unicorn.

"No problem, sweetie. I understand. I just got worried. Well, it was nice to meet you, Nick. Come on, Jenny, let's go grab some lunch," Jenny's mom responds.

Then, as the unicorn struts away, she turns around and calls back to me, "Bye, hun. I never caught your name, but you have a nice summer. And stay cool."

She continues to smile and laughs over her shoulder. A part of me wants to die of mortification, and another part of me wants to live forever in this moment. But once again, I can't find my voice to come up with a response. I can only nod at her retreating form. When she disappears around the corner from view, I'm assuming to go to her car, I finally close my mouth.

Nick is laughing so hard, he has tears rolling down his model-like cheeks. I want to kick him in the stones like I did the pebbles, but I still can't fully function.

After a few minutes, I'm able to ask, more to myself than to Nick, "What was *that*?"

But he answers anyway, "That, my friend, is what ya call a cougar."

I don't know what the hell that term means, but I'm sure going to have to look it up. With my dad being an IT genius, we have more computers at home than any kid I know. Dad is teaching me about the World Wide Web, and AOL is becoming my second best friend.

"Wow!" Is all I reply to Nick.

*** 

Later that day, I looked up what the term means. And much later in life, I would discover that *that* encounter with the unicorn sparked my obsession with cougars, or as I also like to refer to them: *goddesses among us.*

# Chapter 1: Dead End

*Liezel*

February 22, 2018

He's dead. My husband is dead. I know I'm supposed to feel something, but I don't. Maybe if I analyzed my feelings a little more, I could try to feel some sort of guilt, remorse, or sorrow. I would mourn the loss of the father my children no longer have, but he wasn't a good father, so that's a moot point. Come to think of it, he wasn't a good husband either. He was nothing. Just took up space in our house. I made it a home; he made it unbearable.

God, I probably sound like the most evil woman, but I swear I'm not. I feel guilty for not missing him. I feel remorse for not trying to help him more, even though he dug that grave long before the end came for him. And the sorrow? Well, I'm sad that I'm lonely despite having my kids; I have been lonely for years. I don't remember what it's like to feel a man's touch—to feel a man's anything, for that matter.

I've watched a love that continues to grow and strengthen between my boss and his wife for the past few years, and I have been torn sitting on the sidelines. Torn because, on one hand, I am beyond thrilled that he found happiness with the most amazing woman and forged a life he deserves. But on the other hand, I'm jealous of the life he has. For I could not—cannot—give that happy life to myself or my teenage children, and it's eating me alive.

I just attended my husband's funeral, and here I sit on my bed while I imagine everyone is downstairs snacking on the food I prepared for the reception. They probably think I came up here to my bedroom to collect myself because of the grief, but that's not really correct. I'm a monster for not mourning the man himself. But William is not a man I will miss. He left me long ago, not the other way around. *He* is the monster.

The damn bottle became his mistress. The bottle became his only love. The bottle became his life. I was never anything to him. So why did we get married? Good question. I got pregnant, and years ago we thought it was the right thing to do. What I once thought was love was nothing more than infatuation. Our relationship was simply new and exciting. We both quickly realized it was ugly, wrong, and miserable. I coped with work and my kids, and he coped with his mistress.

Our children were nothing to him either. But they are great kids, and even though my self-esteem is in the shitter, I do take credit for their upbringing. All three are teens now, and I can't get over how the time has flown by. Tyler is seventeen and my brightest boy. I'm so in awe of him. Even with his autism, he makes me proud each and every day because of the way he excels in life and perseveres. Kurt is my fifteen-year-old, and he is one tough youngster; shit, does anyone say *youngster* these days? I'm so out of the loop with the youth, even though three teens live in my house. My daughter, Leah, is such an angel at thirteen. I don't feel I deserve to have such a patient, kind, caring, and witty girl. As she gets older, I can see us becoming best friends. However, right now, I have to be more *mom* than anything.

Yup, my kids still have a lot of growing up to do, but they're well on their way. They teach me a lot along the way too. I'm surprised William and I ended up with three kids, actually, considering he and I barely had a relationship—and that applied to sex or any other marital activity. I guess after I had my daughter, that pretty much was it for us. I can't ever remember making love after that. Well, it was never lovemaking anyway; it was always screwing. It was a way to blow off steam and stress, and we used each other. But one day, we stopped using each other for even that.

A knock on my bedroom door alerts me to the fact that I need to get my ass moving and go downstairs. I still have to keep up appearances. The kids have had friends and family all day to occupy their attention, and they knew the inevitable was coming anyway. They are brave pillars of strength in all this. I mean, really, with me being a cardiology nurse, I've known for years what would happen to him—and I've made that fact known all along to prepare us. His liver could only take so much before cirrhosis would claim him, and claim him it did.

*Good riddance! Shit! There I go again. I am a monster.*

I swipe at my cheeks to clear off the tears, but my fingers come back dry. Oh, right. I don't need to cry over William. There is nothing left inside for me to love. I can put on a brave front for my kids, but I have nothing left to offer anyone else. Sure, I wish someone could free me from the loss of love I've been missing for years, but who the hell will take on a forty-four-year-old woman with three teenage kids? There is no one out there up to that task, and quite frankly, I don't know if I could—or would—ever open myself up for a disaster of a relationship again. I had been burned before, and I wasn't about to go there again.

That quickly, I had forgotten about the visitor at the door. A second set of knocks echo through the cold, dark, empty space of my room. I clear my throat and steel myself for whoever could be on the other side of that barrier.

"Come in," I say in a choked voice—again, minus the nonexistent tears.

"I just wanted to check on you, Liz," a very familiar, safe voice speaks to me as a man enters.

It is Dr. Alexi Graham, my boss. The familiar and constant man in my life—not like *that*, so don't get excited. I'd follow him anywhere, though. I had been with him for years. I started with working alongside him at the hospital, then I left to help him open and run his private cardiology practice. I am his favorite nurse, but that didn't make me egotistical. It's just that Alexi knows my checkered history—about my husband. He knows some of my secrets. But Lord, he doesn't know them all—no one does, except for the ghosts of my past, and that is not something I'm willing to get into again.

I was always giving Alexi advice long before he met his wife, Caylan. I look at Alexi like I'm his big sister, and I wanted him to find his other half. When Caylan came into his life, it was like the sun shone on him for the first time, and it brightened his very existence. They have a stunning little girl named Emeline, and Caylan's currently in her second trimester of pregnancy with their second child. We're all hoping for a boy this time. They're the most beautiful family, and I do not begrudge them that. It is a sight to see and witness pure, absolute, and true love between two people.

I have been there for several monumental moments in Alexi's life. Just last week, for example, we celebrated his daughter's first birthday. I was there for important events in his wife's life too. They really embrace me as family, and my kids and I are grateful to extend ours to them as well. I was even lucky to have been one of Caylan's bridesmaids when they married in 2016. The girl sure loves pink—and I must admit I was fortunate I could pull off the pink-shade of dress she put me in.

I know I'm nothing close to a classic beauty, but for my age, I think I still look good. It wasn't about looking good for William, though. No, I want to look good for myself and my kids, and also for my job. I want Alexi to be proud that I'm the epitome of health, a good example for our patients. Watching my late husband drink himself into an urn really made it abundantly clear that I would always eat healthy and exercise, and encourage my kids to do so too. They are all into sports, and I love to go hiking and kayaking with them. It is the four of us, and we are content with that.

I can feel Alexi standing behind me, probably warring with himself over whether or not he should extend the hand I feel hanging in the air and finally place it on my shoulder in a gesture of comfort. The phantom hand means he cares. I don't know if I even want that from him at the moment. The inner turmoil is about all I can handle.

I fidget on the bed, twisting the end of a lock of hair that is hanging in my face. Today, I'm using the hair like a veil or a mask of some sort. If I can't see out behind my hair, then they can't see in—or so I hope. My stick-straight hair comes down past my shoulders, and is a dirty blonde shade. I usually wear it up in a ponytail or twist it into a bun; it's not like I have anyone waiting to run his fingers through it, so it never stays down. But again, today I need the veil.

I have a womanly figure, of course. Who wouldn't after having three kids? But as I said, I keep in shape and look and feel healthy. I was even told I didn't look my age and resembled someone in their thirties, so that was certainly the ultimate compliment. As long as no one calls me a MILF, I'm flattered. I just despise that term and think it's such an insult to women.

Philadelphia, Pennsylvania, is our home. We would not leave it regardless of William's passing. We were both from a small town in Rhode Island, but I would never go back there. I never even went back to visit, and I certainly wasn't going to start now. I have no idea who all might be downstairs waiting for me from our families, and I don't rightly care. At the funeral home, people made their rounds and gave me their condolences. I can't even remember who said what, or who was even present. It is still all a blur.

I sigh, but it doesn't relax me. I have to keep blinking due to the harsh light streaming in from the hallway. I wanted it pitch black in my bedroom; it went well with my mood and the color of dress I had donned for the occasion. The blackout curtains were more for me than they were for William when he was still alive. He didn't work, he just slept all day. He went on disability years ago, and I was only all too happy to get out of the house. I didn't have to worry about the kids because they went to school and had great sitters over the years; now, of course, they are old enough to do their own thing. William and I didn't sleep together because when I got home from work, he would already be gone, off to the bar. When I left for work in the morning, he would just be getting home and passing out on the bed in a drunken stupor.

William and I existed as ships passing each other in the night, and we both liked it that way. He didn't do anything family-oriented. We had a dead-end marriage. I guess I really was just waiting around for him to die. He was already dead to me anyway; he'd missed years and years of opportunities with his kids. So why didn't I kick him out or end it long ago? I couldn't even answer that one.

*I guess I was punishing myself for misdeeds; again, we're not going there. You don't need to be burdened by that sordid past.*

"Thanks for checking on me. You know, you're my rock. You say you wouldn't know what to do without me, but I feel the same. Thanks for being here today. I know I'm not much for company, and I feel bad because the kids have to fend for themselves. I'll be down soon, though, I promise," I tell him, willing him to go away.

I can hear him breathing, and he's running his hand through his hair, trying to judge whether he should really stay or go. In a difficult sign of acquiescence for an alpha male, he simply says, "Okay," and walks out.

The door shuts quietly behind him, his steps retreating down the hallway. I'm in tune with my surroundings again. I listen to the sounds traveling up from the stairway for a little bit. I can't really make out anything, just inconsequential noise. It's comforting, though, and I find myself just sitting here, letting the minutes roll by.

***

Enough is enough. I have probably been sitting here for hours. I figure lots of people have already left. It's time to check on my kids and come back to the land of the living. That didn't just refer to the fact that my husband's ashes are still sitting on my bedside table. I couldn't bring myself to leave *him* downstairs. This is the screwed-up part about me. I didn't want to spread his ashes, nor did I want to leave him on the mantle. I just didn't want to be near him. Jesus, I couldn't force myself to leave him anywhere else, though. It's only fitting that even at the end, he's a slave to a bottle of some sort.

I have really good night vision now, so I can see the urn clearly, resting lonely on my bedside table. My body is stiff from sitting rigidly for so long. I flex my fingers and realize I had balled them into fists at my sides. I stretch my neck from side to side, desperately trying to work out the kinks. I drag my sorry butt up from the bed and make my way down the stairs. There is no one in the living room. I don't hear anything. Where are my kids?

I trudge through the living room and then head into my kitchen. Still no one, so I decide to look out back. We have a nice patio area for hosting, and it is lined with patio heaters for chilly days like this one. I'm just grateful it hasn't snowed recently. Sure enough, my daughter, sons, Alexi, Caylan, their daughter, and Caleb are out there, talking and watching Emeline play.

I suck in my breath when I see Caleb Daniels. It's a shock. I haven't seen him in a few months—not since the last time we were all together for dinner one night at Caylan's house. I just stare through the screen door at him; luckily, no one has noticed me make my approach yet.

I'm grateful I can admire him from afar for a moment. That's another screwed-up thing about me. My husband has just died, and here I am, able to appreciate the male form of another. Okay, this is where the rational part of me won't take a back seat to the feelings I let lie dormant for far too long. Jesus, I'm still a woman. I can, at the very least, admire. I'm no longer married; I'm a widow. Oh God, a widow, at forty-four. It's still so strange.

Besides, it's not like Caleb would ever be interested in *me*. I would be considered a cougar if I ever went for someone like him. He's what, like thirty-four? But my God, he's magnificent. He's successful, devilishly handsome, and so out of my league.

Caleb is a lawyer by profession, and he reminds me of Keanu Reeves in that movie *The Devil's Advocate*. His jaw is strong and confident. The dimple in his chin is sexy and alluring. His brown eyes are soulful, and the manicured brows above his lashes are captivating. He's a man who takes great care with his appearance. But what I appreciate most is how humble he is. It doesn't matter that he is successful, he treats you like a person and never flaunts his affluent background. Caleb is the type of man who would make an excellent father, lover, and companion.

Yup, he would one day make some girl very happy. He really is the ultimate catch. I feel something unfurling in my belly—and it isn't because I haven't eaten. It is because I'm truly and utterly taken with that man. I have seen him at functions over the years, because he is one of Alexi's best friends. But I never looked at him besides being an acquaintance.

I'm confused as to why he is even here tonight. We aren't close by any means. Then I realize he is just once again being a good friend to Alexi and showing support, which in turn is supporting me. I make a groaning kind of sighing noise, the kind you make when you look at something you can't have. Crap, I guess it came out louder than I intended, because all heads turn toward me. That is when Caleb locks gazes with my startled blue eyes.

\*\*\*

*Caleb*

I would know her voice anywhere. I would know her sounds anywhere. I have been studying her for years. I've always been fascinated by Liezel "Liz" Carter. She is a breathtaking woman. She looks like she's thirty. I have a thing for cougars anyway, but she is hardly a cougar. Nevertheless, I'm still drawn to her and cannot fathom one good reason why I shouldn't be.

Her face is angelic, and her body is sinful. And fuck me for even being such a bastard to lust after her when her husband has just died. But I can't help it. I plead temporary insanity. Fuck, no, it's *permanent* insanity when it comes to this woman. I have found myself over the last year finding any excuse to hang out with Alexi, just in the hopes of catching a moment with Liz.

I should feel really guilty about her deceased, selfish prick of a husband, but I know enough about him to realize what he was. Alexi didn't ever betray her confidence, but he apprised me as to the gist of their situation. I knew Liz's marriage was a disaster. I never met her husband, and thankfully I never would have to. He threw away his wife, kids, and ultimately his life.

If Liz and the kids were mine, I'd treasure them. I'd never squander a second of our time. Liz is the kind of woman who deserves to be taken care of for once. She is the ultimate caregiver, but shit, she needs a man in her corner. She needs a man to touch her, caress every inch of her skin, and make her moan. I would gladly be that man for her. I would gladly sign on for a life sentence of being chained to her and giving her everything she needs; she just doesn't know it yet. I'm biding my time, but I'll make my move soon. I'll testify to that.

# Chapter 2: One Bone*r* Fide Cougar

*Caleb*

*The whole lot of my friends can suck my left nut. Ah, hell, they can suck the right one too while I'm at it!*

I'm only saying this because I'm feeling sorry for myself. I just got home from Liz's, and I'm jittery. I normally don't have such dickhead thoughts regarding my friends, but this need to be with Liz is more than getting to me. It's consuming me. I'm the nice guy of our group. Remember, I've always been the sweet, sensitive one. I'm not supposed to be an asshole, so I need to get my shit together.

Imagine, though, going through another night of seeing *her*, and another night of not being able to do a damn thing about my feelings. I know on the surface I have to be patient and take my time.

I. Know. This.

She's been through something I can't begin to understand, but I'm jealous of the life my friends have—I want what they have.

I. Want. Liz.

Out of my best friends, I'm the one who wanted to settle down—they just didn't know it because I never voiced it, so I can't blame them for their good fortune. I've always acted like I was content in skirt-chasing. The truth is, I've been ready to have a family for a long time. I didn't make it to Emeline's birthday party last week because I had an emergency with a client's case. That's why tonight I especially needed to be around Liz and get my fill of her; sadly, it wasn't enough to satisfy me.

My best friends, Alexi, Gil, and Anthony, enjoyed playing the field back in our wild days. And don't get me wrong, I did too, but it got old by the end of my twenties. Now that I'm going to be thirty-five later this year, well, it has me antsy. I don't want to jump into marrying just anybody. I want to marry *the one*. Truly, I'm happy for my friends. Just...jealous.

I made a vow to myself long ago that I'd have certain things in life. So far, I've managed to attain most things on my list. The *muscle gods* finally blessed me at age eighteen. That's when my life changed forever. Once the muscles came, I prowled the local bars and got in with a fake ID; I'd never confess that violation now that I'm a man who upholds justice. Anyway, I trolled for pussy and finally became *a man* at eighteen thanks to my first bona fide cougar—it was paradise being with an older woman. Although, my love for cougars began long before that. I guess it began when I was about fourteen…no, fourteen and a half.

As I said earlier, Liz is barely considered a cougar—we've only got a ten-year difference. And she isn't what you would consider a *classic cougar*. I can't imagine Liz going after a man the way the stereotype leads you to believe—in the context of her being the aggressor. So, I use the term loosely.

God, do I revere older women. I've always connected with them somehow. I'm drawn to them because of their essence, life experience, both personal and professional, and I have an appreciation for their similar tastes and desires, which I find mutually beneficial.

Please don't go thinking this is some kind of a mommy-complex just because my mom wasn't around as I was growing up; that's not it! I don't need the psych babble about my issues stemming from my mom essentially abandoning me because of her going through her own shit. I never felt deprived in life. My mom grieving the loss of my baby brother was warranted. My dad making himself scarce was justified too. I made the life I have. I have no regrets; well, that is, if Liz never reciprocates my feelings.

I'm sitting here in my lonely bedroom with my back propped up against my plush, leather headboard. I didn't even bother to undress out of my suit from the funeral. I had kicked off my dress shoes at least, but can't muster the strength to fully undress. My frustration is wearing on me. Arms crossed, further demonstrating my resolve to be wallowing in self-pity, I lament that no one is here to witness it.

After a few minutes, I rub at my tired eyes. Nah, I'm not sleepy, just worn out mentally. My eyes are tired from trying to make sense of things. I had to take my contacts out and put my glasses on. I'm not a shallow man, but I don't do glasses in front of anyone—it's a weird quirk of mine—I hate glasses on me. The astigmatism in my right eye makes Lasik surgery difficult, and I was told I'm not a good candidate, so I haven't bothered pursuing it further. I stop rubbing my eyes and proceed to massage my temples at the onset of a headache—now I'm giving myself a headache…great!

My bed faces the huge flat-screen TV mounted on the wall, but I

[13]

don't feel like watching anything—not even to escape from reality for a bit. I have a gas fireplace on the wall to my left. My high-rise apartment has the best view, with a balcony entrance directly in my bedroom, which is on the far-right wall. I have a two-bedroom place, but it's not like I ever have visitors; hopefully that soon changes. Yeah, I've had some overnight guests, well companions, but that's just it…I want something *more*.

Family doesn't come to visit. My dad has been dead a few years now. He and my mom stayed together despite the strained relationship. They weren't what I would consider a married couple anyway. My mom passed on a few years before Dad, medicating herself right up until the very end until she overdosed. I'm not shocked my dad outlived her, but his health wasn't ideal either. I suspect Dad's stress level and workaholic tendencies caused his heart attack. The poor man went quickly at least. Even Alexi couldn't have saved him had he been around. Dad's heart was too damaged.

God, I don't want to be my parents. I don't want to have the relationship my parents had. Coexisting with a wife and cohabitating for the sake of functioning in life is no life at all. Liz wouldn't have to want for anything. Liz wouldn't just *coexist* with me. She would be the reason I exist. I'd worship her. I'd put her on a pedestal so high, even I'd have a hard time touching her. Fuck, but touch her I would. I find it increasingly difficult not to tent the front of my pants. Thinking about Liz even in the slightest does this to me.

I notice the little things about her. Hell, I notice everything about her. The long lashes. The legs for days, her lean frame. I can't reiterate enough how she keeps in great shape. *Mmm*, she has such alluring hair, I want to grab and inhale the fragrance. I want her silken tresses to rest against my body and dance across my naked skin. I dream about her eyes boring into mine as I see right into the deepest parts of her. And her generous heart I crave because that's her true beauty. She's the real deal. The total package. The gift that keeps on giving. Name a cliché at this point…she's it!

Shit, I'll definitely need to rub one out here in a second if I keep on going. So, let me get back to addressing more things on that list of accomplishments so I can swim in safer waters and venture out of this sea of lust. Let's see, I've got the career, the finances, the group of friends. Just need to add a woman to the list. I'm the last man standing. I can't fucking believe it! Even Caylan's brother, Brenneth—of all people—is involved. Brent, as we call him, is the one who everyone thought would never take the plunge. Yet, he's engaged! He found Everly before he left for deployment, and the lucky bastard has her forever now.

We had a grenade dropped on us in October when my buddy Gil

announced his engagement. Interestingly, I knew well before everyone else in our circle of friends that he was a goner, but I'm still just as shocked by the news. I guess because, as I said, I'm the last! Up until last spring, I had Gil to go clubbing with and be my go-to friend for bro-time. But, then he turned in his player card for an exclusive one—Addison forever changed him. I never expected to see him like that. Hell, I never expected to see *any* of my friends like that.

Seeing the guys in the condition they're in reminds me of that animated deer movie I watched as a kid. It's the one where all the male cartoon characters were "twitterpated" over the girls—*yeah, I know, it's even more evident that I'm also dubbed the damn sentimental one of the group.* And as for Alexi and Anthony, they've been with their loves for a while. Alexi has Caylan, and Anthony has Shanna. Both women are stunning, and my boys are beyond in love with them—must be nice.

So…Liz Carter…*mmm.* Liz ticks every mark on my hot list. She's everything I've been looking for. I have no damn clue if she'll ever want to get married again. *Hell, that's premature thinking.* I have no idea if she'll ever want a man again in general. I know I'll have to tread carefully. I'm willing to, though, because she's worth it.

I'll also have to tell Alexi of my intentions to pursue Liz. Christ, he's very protective of her. She may act like his big sister—and he does a pretty good job of being her pain in the ass little brother—but he tends to go into big brother mode when need be. I'm sure I'd get his blessing once I explained everything. He knows I'd never hurt her. That's not the kind of man I am. I want to give women the world. Well, I want to give the world to one woman in particular. It's my duty as the *sweet one.*

Don't go thinking I'm sweet in every aspect. Because in the bedroom I come alive—you'd never, ever say I'm *sweet* when you're in bed with me. I'm an animal. I'll make it so you can't walk for a week! I take the cougars, and I become a pussy-poacher, hunting down what I want with my scope. I tame them, claim them, and release them back into the wild. Yeah, you get the picture.

With Liz, I wouldn't be able to release her. It's not about the catch. It's not about the hunt, or the game, or whatever you want to call it. It's so much more. Ever since I was a teen, I've had this deep need to find my unicorn in life. That probably sounds fucked up or cheesy, but I've always considered some women unattainable, hence *unicorn* status. I'd put Liz in that category as a unicorn, but I'm damn sure going to try to claim her and change the *unobtainable* part of the equation. It was hard for me to believe a mythical being, like Liz, even existed. But she's real. I knew from the moment I met her that there was something about her.

It's going to kill me to be patient. I already feel like I've been waiting forever. But Liz was married at the time. Now that she's a widow, I will need to give her some space, a shoulder to cry on, and unwavering support—be a friend. I will gladly be there for emotional and physical support for her and the kids. I need to get to know Liz as a friend first.

I've gone back and forth contemplating my pursuit of her. I keep replaying the evening in my head, when I overheard a conversation between mother and daughter. I didn't mean to eavesdrop on Liz and Leah; I was locked in place when Liz's voice drew me in from the other room—it's natural that she calls to me.

I had gotten up to use the restroom since we were outside on the patio, and Liz and Leah must have moved to the living room to talk. It was a very private and tender moment, which is why I feel like an asshole for listening in when they didn't know I was there.

***

*"Baby, I just have to know if you're okay. You're my strong, beautiful girl, but you know you can talk to me about anything, right?" Liz asks Leah.*

*I rub at my chest hearing Liz's voice catch in her throat here and there. God, what a tough woman and family they are to endure a situation like this. I can't see the ladies talking in the next room; I can only hear them as I'm standing on the other side of the wall that separates the kitchen and living room.*

*"I'm fine, Mom, really. It hurts, and you know I'll love and miss Dad, but he's not like the dads my friends have. You know I've told you before that I wish he moved out a long time ago. I mean, haven't I been saying it since I was like nine? I gave up thinking he'd ever be a 'real dad.' I'm still sad, though, because I never wanted him to die," she confesses.*

*I hold my breath for fear of crying for this little girl. She's so intelligent and insightful—well beyond her young age. I never knew how deep the neglect from Leah's father ran, but somehow she understood it and recognized it, and maybe even accepted it—not even adults can come to terms with concepts of this nature. The amount of courage and strength the kids and Liz have shown whenever I've seen them is awe-inspiring. They're always a happy and positive source to others. It was a shock to find out there were things going on behind closed doors.*

*I hear sniffling, and I'm not sure who's crying—I suspect it's Leah. I haven't seen Liz cry once today.*

*"God, I'm so sorry, baby. If I could change it, I would. I never want you to be*

*hurt or be sad. I'm sorry you were handed this. It's not fair to you. I know your father loved you. He was just too sick with the disease to ever get better. I wish you could've known him in his younger days," Liz explains.*

*I roughly drag my hands up and down my face, trying to wipe away this night. I'm lucky I don't remember my brother's death—I never had to go through it with my parents. There are certain ways to handle grief and loss, and my mom was not one who dealt with it, as I've mentioned. Yet, here Liz and Leah are exhibiting the utmost display of grace and determination. I should walk away now…but I can't. I swallow hard and pull at my tie that's suddenly suffocating me.*

*"Thanks Mom. I love you. I wish Dad would've been different, but it's okay because we've always had you," Leah says, sounding a little more upbeat.*

*"Oh, baby, I hit the jackpot with you and your brothers. And you know I love you more than life itself," she conveys, pausing a little to probably choose her words.*

*I wish I could see her; however, I don't want to make my presence known. I look heavenward and say my sorries for not walking away from their conversation.*

*"The school's going to provide some grief counseling for you guys. Again, you know you can always come to me or someone else. Caylan loves you to pieces. She's also a good listener. Just don't keep anything bottled up, baby," Liz begs of her daughter.*

*"I won't. But I'm worried about you too. You don't ever do anything for yourself. We try to tell you all the time you need to be happy and have a life," Leah imparts.*

*I hear Liz softly chuckle. "Sweetheart, I am happy. You and your brothers make me happy. Why on earth would you think I'm not?"*

*If I was ever lucky enough to have a daughter, God, I'd want one like Leah. How does a thirteen-year-old girl know more about life than I do?*

*"Mom, get real! We know you love us, and we know you're happy as a mom, but you never doing anything outside of us. If I have to go to counseling, then you have to start doing stuff too!" Leah scolds her mother in the sweetest way.*

*I hear Liz sigh as if in amazement, then she questions, "When did you skip ahead from being a kid to being an adult?"*

*Leah lightly laughs and replies, "I have a good teacher."*

*"Oh, baby…," Liz trails off.*

*I imagine she's embracing her daughter, and I finally force myself to leave my spot and rejoin the rest of the group outside. This conversation will stay with me for the rest of my life.*

***

Earlier tonight gutted me. As much as I still feel guilty for invading their privacy, I think as a man and human being I needed to hear it.

Liz's husband's death wasn't *untimely*, though—well, to the outside world it was because no one really *knew* what was going on. Sure, we all speculated, but I never knew to what extent the emotional and mental toll it must have taken on them. Learning recently about his alcoholism was a shock. I always thought he was detached from them by choice—he *was* in the sense that he chose to abandon them by drinking, but when Liz said *disease* it struck a chord. God, I was ignorant. I still hate the guy and most likely always will, of course, but my own family suffered from things that maybe others would be ignorant about too.

It's difficult to fathom the years of disappointments he delivered to Liz and the kids. They must have added up and ultimately made them realize a long time ago what he was.

I'm still grappling with all this. I don't have enough experience in dealing with families. *Fuck, you know mine was the poster for dysfunctional!* I run my hand through my hair. Revisiting the past is daunting, but introspection can be beneficial.

I also don't have experience with romantic relationships. I've mostly dated women for a few weeks at a time, and it was only because the sex was good. Again, I'm not an asshole. The women knew the score before we jumped in bed. It was a mutual thing. It was for fun and nothing more—another thing I appreciate about mature women.

I stare at the painting on my wall. There's nothing super spectacular about it, just an ordinary seascape. But the longer I stare, the longer I picture myself standing on the edge of the craggy cliff wanting to leap off the edge and swim out to greet the sunset over the water. Liz can be that sunset for me. She can be my sunrise too.

My mind is made up. I'm going after Liz sooner rather than later. I will do the friend thing. I suspect I'd be friend-zoned right away anyway, and that's fine. I'll start working on her and worm my way in. I'll work on her mind and body, all the while trying to attain my ultimate goal…her heart.

I'm of the opinion that if you're alone, then it's perfectly normal and sane to talk to yourself; the caveat being that you don't answer back.

I say aloud to the painting, because otherwise it sounds fucking creepy, despite my logic a second ago, "Liz, I'm coming for you. Whether you're ready or not, I'm coming. I'm not stopping. I'll give 'twitterpated' a whole new meaning. I've got my scope set and you in my sights."

*Yeah, I'm not right in the head tonight, but she drives me to it.*

# Chapter 3: He Gets the *Ex* and the Axe

*Caleb*

"So, let me get this straight. You want my permission to date Liz?" Alexi laughs so hard that his mocking tone leaves me pissed.

"Fuck you, man! No, come on, I'm not asking. As a courtesy, I'm telling you," I reaffirm as I give him a hard scowl and shake my head at his behavior.

Alexi continues chuckling and holds up his hands, placating me. I blow out an exasperated breath and shoot him the middle finger. After a few minutes, he finally collects himself enough to carry on an actual conversation with me.

"In all seriousness, don't fuck this up. You know what Liz means to me. I don't want to lecture you on shit I probably have no business to, but I feel like Liz is family. I feel responsible for her somehow. She's not just my trusted employee—she's more. For Christ's sake, I think we're going to name her the godmother of the new baby. Brent and Meg are Em's godparents, of course, but we were going to pick two different ones this time around," he runs a hand through his hair and half-smiles.

I knew Alexi isn't the religious type, but I also knew he liked to do certain things *the right way,* for Caylan's sake. She may not be a religious person either, but from what I've learned about her upbringing, her parents are the traditional sort.

*God, I'd love to be the baby's godfather if I was lucky enough to be chosen.* I keep that thought to myself, though, so as not to pressure my friend.

"That's awesome, man. She'll make an incredible godmother. And I get why you are that way about her. I know you're being protective, and I respect that. But—and there's a big *but*—you needn't worry," I sigh, the wheels turning in my head as I contemplate how to convey things properly.

I continue on, "I want to get to know her the right way. Yeah, my dick is screaming for attention from her, and here's another *but*: but, it's not like that. There's just something about her I can't move on from. I want to see what can grow between us. I know she's an amazing woman and deserves to be treated as such."

Alexi nods in agreement, then I stare off into space and think of her gorgeous face. I close my eyes and savor the image I'm conjuring.

After a few moments, I open my eyes, coming back to reality, and ask my friend, "Have you heard from her since last night?"

He starts to lightly chuckle, and with his right hand he points his thumb, angling it toward the door to tell me, "The woman is crazy because she's here today."

He can see I want to protest as my face transforms into a *what the fuck?* look.

I cannot believe she's here! But the mere mention of her being *here*—in such close proximity to me—already has my groin stirring to life.

He holds up his hands to assure me, "I tried to talk her out of it, believe me. I told her to take time off. Hell, I even tried to plan a trip for her and the kids to get a break. Of course, in typical Liz-fashion, she refused. She said throwing herself into work is the best thing for her. While I'm inclined to disagree, I don't want to push her either. She even baked me cookies. Damn they're good! Except, I don't need the extra calories since I've been skipping the gym lately. Plus, Caylan withholds sex when I bring shit like that home because she doesn't want to gain too much weight with this pregnancy."

He swivels in his chair and looks at me contemplatively. "I get the feeling we're having a boy because she's so different this time around. Her belly is growing waaaayyy faster than last time, and she has odd cravings. Anyway, back to Liz—I think she needs to return to her routine. I imagine William died a long time ago for her. So, my guess is she doesn't need or want a break to grieve."

I shudder at the mention of *his* name. I fucking hate that name. I loathe and detest it. *Why couldn't Liz have met me first before that asswipe?* Then I'm mentally kicking myself in the balls for being an idiot because I would have been a damn teenager when she got together with her ex. Of course, that would have been fine by me, but I'm sure that wouldn't have flown with her, understandably. She's a noble woman and would not have been interested in my boyish self at the time anyway.

I don't want to keep calling her a widow. I don't consider her a widow. In my mind, I consider them divorced. He's her *ex*, end of discussion! He was a shit human being, and I can't look at him differently regardless of the *disease* because he didn't try to get better for the sake of his family, or for himself.

My heart is constricted as I think about what Liz must be going through. Even if what Alexi says is true that he died a long time ago in her eyes, it still doesn't diminish the fact that it must hurt her on some level. This is painful. I imagine she's grieving for the loss of a relationship she never had. At least in my mind, that is what I'm piecing together. That astute and sensitive part of me can be quite in tune with women's feelings at times. Various girlfriends—platonic in nature—have told me over the years that I'm an anomaly among guys; I can live with that distinction.

It's Friday at least, so I hope she takes the weekend to relax. Alexi's practice isn't open on the weekend, and he only goes to the hospital if there's an emergency. Hopefully this means Liz will take the time to decompress. God, what I wouldn't give to be able to make her feel good. I'm not talking about sex. I want to pamper her. I want to treasure her. I want to spoil her.

I'd draw her a bath, massage her all over and relieve the tension, and I'd take away all her hurts and worries—if she'd let me. I rub at the beard scruff that inevitably grows after not shaving for a day, and I can't help but ask myself, *will she ever give me—give us—a chance?*

***

*Liezel*

*Busy, I have to stay busy.*

So, that's what I'm going to do. Coming into work today was the best thing. I'm elated when I take care of patients. Being able to focus on improving the lives of others is something that pulls me from the dark pit I'm in because of the years of despair lodged in my heart.

I can't stop thinking about Caleb, though. Ever since I saw him at my house last night, my brain won't get off the constant loop of images flickering through my head. Images mostly of his handsome face—I can't forget his body in that suit too. *Whew*, I'm fanning myself internally. That man has my veins singing because I need to—and want to—be near him. My skin tingles at the thought of potentially seeing him again at our next group get-together.

I run my hands up and down my arms as if I'm cold, but I'm not. I will the goose pimples that have cropped up to go back down where they came from; they give me away so easily. I feel vulnerable and exposed as if the next person I talk to will be able to see right through me and know I'm like a bitch in heat, lusting after one of my boss's best friends. I'd like to think I'm better than this.

*But don't I deserve to feel something come to life within me after all these years? Shouldn't I feel alive? Shouldn't I feel like a woman?*

I hope I'm not coming off as cold and uncaring. It saddens me to think that others won't understand where I'm coming from.

I berated myself long and hard last night about feeling something when my husband has only been dead for six days. I crawled into bed, and well into the wee hours of the morning, I tossed and turned. But before my alarm went off—which I didn't even need the damn thing for a wakeup call—I came to the miraculous conclusion that my life really isn't all that different from six days ago.

That's why I decided to come into work today. William finally gave me the closure I needed to move on with my life—or that's at least what I'm telling myself. Today is a day in which I'm skipping all the stages of grief and heading right to "acceptance." I'm finding peace. I should be thanking him for that, actually.

I still haven't decided what I'm doing with his urn yet, but I'll eventually figure it out. I moved him into my bedroom closet last night because I couldn't look at it anymore. He was always closed off from us and kept locked up in the dark in his own little world, so my solution seemed fitting.

What I wrote for his eulogy made me feel somewhat guilty. It was short and not sweet. He died on a Saturday…end of story. Well, it was the morning after Emeline's first birthday. Alexi was the first person I called after receiving the news. I had to find out from the police. The cops were dispatched to the seedy bar where William frequented. There was no saving him even after the cavalry showed up.

He apparently went quietly because he slumped over and the bar patrons thought he passed out—it was a few hours before anyone noticed he wasn't breathing. The medical examiner pronounced him dead at the scene. The initial autopsy and toxicology reports cited a classic case of alcoholism, and there was no foul play suspected. Therefore, we were able to proceed with a funeral.

The cirrhosis that I already knew existed is what ultimately became his end. He never once got treatment for his liver, and *it* had finally had enough. He treated that poor organ even worse than he treated me.

"I should've had a funeral for his poor liver," I mumble to myself. Then I roll my eyes at my absurdity.

I pick up the patient chart I had set down on the counter in the exam room I had been tidying up and prepping for the next patient. It's been a slow day for the most part. Alexi had rescheduled most of his patients for next week in the event he needed to be there for me.

I know I'm a lucky lady to have such a caring, attentive boss and friend. I really need a friend more than anything. However, I don't like leaning too far on Alexi because—not that Caylan has ever been the jealous type—I don't want to cause any issues in his marriage. I've been on my own for so long that I certainly thrive on it. But admittedly, it would be nice to have someone to prop myself up against and say, "Yes, I'll take the help you're offering."

*I wish there was someone who could do that for me.*

I'm suddenly brought back to that pit of despair, thinking how I never had *that* with William, and I recall the words at his funeral. It was rather pathetic, because really, what could I say about my husband?

***

*"Thank you all for being here," I say to the small group of friends and relatives gathered at the funeral parlor.*

*"William was a husband and father. He was a son and had a best friend who really comforted him in his time of need." I take a shaky breath as I'm speaking into the mic. I have no idea if anyone realizes my euphemism for "friend" is really referring to his mistress, the bottle. He didn't have any actual friends.*

*I want to use my hair to hide behind because I wore it down, but I know I can't. I have to do this. I will do this. I will be strong for my wonderful children seated in the front row, staring at me with tears shimmering in their eyes. This is torture! I tuck my hair behind my ears and decide I will show William I'm the strong woman he married and the strong woman he essentially left.*

*"We will remember William for the three beautiful, talented, amazing children he left behind. Tyler, Kurt, and Leah are the epitome of grace, faith, strength, and beauty. They are a mountain no one can chip away at. I am in awe of their character and perseverance. William's passing will not cripple our family, but cause us to bind ourselves together even more tightly." I finally look up from the yellow notebook paper I scrawled his eulogy onto.*

*There's not much more I can say at this point because my mother always said, "If you can't say anything nice, don't say anything at all."*

***

I come back to the present and decide to put the funeral behind me.

Some parts of last night are still jumbled for me. But what remains perfectly clear is William definitely belongs in that closet!

With my chart in hand, I head to Alexi's office to converse with him about our last patient of the day, who should be arriving in the next hour. I know I don't have to dry my eyes because there are still no tears. I made sure I put some makeup on today just in case I needed a layer of courage, and Leah twisted my hair into a nice updo with curls cascading down the back. She loves to play with my hair, and I swear that girl could be a hairdresser to the stars one day.

Leah revealed to me last night that I basically need to *start living*. It's easier said than done, but I'll try. Leah is my light when I'm walking through darkness. She should be a kid, though, and not have to worry so much about me. So, I will have to make the effort and try to *live*!

Alexi's door is shut, so I knock softly. After hearing his invitation to come in, I open the door and freeze in the entrance when those two brown eyes I swoon over are staring me down.

"Caleb!" Is all I can manage to squeak out.

Oh shit, twice in two days I get to see him. Thank God my boss is a cardiologist because I think my heart just stopped!

# Chapter 4: Cookies and Cream

*Caleb*

As I'm casually lounging in one of Alexi's comfortable, plush leather office chairs talking away, someone knocks on the door. Alexi tells whoever it is to enter, and in walks Liz.

"Caleb," she says in a shocked tone. But I could swear there's a hint of breathiness to it.

My hands, which were resting easily on the arms of the chair, begin to grip the leather tightly at seeing her. She stirs something fierce inside me. I want to beat my chest like a wild man. I want to throw her over my shoulder and run into the nearest exam room to have my wicked way with her. I know I laid eyes on her last night, but it doesn't matter. I could see her every damn minute of every damn day, and I'd still have the same reaction. She does this to me, and she doesn't even realize it.

The scrubs she dons would be pajamas on anyone else, but somehow she makes them look so damn sexy—I don't know how she does it. I want to lick her collarbone that is peeking out from the V-neck of her top. Her hair, twisted up in an elaborate style, is begging to be taken down and be wrapped around my fingers—the few pieces floating around her face are such a damn tease. Her beautiful mouth is slightly agape, asking me to stick my tongue in so deep that I can taste every part of her. I want to savor every flavor on her body, inside and out.

Alexi might have to use the defibrillator on my heart because it feels like it's pounding abnormally. I've never reacted so strongly to a woman in my life, and that's why I know she's *it* for me. I want her now more than ever. Every single time I see her, the attraction gets stronger and stronger. It's ticked up a notch each time, and it's hard to describe, but I'll do my damnedest.

My longing for her becomes fiercer and fiercer. And I know it will not wane even once I finally have her. She will fill a void in me, but the feelings will always be there, as if it's the first time every time. She's the woman I was meant to be with, and I feel it in the depths of my soul.

I lick my lips and deliver a wolfish grin that's perfect for trying to ensnare my prey. I don't know what to say yet, but something will come to mind. I want to see if I can make her squirm a minute longer.

She puts her hand to her throat, breathing heavily, and all that action does is make me want to focus my attention on sucking her beautiful skin. Fuck, she must smell so heavenly. I will need to save her from herself, it seems, since she appears to be so startled by my presence here. I think I'm going to take this as a good sign. The fact that I can make her feel anything other than the grief or guilt I imagine she'd be feeling after yesterday is a definite start.

"Liz," I say in greeting, nodding in her direction. I then give her another smile.

After all, she said my name, so it's only fair I say hers back. I mentally slap myself at how coy I'm being in this moment. That simply won't do. I'm taking control of this!

"Where are *my* cookies?" I chuckle and wink at her.

She seems confused at first, as if maybe I'm referring to something else, and then that look of realization hits her.

"Oh my goodness, how rude of me. I should've baked you some too. I had no idea you'd be here. I mean, I know I saw you last night, but I don't think you mentioned coming here today," she stammers, then bites her bottom lip as if she's embarrassed.

I smile and shake my head, reassuring her, "I'm just teasing you. Although, I'd love to try your cookies some time. Each occasion you make them, either this guy over here eats them before anyone else can have a taste, or they're scarfed up by everyone else." I point an accusatory finger Alexi's way.

"Hey! I don't eat all of them!" Alexi complains.

Liz blushes at my words. I know everyone raves about what a damn good baker she is. I get by all right with making some basic meals for myself, but neither baking, nor cooking, is really something I've tried my hand at. The few times I've attempted something fancy by following the step-by-step directions per the TV cooking show, it's turned out like primordial soup. Whipping something up in the kitchen could be fun, though, if it involves her. She's the only sweet treat I need to taste anyway.

"Well, maybe you can teach me some time," I suggest.

She smiles at my words. "I'd love to. I make a mean sugar cookie. The vanilla flavor and scent just hits you right. I've taught the kids how to make them, yet they're not really fans. It would be nice to teach someone with some enthusiasm about it," she giggles.

I love hearing that lyrical sound. You would think this woman would have nothing to smile about or be happy about right now, but that's Liz. Her heart and personality are infectious. It's intoxicating being around her. She seems to always be in good spirits, even if the situation calls for the exact opposite.

"Just say the word, and I'll be there...even tonight," I offer in return. I'm hoping a lesson would further help take her mind off things.

She chews at her bottom lip again and smoothes the front part of her hair back to the nape of her neck, clearly contemplating my words.

"Erm, I'm going to be pretty busy this evening trying to play plumber. I have to replace the wax seal in the downstairs bathroom, so that should be fun," she says, rolling her eyes.

And that's when lightning strikes and gives me a genius idea. She just opened the door for me to come in all alpha-male, rescue-me, knight-in-shining-armor style. I know she didn't ask me for help, and even if she can do it on her own, I still want to help. The least I can do is lift the damn toilet up. I may not know much about toilets, but I know the seal is at the base.

"I'd love to help you if I may. I'm a whiz at changing those things. That is, if you and the kids don't mind company and my assistance?" I reply, crossing my fingers and toes in the hopes she'll accept.

"Wow! I don't know what to say. I'd love the help. As far as the kids, well, William's parents are here for another night, so they're staying at Bill and Anna's hotel with them to get one more night of family time in. I would've had his parents stay with me, but they don't—well, they never have, actually—liked me. Despite that, I'd never let it ruin any relationship they have with their grandchildren," she says sadly.

So many things are buzzing in my head at the moment because of her words. First, Liz is an incredible woman—that goes without saying. She's always putting her feelings aside or last, for the sake of others, the ultimate giver in every respect. I don't know how *anyone* wouldn't love her.

*There must be some kind of dark history in the family or drama, I imagine, to have caused this apparent rift.*

Secondly, I'm internally panicking because I don't know the first fucking thing about changing a seal. I admit I'm not a handy guy, but damnit, now I wish I was! I want to be the guy who can help her with this kind of shit. I'll watch YouTube or something and figure it out. Really, how hard can it be?

And lastly, but surely the most important notion, is that she'll be kid-free tonight. I'm a lucky SOB to have managed to score some alone time already. I thought it would take weeks, possibly longer, to have her alone. I'm rubbing my hands together in my mind in a conspiratorial manner. With my plan in place, I will take every opportunity to wear her down until she's mine.

I've said it before, but I'll reiterate, I won't be an asshole about it. Even if on the surface she seems fine, I can still recognize that she needs time to heal from her marriage, and I'm sure the last thing she needs or wants is to jump into something new. Fuck, I don't even know if she even likes me like *that*. Now I sound like I'm twelve and passing a note in study hall asking her to circle "yes" or "no" if she'll be my girlfriend.

Anyway, I'm going to try damn hard to feel her out tonight so I know where I semi-stand. Knowing what she's thinking and feeling is important, and her emotions will be the key in all of this. God, I want to be there to catch her if she stumbles along the way. As they say, *you must learn to walk before you can run*. And even if she runs...I'm just going to have to sprint after her.

"Well, what time do you want me to come by? I can bring dinner if you'd like," I propose, delivering my words with one of the best devilish smiles I have in my arsenal.

"Umm, six o'clock, I guess. I have tons of food left over from all the friends and neighbors dropping stuff to the house over the last week. I think I have enough casseroles to feed an army. I had to put so much stuff in the freezer so it wouldn't go to waste. Normally I eat salads or stir fries. But, I can certainly pop a casserole in the oven. And if there's time after fixing the seal, maybe I can let you in on my cookie baking secrets," she counters with a wide grin that has my heart racing again.

"That sounds great! Six it is, then. And Liz...I'll eat whatever you put in front of me." I say the last part while staring her down and putting as much heat as I can into what I'm saying.

I see and hear her very audible intake of breath, watching with rapt attention as her pupils dilate at my words. This reaction does things to me. I want to growl, and I don't even care that Alexi is only sitting a few feet away from me at his desk.

She swallows. Seeing her throat work makes me want to put something else in it. I can't help my overly dirty thoughts no matter how much I want to shove them down and handle her with kid gloves.

She shakes her head as if to clear it and responds with, "Okay, see you then," and scurries out the door, shutting it behind her before I can say anything more.

Alexi once again is laughing. This time I'm not sure at what.

"That's the first time I've ever seen Liz distracted enough at work that she didn't even tell me what she came in here for. It's as if I wasn't even here," he says sarcastically.

Then he continues on, "But you can take that as a positive. That woman is *never* distracted at work. She never lets her personal life in here. I'd say you have a pretty damn good chance because, man, did you lay it on thick," he ribs me.

"I had to do something," is all I come back with.

"Dude, do you even know how the fuck to change that wax thing on the toilet?" He questions as his brows lift in suspicion over my alleged lack of knowledge.

"That's what YouTube is for," I quip.

He's laughing his ass off again, and that's my cue to leave. I nod in his direction, indicating my "goodbye," and take my leave. I know he means well, but sometimes he can be a dick. I roll my eyes as I'm walking down the hall to exit his clinic, thinking, *I don't know how Caylan, or Liz, put up with him on a daily basis.*

But I don't need to, or want to, think about my friend anymore as I have someone else to think about. Before I have a date—*date...I wish*—with Liz tonight, I've got a date with my computer so I can take a crash course on toilet repairs.

*How romantic,* I chuckle to myself. Well, whatever gets my foot in the door at this point, right?

# Chapter 5: Seal the Deal

*Caleb*

I arrived at her house promptly at six. I brought her a plant as a gesture because I wanted to be gentlemanly. Golden rule is to never show up empty-handed; I believe chivalry is not dead, despite what others may think.

Flowers, chocolates, and wine would have been too forward, and I don't need any aphrodisiacs to be lusting after her—yup, no help needed in that department. And I don't want her to need those things in order to want me; of course, I'd give her anything and everything in this world, including flowers, chocolates, and wine, but I'm hoping I'm enough to satisfy her. I need to take baby steps here, and I'll try not to put the cart before the horse.

I did what I said I'd do and watched a few videos before arriving to ensure I could *fake it until I make it* with the plumber skills. After viewing them, I think it will be quite easy to do the project. I've always been a quick study, so this should be a walk in the park. I'm glad I can help Liz. This is not something she should be doing on her own. Having to remove the toilet from the floor would be too much for her to handle on her own, so cue the knight-in-shining-armor music as I strut into her place. I'm not being chauvinistic either; she needs some added muscle for this task.

When she answered the door, I was instantly hard. *Who am I kidding?* I was hard on the drive over. She just intensified the sensation of my dick straining against the zipper to my jeans; he wants to come out and say "hello" too.

She looks adorable wearing a pair of faded skin-tight blue jeans with a plain white T-shirt, the look completed with a pair of sneakers. I love that she's a no-fuss kind of woman. She can rock anything, and this ensemble is just as gorgeous as others. Oh, I've seen her dressed up at events and believe me, she's a beauty. Hell, I couldn't take my eyes off her the day of Alexi's wedding. Now with Brent's wedding coming up in three weeks, I can't wait to see her in formal-wear again with some sexy heels. I'm hoping I can be her date—but maybe that's premature thinking again.

Thankfully, she picked up all the supplies at the hardware store on her way home from work; shit, I didn't even think about suggesting I pick up the stuff for her. I refrained from laughing and thereby outing myself when she informed me she "watched a few YouTube videos" to prepare herself. See, great minds think alike!

She told me the staff at the local store was only all too happy to help her with her lot, and even offered to come over to assist with the installation. As she's telling me this, I'm gripping the caulk so hard in my hand, I'm surprised the tip didn't blow off, creating a mess. I can't hold back my feelings of jealously and possessiveness over her. She has no idea of her appeal to men—and probably women—and that makes her even sexier.

Since we're on the subject, I have to ask her, "So, what made you want to do this on your own instead of hiring someone? I mean, don't get me wrong, I'm delighted to help you; I'm just curious."

She blinks and smiles shyly at me as we're crouched on her bathroom floor putting the finishing touches on the caulk job—*fuck, I wish it was a cock job.*

I love that she can be so shy sometimes. From the little I know, she'd been with her ex for so long, I gather it's a new thing for her being around a man—well, other than friendship with Alexi, of course.

"I like doing things myself. I admit that for bigger things I usually hire someone, but when I noticed the seal leaking and googled it, it didn't seem that difficult. Plus, it's giving me something to do to take my mind off everything. There's nothing like some good ole elbow grease to do the job. Does that sound ridiculous?" She asks sheepishly.

I'm sure I have this mystified look in my eyes as I stare at her, but I can't help it. She amazes me. She's so independent and hardworking, and I can't get over the fact that a woman like her is in front of me. I want so badly to reach out and stroke her beautiful cheek that's flushed with a little rose tint to it.

"You're so beautiful," I practically whisper.

She swallows and tucks a strand of hair behind her ear that escaped from her ponytail and mumbles a "thanks."

I realize saying it is probably a colossal mistake because I made her uncomfortable. I couldn't hold back the words because she has me hypnotized by her inner and outer beauty. *Damn I'm an idiot.* I knew I had to take this slow.

***

*Liezel*

*Beautiful? Me? What?*

No one ever calls me beautiful. Well, Tyler does because we're each other's adoring fans. He's definitely a mama's boy, and I don't think it's because of the autism; he's high-functioning and completely verbal, and I'm very lucky that's the case. I think Tyler is attached to me because I'm the only one who seems to understand him outside of his brother and sister.

William never called me beautiful, not even on our wedding day. I can't believe it came from another man's lips. I feel like a twit for just telling him "thanks." *Ugh, I was caught off guard.* The fact that *this* man would say such a thing like that to me is plain crazy!

*He's* the beautiful one! Can men be described as beautiful? I suppose they can because there's no other way to describe Caleb. He's so strong, handsome, and incredibly giving. I can tell he's a genuine person with a deep soul. I think we can be great friends. Alexi is really the only platonic relationship I have with the opposite sex, so it will be nice to add another friend to my list. I love the girls in our group too, and it's amazing how it's grown over the years starting back when Caylan entered the picture.

When Caleb first asked me about a baking lesson earlier today, I wanted so much to take him up on it for tonight. I kept thinking I need to *live, live, live.* A chant I will have to repeat since I promised my daughter I'd "do something for myself." When the opportunity presented itself in regard to help with the repair, well, I had to go for it. Lightning wasn't going to strike twice. *Thank you toilet!*

I still can't believe he's here helping me with plumbing of all things. A part of me feels like I should be embarrassed, and then another part—the long ignored woman in me—wants to be near him no matter what we're doing. I feel like I *need* to be near him. I'm drawn to him, and I can't deny that. Once again, a small twinge of guilt assails me; I should probably remain in denial because I haven't done *anything* wrong.

Sure, I agonized over what to wear tonight and whether to put my hair into a simple ponytail. Then I had to keep reminding myself through fits of laughter that *this is not a date*. So, I settled on something comfortable and appropriate for working on my damn toilet! He hasn't said anything else, so I should probably make small talk. I do want to know more about him. Even if I can never have *him*, or a man like him, I still want to know more.

I go for the lame opener, "Erm, what's your favorite type of music to listen to?"

"I have eclectic taste. But I'd say I grew up listening to the stuff my parents would have playing throughout the house. I love Fleetwood Mac, REO Speedwagon, Journey, and Billy Joel," he says with a panty-drenching smile that does things to my inner core.

*God, does he realize how sexy he is without even trying?*

"Oh my God, I love Billy Joel! He's one of my favorite musicians. I saw him in concert years ago with Elton John during their Face to Face tour. It was epic!" I know I'm beaming at the fact that we have this in common. It's silly, but it still means something to me.

"My turn," he says.

I'm confused for a second, but then he starts talking, and I soon realize we're doing the question game.

"Do you collect anything? I used to collect Pogs as a kid but not anything in my adult years," he chuckles.

"Wow, I remember those things. I think the big, metal, heavy one was called the slammer or something like that." I bite my lip and giggle at the memory of seeing everyone playing them in my mind. I personally didn't play with them, but many people did back then.

"Oh yeah, the slammer was where it was at!" He winks at me.

I clear my throat because I don't like reading into anything he says or does since he couldn't possibly be flirting with me, could he?

I put us back on track, "Umm, I collect owls. I have so much owl stuff around the house I'm surprised you didn't notice. But I guess I didn't even give you the grand tour, so I'll have to rectify that after we're done with this. I suppose the only time you've been here was last night. But upstairs in my bedroom it looks like someone vomited owls everywhere."

My cheeks must be ten shades of red, and I feel my face flaming realizing I mentioned my bedroom to him. I'm mortified, but all he does is smile and stare at me like he's trying to read something in my features. I blow out a breath and discover I probably shouldn't take him into my bedroom. I mean, for God's sake, he doesn't need the tour of that! He'll think I'm some kind of hussy if I invite him in there.

"A tour would be great when we're done. You have a fantastic home, Liz. I like owls too. I consider them intelligent and valiant creatures. I can see why you collect them," he speaks in earnest.

*Must not read into anything. Must not read into anything.* If I say it enough, maybe I'll believe it.

"So, is it my turn for a question, or yours?" I ask.

"Yours," he says as he makes a grand sweeping gesture with his hand to indicate I have the floor.

He's adorable, and so sweet, and so…gah!

"Okay, so what's your guilty pleasure? I'll tell you mine if you tell me yours," I hedge, raising my eyebrows to show it could be all manner of things from something sinister to something spicy. Of course, I'm joking and attempting to be flirtatious, but I'm sure I'm failing miserably. It's so easy to want to flirt with him.

I swear his eyes darken at my words. In my peripheral vision I see him grip the tube of caulk. I recall he did that earlier, but at the time I thought it was a figment of my imagination. He better be careful squeezing that thing or it will blow!

"Don't strangle your cock," I warn, trying to be funny, and then I realize what I said. I meant "caulk," damnit! Well, if that isn't a Freudian slip, I don't know what is.

*Kill me now, oh my God, just kill me now!*

I know I have shock and awe written all over my face as I scramble to formulate something to recover from my monumental fumble.

"Caulk! I mean the *caulk*. Sorry about that!" I respond and shut my eyes tight like I'm a little girl and wishing away the Boogeyman.

I hear him breathing heavily, but I don't dare look. I'm a coward, and I'm okay with that because if I look at him and start thinking things, then I might want to tackle him to the floor. I would pounce on him so easily. I don't truly consider myself a cougar, but Lord, I'd definitely pounce on him and rub up against him like a wild animal—so, I'd take the title if it means I get to be with him.

After what I'm sure is only a few moments but feels more like an eternity, I finally take a quick peek. I look at the floor first because I'm living up to my coward status, and oh boy, there's caulk—see, I said it correctly this time in my mind—all over my tiled floor.

"Shit," is all I end up saying to this man.

# Chapter 6: Cookie or Nookie?

*Liezel*

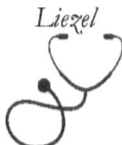

We cleaned up the mess from the tube incident and had a good laugh about it once the moment passed us by. I had to admire our handiwork when all was said and done. I thanked him profusely for helping me. I don't think I could have managed to lift the toilet off the floor and place it back over the seal in order to seat it properly had he not been there. Sometimes I bite off more than I can chew, so I'm grateful for the assistance.

As promised, I gave him a tour of my house. He seemed to think my owl obsession sprinkled throughout all the rooms is endearing, and I find his reaction quite exhilarating. We avoided my bedroom, and that is a good thing because if I was anywhere near my bed, I couldn't be held accountable for my actions.

He shouldn't be so yummy. He shouldn't be allowed to walk the earth and not expect women to throw themselves at him. I'm sure I'm on a long list of willing participants. He's so easy to be with and that makes him dangerous because if he were an asshole, then I could accept that I shouldn't develop feelings for him. But when he's so amazing like this, well, that adds a whole new level of complications to my life.

We're now standing in my cozy kitchen, and I'm thinking about when I watched his muscles flex during the heavy lifting—a titillating sight indeed. *Mmm,* him in that gray T-shirt he's wearing can't house all the ridges on his delicious biceps, and it makes my belly flip while reminiscing. If he had shown plumber's crack, it would have been totally hot on him—believe me, seeing his ass should be considered a gift from heaven.

I've taken stock of every part of his body tonight. He's got those thick thighs accentuated by the denim, along with a perfectly sculpted body that can't be denied, even in clothes. And his incredible behind needs to be squeezed—I'm not into butts, but his is the exception. Oh Lord, I need to fan myself again. I'm still a little too young to have hot flashes, so I know it's not that—even though it definitely can happen in your forties. Ugh, I'm so not ready for *the change*.

Caleb is causing my body to experience things I haven't felt in ages. I'm not used to having these passion-filled emotions about a man.

I also love that he's wearing work boots. I've seen him in suits, but this rugged, domestic look is so damn sexy. My nipples are hard fantasizing about him running his hands up and down my body. I want to moan just thinking about it. Instead, I bite my lip to keep that sound from escaping.

I almost drop a glass from the cabinet when I go to get him a drink of water because he has me so jittery. I practically forgot my hosting manners, but luckily remembered at one point; all he wanted was water. I'm not hungry and neither is he, so the casserole I heated up earlier will have to sit there until we develop an appetite.

I hand him the ice-cold glass of water, and our fingers graze one another as I pass it to him. I shiver in response. Of course, it's not the glass causing this response—oh no, that's due to this man. *Ahh*, I shiver because his skin scorches mine from the sexiness and power he exudes. It's an exciting duality that exists within him. See, he's the sweetest man, but also has this magnetism—I know in the very depths of my being that he's pure alpha male. I can't help but wonder if I'll somehow end up submitting to his every whim.

If he notices my staring and my stupidity of being frozen in place by the brief contact, he doesn't say anything or do anything—*damn!* He starts chugging the water, and I'm watching his Adam's apple work up and down in his delicious throat as he swallows the cool liquid. I'm so transfixed by the display before me.

*How the hell can the sight of him drinking a glass of water be so sexy?*

A small drop of liquid escapes from his mouth and runs down his neck. I'm tightly balling my fists at my sides to resist from reaching out and grabbing him. God, I want to pull him to me to lick off the drop. Ugh, I can't look anymore; it's too much! Hearing a *thunk* as he sets down the glass on my black granite countertop, I turn my head and clear my throat. Out of the corner of my eye, I watch as he wipes his mouth with the back of his hand. I squirm in place as I feel every girly part within me clench.

"So, we never told each other our guilty pleasures," he reminds me in a sexually charged low tone.

I'm assembling the ingredients for nookie-making. *Ugh!* I mean cookie-making. I blow out an exasperated breath. I don't trust myself with speech right now because I'll flub it up again. I opt to reply with a simple "hmm," indicating that I acknowledge what he's saying—I can't fully give an answer as I'm sure you understand.

I hear him laugh softly. Maybe he knows what he's doing to me.

"Okay, mine is a bit cheesy, but I'll go first. My guilty pleasure is binge-watching episodes of *The Golden Girls* every chance I get," he confides.

*Thank you, sweet baby Jesus!* He broke the spell momentarily as I burst out laughing. God, I haven't laughed this hard in so long at the hands of another man besides my awesome boss. Yeah, my kids make me laugh; however, it's not the same thing. They say laughter is the best medicine; well, as a nurse I recommend this type of humor at every opportunity. He keeps the humor going by telling a joke.

"At the risk of mocking my own profession, stop me if you've heard this one…. So, how does an attorney sleep at night?"

*In my bed*, is what I want to say, ha! Clearly I don't say it, biting my lip instead to quell the thoughts. I give him the universal non-committal shrug for not having prior knowledge of the punch line.

He tuts and delivers it effectively, "First he lies on one side, and then he lies on the other."

We begin laughing all over again, and I turn to face him. I have big ole tears rolling down my face that I should be shielding. I'm doubled over, holding my stomach because it hurts so much. In this moment, I want to kiss him more than ever for making me feel things I *should* be feeling as a woman. I need this!

He stares into my eyes, and both of us become silent. I feel like he wants to say something, but he refrains from doing so. Probably because he doesn't think I'll want to hear it. Earlier in the bathroom, I didn't know how to respond to the *beautiful* comment, so I can appreciate his dilemma. His eyes are saying something, and I want to believe they're telling me "I'll never lie to you." God, if he told me again that I'm beautiful, I'd definitely know how to respond this time—except it wouldn't be with words.

He reaches out a tentative hand, and as much as I want to close my eyes to savor whatever he's about to do, I can't close them. I need to watch. I need to burn this into my brain so it's there…forever. He strokes my left cheek with his right hand, moving his thumb back and forth. This small touch feels so good and means the world. It's thrilling having him touch me in any small way. I thought the brush of our fingers on the cup was electrifying to my system, but this takes the cake…or the cookie, I should say.

*Please kiss me. Please kiss me.* I'm willing him to do so.

He continues stroking and explains, "You had some flour on your cheek."

*Oh, is that all?* I want to blow the piece of hair hanging in my face out of the way in a sign of frustration. Gosh, here I was thinking it was something *more*. It felt like something more. He removes his hand from my face and steps back, but doesn't break eye contact with me.

"So, you never said what *your* guilty pleasure is," he says cheekily.

*You!* is what I want to say. Sadly, I'm still a coward.

\*\*\*

*Caleb*

I wanted so badly to tell her my guilty pleasure is *her*. I went for something safe—the TV show—not wanting to spook her. There have been a few times I would bet my life that Liz wanted me to make a move. When our fingers touched on the glass, I wanted so badly to clear the counter and throw her down on it.

Then when I took a drink of my water, I could feel the heat from her gaze watching my every move. I needed to cool down because she had me burning everywhere for her. I had an appetite all right, but it wasn't for food. I wanted to take the ice in my glass, run it along her skin and watch her nipples pucker from the sensation. Doing a wet T-shirt contest with her would be my wet dream.

Finally, I stroked her cheek to test her one more time, I needed an excuse to touch her. Of course, there was no flour on her face—*shh…that's our little secret*. I was delighted when she reacted to me, so I know I'm making progress. I'm still waiting for her to respond to my question; she's been contemplating her response for a long time, and I wish that *I* was her answer.

"Hmm, I guess watching eighties B-rated horror films. Have you ever seen *Motel Hell?* That movie haunts me, but I still scour the internet for it every once in a while," she finally says, merriment laced throughout her confession.

I'm grinning like a fool and shake my head because I've never even heard of the movie.

"Okay, well, you're missing out. We'll have to watch it together some time," she offers, then bites her juicy bottom lip.

And just like that…I'm back in the game!

"Most definitely! I'd like that very much. You just tell me when and where, and I'll be there. I enjoy spending time with you, Liz. You're a remarkable woman," I proclaim.

"Thank you, Caleb. Hearing you say that…I can't tell you how moved I am. I feel so blessed to have so many incredible friends in my life," she says warmly.

*Fuck! Was I just friend-zoned?* I knew it would be a possibility.

I'll table that for now because I'm not giving up that easily. I don't know if she's scared, or if she thinks I'm not interested, or if it's something else entirely. I'm sure the obvious thing would be to come out and ask her, but I get the feeling it's way too soon. For God's sake, I need to keep reminding myself the funeral was only yesterday!

"What's your favorite food?" I sincerely wonder as I smile her way.

"Hmm, I guess I love anything with quinoa. Throw it on a salad, or put it in any dish, and it tastes great. What about you?" She asks innocently.

"I would have to say burgers," I tell her.

Of course, she doesn't know that my preference is *fur burgers*. I'm getting hard thinking about *hers*. And for dessert, hair pie. Yup, a double round of pussy for me, please!

"Ooo yeah, there are some really good burger places in the area. Do you like to eat out a lot?" She asks in turn.

*Oh baby, if you only knew.*

"I do indeed, because why eat in when you can eat out?" I respond.

My words are dripping with sexual references. Although, I'm not sure she has any idea as to exactly what I'm insinuating, and as to what kind of *eating out* I want to do…on her. Fuck, she's innocent and sweet. And it's probably best she doesn't get my meaning because it's all kinds of wrong. Okay, subject-changer time in three, two, one, go!

"Well, Liezel, you ready to show me how to make these famous cookies?" I decide to ask to get my mind on something else.

"Wow, I haven't heard anyone use my full name in so long. I didn't even realize you knew it, to be honest," she replies.

"I know many things about you. Especially your beautiful name," I confess and then roll my eyes in my mind because I went *there* again with flirting. It's easy to do with her, and I'm a damn natural flirt anyway.

"I will tell you my mom had a thing for *The Sound of Music*. One of the Von Trapp kids was named Liezel, just had a different spelling, and so she fell in love with it. I could never really buy into the name, unfortunately. You know what's ironic, though? I go by Liz, and yet I didn't ever shorten William's name. His dad goes by Bill. And I guess giving him a nickname like Will would've been too intimate. I swear sometimes we were more strangers than a married couple," she whispers. Then she stares off, looking somewhere in the distance, clearly seeing something in her mind's eye that I cannot.

She shakes her head as if to clear it and continues, "Sorry about that. I didn't mean to get so personal about my marriage. I've never revealed that to anyone. I don't know why I just did now."

I grab her hand and squeeze it. She looks down at our joined hands, and I tell her, "God, don't be sorry. I can't imagine what you're going through. Just know I'm here. Whatever you want to talk about, I'm here to listen. That extends to the kids as well. I know you have Alexi, but I hope you know you can count on me for anything and everything too." I want to add *forever* to my impassioned speech.

She swallows and finally gazes up into my eyes, and there are tears shimmering in her hypnotic blue gems. I pull her into me without even thinking twice about it. I embrace her and envelop her like I'll never let her go. I can't help myself as I move my right hand into her hair and massage the back of her head. *God, I wish her hair were down so I could stroke her gorgeous locks.*

This will have to be enough for now. I won't push her any further than this. The fact that I get to touch her again in any capacity will have to sustain me. There's so much more I want to tell her. There are so many unspoken things between us, starting with the fact that I'm not going anywhere…ever. It can all wait. I have to hope and believe we'll get there in time.

After a few minutes, she finally pulls away. I can feel a few drops of tears have soaked into my shirt, but they feel amazing against my skin as it's confirmation that she let me hold her.

She clears her throat, wipes her eyes and smiles. "Okay, let's get started!"

*Oh my beautiful woman…I'm ready for this baking lesson, and I hope one day you'll be ready for me.*

# Chapter 7: In the Right Con*text*

*Caleb*

It's Saturday morning, and I'm still thinking about last night with Liz. I woke up super early because I couldn't sleep. We made the most delicious sugar cookies. They practically melted in my mouth. I think I made every erotic sound known to man while devouring her baked goods. They are sinful and seductive like her. I was a good student and thoroughly enjoyed the lesson.

The best part about the whole experience was getting to know more about her and the kids. She told me all about their likes and dislikes, and how their upbringing went. I already knew she was a great mother, but getting to hear about her schooling to become a nurse and raising three children on her own, well, it's a real testament to her strength.

*I think I'm already falling.*

*No, I've already fallen.*

I've fallen hard and fast, and there's no point of return on this one-way ticket to love. I will have to keep these feelings to myself, though—I imagine that will be the case for quite some time.

And my God, she's a dream in the kitchen as well as everywhere else. I love that her home is so warm and inviting. I felt so comfortable there. I can't wait until I'm invited back again. Her place screams of everything soothing and generous in the world. The soft tan tones of the patterned backsplash against the dark black granite counters made me want to sit down and never leave. Her kitchen island must get a lot of love and attention, and I want to be there to cook meals with her and watch her busy herself doing even the most mundane of tasks. Those small domestic actions will be more meaningful to me than anything I've done in my life.

Fuck, my heart broke for her when she mentioned her marriage being so cold and distant. It was hard for me to know how to react because

I've never had to deal with emotions of this magnitude. That's why I want to show her how it can be between *us*, and ultimately how it can be when a real man appreciates her and knows her worth.

We didn't make plans to see each other again, but I'm about to remedy that. I didn't want to overwhelm her last night and push my luck. But since she mentioned watching that horror movie, I fully intend to put a plan into place. We did, however, exchange numbers, and I made her promise to call me anytime, especially whenever she needs help with a project.

As I sit here at my breakfast bar in my kitchen drinking my energy drink and vaping—I vape when I'm anxious because somehow the flavor settles me—I'm warring with myself over one thing.

*To call or text, that is the question. Hmm.*

I chose vanilla flavor juice—for obvious reasons—as I blow out the vapor in a huge plume of smoke. It soothes me while sitting weighted on my tongue and reminding me of last night. It's a poor substitute for anything resembling her, but it will have to do.

I hold my cell in my hand, and I'm about to push unlock. I think I'll go with a text for starters. A text is harmless and innocent enough, and she can choose to respond or not. Sure, she can do the same with a phone call—accept or deny—yet, the text keeps it more casual and light. I'm not a pussy! I'm not afraid to call her. More than anything I want to hear her captivating voice come across the line. But, what keeps coming back to me is that I need to take baby steps.

Another thing niggling at me is the fact that I should be working on my cases; one in particular needs my attention. I thought the damn thing was settled last year when I went to New York City to meet with my client, but oh how wrong I was. That's actually the same weekend I met Gil's fiancée, Addison. It's interesting how things have changed in a year.

Anyway, this client's divorce has been long and drawn-out, more so than most, and a messy one at that. The players involved are high-profile and require my dedication. My client, Mrs. Yvette Price, is taking on her filthy-rich, unfaithful husband, Darron Price—yeah, there's a price in this, all right.

Mrs. Price is the kind of woman with the highest pedigree, one who runs in the most elite circles. She is contending that her husband had relations with his secretary. These cases can be rather sticky, and I wish I would have had this wrapped up months ago, but recently they're contesting everything.

Her perfectly manicured hands, superb style of dress and accessories, olive skin, and impeccable facelift would never betray her age. I know from her file that she's forty-eight years old, but honestly she could probably pass for mid-thirties. Her expertly arched brows always look waxed to their finest, and her dark eyes complement her dark hair. There's no interest on my end, though. I cringe when I see or talk to her these days.

Darron runs a successful real estate company. He's the mogul of the New York City market, and anybody who's anybody seeks his company's talent when acquiring property. You would think I'd be nervous handling this divorce because of their marital assets, but I'm not. This is where I usually shine because money doesn't intimidate me; it never has and it never will. That's not what motivates me in life, unlike most people.

I never let my personal life interfere with my career but in this instance, Liz occupies every thought and action, so I'm shit for working at present.

My law firm would certainly not appreciate my lack of concentration; they'll have to get over it because I've made Goldberg & Barrish a more lucrative and profitable business since my joining. The Philadelphia-based firm specializes in domestic litigation, and I expect to make partner in the near future. If I don't get my act together as of late, then that prospect won't ever come to fruition.

At one point during law school when I settled on what form I wanted to practice, I couldn't help but feel I was led to this path because I felt my parents should have gotten divorced. I like to help people take that next step in their life to move on from damaged and broken relationships. Sometimes it just doesn't work no matter how hard you try. I get why some people stay together, but happiness is just as important as the plethora of excuses I've heard over the years from those I fight for—believe me, I've heard them all: financial, legal, convenience, kids, loneliness, abuse, and so forth.

I would have been in Liz's corner had she ever attempted to divorce that lowlife. I know Alexi would have referred her to me had the opportunity presented itself. I never judge—okay, you should laugh at that pun given my profession—but seriously, I try to be understanding and open-minded about situations. I somewhat understood before why she didn't divorce him, but more and more of the pieces are falling into place of the puzzle that is her life. And, boy, it's a beautiful life despite being touched by pain and sadness.

I finally unlock my phone and start to type out what I want to say. Again, I'll keep it casual so I don't exert too much pressure. I key in the following:

> *Morning sweetness! You and the kids game for movie night at my place? Motel Hell safe for them to watch? I'll cook dinner as an added bonus. By the way...I'm still thinking about*

*your cookies ;)*

Okay, sue me for saying I'd keep it casual. Look, I had to get a little flirty. I'm a fucking dude! It's pretty much encoded in our DNA.

I'll sit here and wait for a reply as long as it takes. *God, I hope she comes over!*

\*\*\*

*Liezel*

*Oh my God, I'm going to come soon!*

I have my fingers working feverishly on my clit as I'm so close to shooting off into space. The only thing in my mind about to bring me to the best orgasm I've ever given myself is envisioning Caleb. His sexy face and perfect body have me right there on the edge. I've become a master at pleasuring myself since I've resorted to that route for the last twelve years. I've always used celebrities for my material, or inspiration, I should say, but not today—today I have an image better than all the actors in Hollywood.

I haven't masturbated in weeks. This is what I need to help alleviate my stress. God, I would kill to have the real thing, though. I still feel ashamed for lusting after someone that's possibly too young for me. He said he'll be thirty-five in September, so at least there's just the ten year difference. I realize that number should not mean a hill of beans at our respective stages of life, but somehow I feel it does. I've already *been there, done that*—shouldn't he just be beginning that part of his life? Why would he want someone like me? Wouldn't he think he'd be saddled with too many problems?

Okay, I talk too much even in my own mind. I'm starting to slip further away from reaching the edge where I'll tip over into ecstasy. A climax was imminent until I had to go do that self-deprecating thing I do so well. I know men don't find low self-esteem sexy and tend to respond to more confident women; it's something I clearly need to work on.

So, I'll put all my worries, fears, apprehensions, and embarrassment to the back of my mind and start small by trying to be confident in my fantasies. For now, this will have to suffice. Because in this fantasy, Caleb wants me the way I want him. In this fantasy, Caleb is very much here and making me burn hotter than I've ever been in my life. In this world, he's rubbing my nipples and pinching my clit to the point I'm moaning so loud that I thank God I'm home alone.

As I continue to work myself and finger my slick channel, Caleb's scent washes over me. I relive him being in my house last night and being near him. The delicious cologne he wore smelled like sin. I wanted to rub him all over my body like a loofah. I'm trembling from the feelings of passion swirling around in my body, centering right in my very core.

Normally I need some type of lubricant to aid me in my quest for release. This isn't the case with that god invading my mind and overtaking my body as if he were standing before me. I'm soaking wet, and if he were here, I'd drench his shaft easily with all my juices. I lift my finger to my mouth and suck on it, tasting myself. I wish he was licking me, sucking my flesh and tasting my cum—I rarely taste myself, but I'm so lost in the moment.

I'm quivering because I know his naked body will be magnificent commanding mine to do his bidding. I want so badly to touch him, taste him, hear him, feel him. He engages all my senses and turns me into a trembling mess of ecstasy.

While I continue to rub at the nub of nerves with my right hand, I pinch one of my nipples with my left hand. I bend my knees and open myself a little wider so I can feel every sensation. There's nothing better than that sensation of fullness and being stretched out over someone's cock. I desperately want Caleb to fill that void in more ways than one.

I concentrate once again on his image and picture him moving over me in the most delicious rhythmic motion. I imagine him satisfying me the way I know he can. I rasp out his name when the images overwhelm me, and I finally come with a shudder in an explosive rush. My heart is racing with the speed of a thousand galloping horses, and that telltale sign of euphoria invades every crevice in my body and brain.

I lie there practically passed out on my bed. I'm spent. I don't know how that's possible when the deed was done by my own hand, yet I know why, and that it is, in fact, possible. Caleb is a talented man, and he doesn't even have to physically be here. The fact that he even walks the earth is enough to shoot beams of horniness to parts of me I didn't even know I could experience.

Surely, Caleb will be the most generous lover. I know that if he gave me a chance for even one night of passion, it would be glorious, like the linking of two souls. I'm a little rusty in that department, but it's like riding a bike—I don't even think I'll need the training wheels.

*Am I really trying to convince myself that I have a chance with him?* Or really the question should be, *am I going to try to make a move on Caleb?*

Yes, I guess I am—yes to both questions.

I'm a grown woman and can do what I want. Wow, I didn't even cringe that time when I thought about how much of a *grown* woman I am. Maybe this whole thing will work, and I'll be able to accept that I'm older and that it's no big deal.

My heart finally calms, and I close my eyes and breathe deeply. It feels so good to take control of my life and have a clear direction to head. Caleb gave me his number last night, and I'm so tempted to use it. I told myself I'd only reach out to him if I was desperate and needed help with something. Now…well, now I'm desperate for something, and it's a project of a delicate nature.

I actually have the blackout curtains pulled back for once, and light is streaming in and warms me. I can clearly see the owls all around the room, and my space seems more lively and vibrant. I changed my sheets and comforter last night to a cheery patterned white set. I realize the white represents purity and innocence, but to me it also represents a new beginning of sorts.

"Caleb can be my new beginning," I say aloud.

I open my eyes and turn my head to look at my phone sitting on the nightstand. I'm going to pick it up and text him. I'm too chickenshit to call, even with my newfound bravery. I reach for it, and as I pull my arm back to look at the screen, I hear it chime as it vibrates against my skin to indicate I have an incoming message.

I look at the screen, and the biggest grin crosses my face. It's a text from the man himself. Now I have to think of a flirtatious reply. He mentioned my cookies; well, I'll let him take a bite!

# Chapter 8: You Forgot the "R"

*Caleb*

Hot damn! Her reply came fast. I wasn't expecting that, but it's the most welcome thing knowing she's holding the phone at the same time. Is that some corny shit or what?

> *The kids don't come home until tonight. I promised them some MT. That means mom time, LOL. Raincheck for the kids, but I'm available this afternoon if we can do it then? And you can taste my cookies anytime you'd like ;)*

M. O. T. H. E. R. F. U. C. K. E. R!

If she's teasing me, well, she truly is the queen of it. My balls tighten up painfully at the thought of tasting anything on her. My dick is twitching so much in my pants, it's probably wagging like a damn dog's tail. I close my eyes to take a minute to collect myself.

I love that she's flirting. This is what I needed to know. There were those few times last night I thought there could be something, so this confirms it. I'm looking forward to being alone with her again, but of course it would have been fun with the kids. I hope there are plenty of opportunities in the future for a more family-oriented visit.

I realize I haven't responded. I scold myself by doing an internal tongue-lashing for being an idiot in keeping her waiting. My fingers move across the screen, but my hands are sweaty, making the damn screen protector even more slippery. I high-five myself as I hit send for being such a smooth operator.

> *Whatever flavor you give me, I'll try. Look forward to seeing you. Noon work? I'll make lunch. I know my place can be a pain to get to given the traffic. Pick you up, or you want to*

*drive here?*

I'm hoping she'll want me to pick her up, but I also want to present her with an easy *out* in case it's a comfort thing to come on her own. I see the dots moving on the screen, so I know she's writing something.

> *I'll come there if you don't mind. I'm used to driving in city traffic, silly. Remember, Alexi didn't always have his own practice, LOL.*

Ah, yes, she got me there. She's probably just as familiar with the ins and outs of Philadelphia as I am.

> *How easily I forget, that's not like me. Something must have bewitched me. Think there's a cure for that? My address is 25801 Marketing Street, 14th floor, Apt. 2. I have a guest parking spot in basement, No. 36. Drive safe, Betty Cocker!*

I'm waiting to see if she says anything else, and while I'm waiting, I reread my text. *Oh shit!* I forgot an "r," didn't I? *Yeah, some smooth operator I am.* I feel like a jackass, and that wasn't any type of Freudian slip of the fingers. I'm really worried I crossed a line when she doesn't immediately reply. But finally it arrives.

She uses the laughing emoji and the letters "LOL." I blow out a grateful breath and realize she took it the best way. I don't deserve her.

*Is it possible to fall more in love with someone over a text?*

Lunch can't come soon enough. I have to figure out something quick and simple to make. It's only nine o'clock, so I still have time to run somewhere; yeah, that's what I'll do. Three hours till show time!

\*\*\*

*Liezel*

When I arrive, I can't help but admire the building. I love how the glass on the outside glistens in the sun; you wouldn't think it's such a chilly day out. I'm nervous as hell as I head into the basement and park my car in spot thirty-six like he instructed.

I'm trying not to focus too hard on the source of my nerves. I get out of my car and head toward the elevators to go up to the lobby. Upon arrival, the doorman gives me a friendly greeting. The man has a kind, warm face with trusting eyes, and I relax marginally. Clearly, he's expecting me as he directs me to the next bank of elevators to go up to the fourteenth floor to Caleb's apartment.

As I'm ascending, I'm once again thinking about how it's such a lovely building I'm in—I'm employing a distraction tactic, of course. Even though I've driven in the area plenty of times on my way to the University Hospital of South Philadelphia when I worked there with Alexi, I never really noticed this high-rise structure.

I clutch the strap to my shoulder bag more tightly as I become nervous again. When I masturbated a few hours ago, I was revved up and ready to go make my move on him. Now that I'm so close to making that final lap, it's intimidating. Thinking about doing something and actually doing it are two entirely different things.

The elevator chime sounds, and I walk out. I take two steps and freeze. I fidget and pull at my jacket, trying to decide if what I'm wearing is attractive enough. I smooth out the nonexistent wrinkles on my shirt. I purposely left my hair down to give a different look today. I run my fingers through it. I don't need it as a shield—well, maybe he'll need it as a shield from me. I so want to attack him on sight, but I'll restrain myself...*are you tired yet of the back and forth with my emotions?* Yeah, me too.

I'm wearing my favorite pair of dark-washed skinny jeans. I feel sexy in them, and they make my ass look fabulous. I have on my adorable brown ankle boots that have a cute design with studs on the strap that run up the sides. I'm also sporting a cotton V-neck long-sleeved top. It's a nice royal blue shade that brings out my eyes.

My black pea coat gives me a sophisticated edge, I think, but I still believe I look youthful. I'm wearing a white infinity scarf decked out with brightly-colored cartoonish owls—okay, I realize I'm probably going into the category of *too youthful* on this one, but I love scarves, and ya know I love my owls. I borrowed this one from Leah. I'm lucky she's my buddy and doesn't mind sharing, and I gladly reciprocate with my wardrobe.

I decide it's now or never, so I make my body move—I like to be prompt. As I round the corner to his apartment door, I glance at the silver watch on my left wrist and realize it's noon on the dot. I shake out my remaining jitters and rap three times on the door in quick succession. I'm telling my heart to stop pounding, but it has a mind of its own—surely Caleb can hear it on the other side of the door.

I pick up on movement as locks are turning, and then the handle jangles. He wrenches the door open with—dare I say—enthusiasm. At first, I look down at the floor, then slowly work my way up his figure until I get to his gorgeous face. My skin immediately heats, and I'm going to sweat through my jacket if I don't take it off soon. He isn't wearing shoes, and his white socks suggest he's comfortable and inviting. I sigh with relief. The sock thing is adorable. But now I'm worrying this is a friend-thing and not a potential passion-thing.

*Stop it,* I scold myself.

His text was flirty, so I'm going to roll with it. He's donning a pair of jeans too, but his look well-worn and loose-fitting—they must be his favorite pair. The last piece of clothing is a black fitted T-shirt, which stretches nicely across his broad chest and shows off his muscular arms. *Yup, getting really hot in here.* But the final element that completes the look is his glasses. I had no idea he wore glasses…and, oh my God, yum!

Ladies, this man can wear glasses. It's like seeing Clark Kent, but somehow Clark is hotter than the man with the big "S" on his costume. However, there's a letter Caleb should wear, and it would be "C"—surely you realize the big "C" doesn't stand for Caleb, ha ha.

He's grinning ear to ear, and I'm about to melt on the floor before I even make it inside. I clear my throat and start pulling at my jacket.

"Liz, you look stunning," he says in a rush. Then he continues, "Please come in. Let me take your coat."

"Thank you," I say as I slip my jacket off and hand it to him.

He hangs it up on the wall hook. I set my purse down on his entryway table as he closes the door. Then, I unwind the scarf from around my neck and set that down with my purse as well. I hear him chuckle at the sight of the owls. Finally, I hike up my sleeves to make them three-quarter length, giving more skin a chance to breathe.

"Are you comfortable?" He asks, genuinely bemused by my flustered state.

"Oh, yes, sorry. I'm fine, thanks. Just a little warm. Your building is phenomenal. I love the architecture. Mind if I take my shoes off? If you're going shoeless, then I suppose it's only fair," I giggle.

"I wouldn't have it any other way. Take off whatever you need to," he says with a scorching gaze.

Now I'm completely aroused. *How does he do that?* I don't know how he manages to drench my panties in a split second. I've never seen anything like it, and he's not even freaking trying!

I unzip my boots and pull them off, then place them under the table by my purse. He gestures for me to have a seat on his couch. I sit while he stands. I love his place. He has the perfect city view, and the entire wall of windows is the kind of glass that's tinted so you don't need curtains. It appears he has bamboo flooring, and the gray couches with blue accent pillows are such a nice contrast. The walls are white, which I love, because everything looks clean and fresh and so open.

"Wow, I love your apartment," I gush in wonderment as I look left and right and marvel at the area.

"Well, let me give you the grand tour," he says cheekily.

I pop up from my seat and dutifully follow him around for a thorough tour. I even saw his bedroom—I didn't show him mine, so I was surprised when he showed me his. I couldn't get over the painting in his bedroom. That seascape is to die for.

*I wish I could be there with Caleb inside that painting,* I remark only to myself.

He catches me staring at it. After a few minutes, we move on to the rest of the rooms. Once we're done with the tour, we end up in the kitchen, and I sit down at his breakfast bar.

"So, can I help with anything?" I ask sweetly as he makes his way over to the stove.

"No, thanks. You just sit your gorgeous self down and relax, and let me take care of everything. The food's actually done; I was just keeping it warm," he explains.

He offers me a beverage, but I decline for now, opting to wait until we're ready to eat. I glance over at the crock pot sitting to the side of the stove and wonder what he made.

"I take it you made something in the *cock* pot?" I ask.

And then I'm sure a look of terror and humiliation crosses my face as he stands there open-mouthed at my question.

*Oh my freaking God!*

I did it again with misspeaking. I forgot the dang "r." You would think that with him doing that earlier in his text, I could have avoided that potential pitfall. He shows me mercy and starts laughing so hard. I burst out laughing too, and for the second time I've laughed harder in two days than I've done in years.

This friendship and attraction are becoming addictive too quickly. It's no secret that I desire him, but I'm enjoying being with him as a friend. It's unbelievable to have both things with someone. This man is so magnificent, and I can't keep saying it enough. If I didn't know any better, I'd say I'm falling for him.

*That's absolutely ridiculous, and absurd, and unheard of to have developed feelings so soon,* I remind myself.

Plus, let's not forget the fact I recently stuffed my husband's ashes in the closet. Ugh, now my laughter has left me. Anytime I think of William, I'm immediately brought down; he still haunts me and rules my mood somehow, even from his resting place.

Caleb takes off his glasses to rub at his eyes since his lashes are coated in tears from laughing so hard. Then, he examines his glasses with a shocked look.

"What's wrong?" I question, thinking there has to be something to cause him visible distress.

"I can't believe I'm still wearing my glasses. I never leave them on. No one ever sees me in them. Clearly you're special, Liz Carter. And evidently I'm very distracted these days," he admits more to himself than to me.

My breath hitches at his words. He puts his hands on the counter of his kitchen island and stares at me, as I'm sitting across the way at his breakfast bar. We hold each other's gazes in an electric storm. You can practically see the currents moving back and forth between us. I don't say or move for fear of being zapped.

He breaks it first by shaking his head as if to snap out of it, then turns back to the stove to tend to his cooking. I bite my lower lip, wishing he'd walk over to me and attack me already.

*God, I want him to throw me down on the counter, or the floor, or anywhere— pick a damn surface!*

I need him. But the moment has passed us by. It's okay, though. I guess I can always make the first move—I don't do it right now, but maybe I can work up to it later.

"Touché by the way on the 'cock pot' comment. You're too much, you know that?" He conveys in an amused tone while arching a well-groomed, although manly, brow.

"I didn't mean to say it. It just came out," I plead.

"Sure it did," he replies with a wink.

A wink, I got another wink from him—that's like his third! I could never pull off a wink, but this guy right here can pull off anything. I hike up my sleeves a little more—this damn thing will be a tank top soon enough at this rate. How did I think I could survive him? I can't even make it through the first fifteen minutes of being here.

As he sets out silverware and the plates for our meal, I still can't believe I'm at his place—in socks, no less, just hanging out. I also can't believe he's never worn glasses in front of anyone before. He's so foxy in them that he should never be ashamed to wear those bad boys. Better yet, I hope he doesn't show anyone else because I love that I'm the only one. It's idiotic that such a small thing makes me feel special, but it does. I especially don't want any other woman to see him like this.

We eat our meal, chatting and laughing away in his kitchen. We both chose water to drink, and he served us salad, grilled chicken with mixed vegetables, and quinoa—he remembered my quinoa! I appreciate that this is a delicious, healthy meal. I would have eaten it anyway to be polite, but obviously he takes care of his body like I do. So, it's yet another thing we have in common and can both respect about one another.

We finish our meal, and I help him tidy up. I can feel his eyes on me the whole time, and I give him side-eye every now and then. I'm trying not to be too transparent about it. It feels so good to do the flirting thing since it's been ages for me. I thought I'd be terrible, but it turns out I'm pretty good at it.

We head over to his couch and plop down. We're at opposite ends, and I cross my legs, sitting primly. He throws his legs up on the couch which he stretches out near me in challenge. I wasn't expecting things to be so laidback like this. I return the challenge and mimic his position. I'm way too comfortable now, but I suppose that's the idea.

He smirks and says, "Now that's more like it."

I flex my legs and feet, and it does feel damn good to stretch out. I don't always get to do this because I'm up and down getting stuff for the kids, or at work, or doing things around the house. This is nice, and so very much needed.

He lifts up my left foot and starts massaging it. At first I'm startled, but he playfully pinches my big toe in an effort to tell me, "Don't protest and just enjoy." I acquiesce to his powerful, manly hands, letting him do as he pleases.

*Holy crap!* It feels unbelievable. He has an incredible kneading technique and expertly exerts the right amount of pressure and tenderness to the right spots—what a talent! I'm moaning loudly, and I don't care. After a few minutes, he puts my foot down and switches to the other one. It starts all over again, resulting in more moaning, and I'm not embarrassed because it feels too damn good. I close my eyes and let every sensation seep into my body. He is taking such good care of me. I didn't even have to ask him; he's doing it on his own. I want to cry because it's hard to accept that this beautiful man is being the way he is with me.

He finally releases my foot and squeezes my leg. I slowly open my eyes, and he's looking at me, smiling so serenely. I gaze at him with that dreamy-eyed look.

"Okay sweetness, I'm prepared now to be dazzled by the amazing cinematography that is *Motel Hell*," he declares.

I want to groan because now I'm rethinking the movie choice and wondering if it's too late to switch to porn.

# Chapter 9: A Case of Virgo

*Caleb*

We're about thirty minutes into watching the film. Every now and then I brush up against her legs with my feet or hands. I haven't massaged her again, but of course I want to. I wanted to keep massaging my way up until I reached the juncture of her thighs where I could really get to know her better.

So far, I've kept the promise I made to myself to be as patient as I can be. I have no doubt now that she wants me as much as I want her. I can easily turn her on, and she does the same to me. I want this friendship to continue to blossom a little more before I go all in—*two days of friendship does not equal any type of relationship*. Besides, I don't want her to feel that a romp in the sheets is my version of valuing and respecting her as a woman.

*There's something between us, though.*

She looks delectable in her outfit. Her long legs have those skin-tight pants hugging every curve. Her ass is something I want to take a bite out of. It's such a tease—and one I brought on myself—every time she moves, knowing I'm just going to sit here and do nothing about it. When she let me massage her feet, there was such acceptance, trust, and gratefulness on her end. It only strengthened my resolve to want to take my time with her. We'll have plenty of chances to get to passion and ecstasy. Liz was robbed of such a level of intimacy during her marriage—I will give her all of it and not fail her.

The movie is an interesting choice and not one I expected her to like. I can see why she finds it appealing. The fact that this psycho farmer in the film is planting people in the ground to harvest them, is an equally intriguing and disturbing plot twist. The noises the captives buried in the ground make, though, will torment me for years to come. It's almost like that sound the creepy ghost chick makes in *The Grudge*—another terribly awesome movie.

I still have to think of how to broach the subject of Brent's wedding and wanting her as my date. I also think I'm going to talk to Alexi and devise a plan for us all to get together at one of our favorite restaurants called *Tai-Phoon*. It used to be the place where Alexi, Anthony, Gil, and I would frequent; now it's a place for our entire family. I definitely consider our group a family, and it's remarkable how it's expanded the last couple of years.

Dare I admit that I have another dorky side to me that not everyone knows? Besides being intelligent, good with computers, and possessing a certain magnetism with clients, I actually check out the daily horoscopes. Dork or not—I'll let you decide. I never really gave it much thought before today; I've read them over the years for shits and giggles. This morning while I was waiting for my coffee to brew—because, believe it or not, I don't do the one-cup contraption thing—I wandered over to the app on my phone to see what today would bring.

Liz told me her birthday is April 16th, which will be here in less than two months. So, I know Aries are typically go-getters; she possesses that spirit, and it's evident in the way she takes care of her family. The element symbol commonly associated with her zodiac sign is fire. I'm not surprised by this considering she's a burning ball of energy and scorches me with just a look.

With my birthday falling on September 19th, I happen to be a Virgo. We tend to have a sense of duty and operate under efficiency. My element is earth. I still have a hard time understanding the difference or relationship between zodiac, astrological, and elemental signs and whatnot, but I imagine there's some truth to it all.

As I think back to the passage about her sign I perused earlier, her horoscope read as follows:

> *Aries*
> *You're feeling light today, and surprises will arrive this afternoon. Tonight, you'll be in a euphoric mood as the moon illuminates a sector of your chart that rules home and family.*
> *Your lucky number is 10.*

Then, when I looked at mine, it was kismet. It read as such:

> *Virgo*
> *Your focus should be on work most of the day, but as the moon travels, this evening will bring light to the friendship sector. It will also bring exciting plans for the future and cause you to dream up new opportunities.*

*Your lucky number is 5.*

This morning these passages didn't really align and make sense, but now, thinking back, there has to be a shift going on. It's all pointing to one thing…Liz and I are meant to be, and that I should stay on this path and see where it leads.

I didn't realize the movie is over as the credits roll across the screen. I was lost in thought all this time, and seventy minutes flew by in the blink of an eye. I turn my head to look at Liz, and she's peacefully asleep on my couch as if she's always been here with me. God, she looks so fucking beautiful, it's making my chest ache. Her soft snores are adorable.

Her one arm is propped behind her head, and the other is positioned comfortably across her body. A piece of hair has fallen upon her face, and I'd really have to stretch across her to tuck it back behind her ear. So, I'll leave that wayward tendril alone—kind of like I'll leave her alone, but all I want to do is touch. I want to touch so badly that I may go insane.

Her hair is alluring since she left it down today. I flex my fingers, which are tingling to reach out and take what's mine. There are no two ways about it—she is mine in every way possible, and there's no convincing me otherwise by anyone or anything. I'm going to have to jack off for hours in order to alleviate some of this pent-up need and desire.

I let her sleep for a little bit longer and just watch. She has the most captivating features even in sleep. I imagine she's exhausted—mentally, emotionally, and physically drained. After all, she's been through hell and back over the years trying to hold on to her family at all costs.

After some inner debate, I finally decide it's time to wake her up. She said the kids are coming back tonight, but I don't exactly know what time that will be. I gently shake her, and she yawns and stretches out her slim form. Then she suddenly realizes where she is as she's startled fully awake. She jolts and sits up, and all it does is make her breasts jiggle practically in my face, and I groan to myself.

I swing my legs over to the floor. I grab her hand in mine, and she looks at me sheepishly and pulls it away. I try not to act hurt, but it stings.

"Sorry about that. Gosh, I didn't even realize I was tired," she confesses and pulls her sleeves down from the spot they were at on her elbow; I guess she's not hot anymore—*damn!*

"Please don't be sorry. Clearly, you needed it. I didn't have the heart to wake you sooner, but it's about four o'clock now. You didn't say what time the kids are coming home, and I know you'd be mad at yourself if you weren't there to greet them. Believe me, I'd want nothing more than for you to stay, but your priority is Tyler, Kurt, and Leah," I convey meaningfully.

I was so glad I got to watch over her while she slept. I felt like her

[57]

protector. It seems natural to serve in this capacity for her. Maybe some people aren't content sitting here with someone watching them sleep, but I am and would do it any day, at any time.

She does one more stretch, and I watch her beautiful blue eyes search mine as she swings her feet over too and faces me.

"You're so thoughtful and sweet. I wish I could stay as well. You're absolutely right…I want to be home with the kids tonight. They need me. I appreciate your understanding because the truth is, I need them too. It's always been the four of us. I had fun today, though, thank you. You spoiled me with a delicious meal and an even more delicious foot rub. Is there anything I can do to return the favor?" She asks, all the while beaming with a Cheshire Cat-like look.

Fuck me, she has the most sensual mouth. I think I just creamed my pants. My thoughts are dirty and wicked as I conjure all kinds of things that would surely curl her enticing blonde hair. I long for the day when I'll have her in my bed—beneath me, above me, in front of me. I want to see her writhing with desire and uninhibited. *All in due time*, I remind myself.

I rub at my scruff-lined chin in a mischievous way, letting her know just how dark my thoughts are running. Her pupils dilate. Oh yeah, she's picking up what I'm putting down. I can't respond…not yet. I need this time to figure out how I want to proceed because I can't very well tell her what I yearn for most. I know she'll probably be a naughty minx between the sheets, but as I've said—and will keep repeating to myself so I don't renege on my word—*we're not going there yet.*

I give her a saucy grin with my *favor* in mind, "Another date then?"

"Is that what this was?" She asks in part hope and part disbelief.

"I'd like to think so," I offer in affirmation.

She fidgets slightly and tucks her hair behind her ear, baring that delicate expanse of skin at her neck to me. She has the most slender and glorious throat. The column of her neck even turns me on, making me think devilish and dastardly thoughts.

*Fuck, she'll look splendid taking my dick deep all the way to the back of her throat.* I'll be holding her hair in place so it doesn't obstruct my view. After all, I need to watch the show.

"Okay then. Another date it is. I'll call you so we can set something up," she replies.

It almost feels like a brush-off, but I somewhat expected this. I probably spooked her. At least she said *yes* to another one and recognized that today was a date; that's a start. I firmly believe if she didn't want to see me again in that respect, then she wouldn't have agreed to another.

"That sounds great. I look forward to the next time I hear from you. Thanks for coming over, and please know you're welcome here anytime. It's been the best day." I grab her hand and squeeze it.

She pulls hers out from mine. I think she's giving me the brush-off again with refusing my hand, but instead grabs mine in return for a reciprocal squeeze. I love that she sometimes surprises me. I don't mind the hot and cold with her either. I have her burning one moment, and then the next it's like I dumped a bucket of ice on her. I'll keep saying it until I'm blue in the face, *I get it*. This is uncharted territory for her—I lump myself into that category too since I've never tried so hard with a woman.

She stands up to leave and puts her boots back on, her scarf in place, and I retrieve her coat. I help her get into her jacket, then she reaches for her purse and places it on her shoulder. I open the front door for her, and she walks out, but turns back around.

I'm looming in the doorway propped up against the frame because, as much as I don't want to see her walk away, I certainly don't mind watching her fine behind make an exit down the hall.

She leans into me, and I don't move for fear of spooking her in some way again. She kisses my cheek and lingers, and as she pulls away I turn my head quickly enough to catch the corner of her lips on mine. *Fuck, I want more.* Her taste and scent is lethal enough with just that morsel of a peck.

"Until next time…see you later, alligator," she says and spins around, leaving me with a hint of her floral scent.

I see what she did there, though. She opened it up for the perfect reply. She's a devilishly clever woman.

"In a while, *cocodile*," I remark withholding the "r," of course.

I hear her tinkling laughter echo down the hallway, and I wait to shut my door until she disappears from sight. I'll definitely be texting her later to make sure she got home all right. I'm ever a gentleman. I'll remind you, I'm the *sweet one*, but sweet ones can sometimes turn spicy…. Bring on the heat!

# Chapter 10: The Sweetest Torture

*Liezel*

I got home right before the kids arrived. Boy, did I miss them. I know it was only one night they were away, but they're my life. William's parents didn't even come to the door; I shouldn't have expected anything different. They refused to come back here, even after the funeral. We've got years of bad blood. I'm as cordial as I can be—I can't say the same for them. I'm grateful they love their grandchildren, but they think of me as a demon sent straight from hell.

I'm in the kitchen getting snacks together for the kids and me. I take the mom thing very seriously no matter how old they get. I don't spoil them; they pick up after themselves and are respectful in their independence. It's just, I still like being their caregiver since it always brings me comfort. I, of course, will accept the day when they each spread their wings and go off to college or whatever they want to pursue—for now, I can live in my bubble space of knowing they're with me.

I have a feeling Kurt will go into the military after high school. Not sure which branch he'll choose, though. He has really taken a liking to Brent—he's a Master Sergeant in the Air Force. That man is a hero in my book, having been deployed numerous times and serving for seventeen years. I know my kids need a man like him in their lives.

I'm in awe of the fact they have so many positive male figures. Since our circle of friends has grown, my kids have been exposed to the many successful men and women who make up the couples of our group. Before Anthony, Gil, and Alexi found their soul mates, I never hung out with any of them.

A wave of failure hits me right in the heart as I think of how I—no, how William—let them down in the family department. I typically blame myself only because I'm the one who went and married the damn man! However, I have to always stop and remind myself I wouldn't have these kids if I didn't end up with my late husband.

*God, Liz, let go of this crap already! You're being pathetic*, I scream at myself.

I finish assembling the snacks and start getting together drinks. I can't wait for better weather so the kids and I can do more outdoorsy stuff. I'm going to have cabin fever if this is a long winter; obviously I'm praying for an early spring. Because of the cold, we'll have to stay in tonight—even the patio heaters aren't enough in this weather. It will either have to be board games, or maybe we'll watch a movie, especially since I missed movie time earlier with Caleb.

I can't believe I fell asleep on him. It was my prime chance to talk to him or even sit there and gaze at his figure. I got cold feet—hard to believe with the foot massage—but seriously, the expression applies. I chickened out the few times he made a move. You wouldn't think I was such a brazen creature this morning in my bedroom given the opposite behavior I displayed this afternoon—my morning was a solo thing, though, so it was easy to get lost in a fantasy.

Good Lord, did that man's lips feel good as they quickly slid against mine when I gave him a kiss goodbye on the cheek. I can't wait to feel the real thing; that was only a little kernel, but I want the whole bowl of popcorn! I know eventually I'll work my way up to the big moment—I hope he'll still be around. Life is too short not to go for what you want.

I know you must think I'm going bonkers for overanalyzing every little detail and being so wishy-washy. If you've experienced what I have recently, you'd understand I'm in a fragile state. Hell, being a nurse I can recognize the fragility even in myself.

That's the whole thing, though. *I know I have to nurse myself back to where I need to be.* Sure, it wouldn't hurt to have Caleb help in the process, but he's not the end-all solution…*I am.* I have to do this for myself.

"Mom! You coming?" Leah calls from the living room.

"Yeah, sweetheart, I'll be right there," I yell back.

I run the snacks to the kids, then Tyler returns with me to the kitchen to help grab the drinks. He gives me a hug, and in true Tyler form tells me I'm *beautiful*. I pat his cheek and give him a kiss on the forehead.

"And you're my handsome guy. I love you buddy," I tell him and give him my warmest, most motherly smile—he always makes me smile.

As I head back out to the living room, I realize I forgot something. I tell them to give me another minute because I want to throw a lemon in my water—gotta keep those kidneys in working order. As I enter the kitchen, my phone buzzes in my pants pocket. I pull it out and look at the screen, and I'm elated to see what it says and who it's from.

*Hey sweetness! I wanted to make sure you got home safely. Thanks again for today. I look forward to the next time. Say hi to the kids for me and have a good night. BTW, you're an amazing mother.*

I type out a quick reply thanking him and letting him know I'm home safe and sound. I don't give any hint of getting together soon. So, whether it's right or wrong, I'm going to let this heat between us simmer for a few days and see if it has any staying power. When I eventually reach out to him again, and if he's still interested, then maybe I can let my heart unfurl a little more. Otherwise, that bitch is locked up tight until further notice—I have to protect my heart in all this, or I won't survive.

I want so badly to trust a man again and let him into my life. I believe Caleb can be that man. I've already admitted that I'm practically falling in love with him—as unrealistic as it may seem to outsiders looking in. I have to stop second-guessing myself at every turn and go with my gut. Maybe in a few days my worries will have dissipated.

I need to put everything in my mind to the side. My focus right now is my kids, and that's why I also need to tread carefully no matter which path—and no matter with who—that may entail. I walk out to my living room, smiling for my troupers. They're the best thing that ever happened to me in life!

*** 

*Caleb*

Liz's hands are running up and down my pectorals as she's straddling my lap. We're on my bed, and I'm witnessing the most erotic show I've ever seen. I feel like a fucking ringmaster trying to tame my cougar. You have ringside seats along with me for this wild ride. But if a clown pops out from somewhere, then I'm out—those fuckers terrify me!

Anyway, let's get back on track here. Her eyes are hungry, and mine are just as greedy and eager as I stare at her body, imagining what I'm going to do to her. I can smell the floral scent on her skin, and the sweet honey between her legs. She still has her panties on, so it's such a tease not being able to freely rub up against her most sensitive, luscious flesh.

She's torturing me. My dick is hanging out, bare of course, because

I'm naked as a jaybird. The big fella is standing tall and proud, waiting for her to slide down and sheath me all the way to the base—whether it be her mouth or pussy, it doesn't matter, because both are equally a slice of wet heaven.

I palm her beautiful creamy tits, and she throws her head back while the blonde strands cascade behind her. She arches, and her chest juts forward as an offering to keep me stroking what is mine. Her moans are fueling my desires, and I pinch her pretty pink nipples. She responds so deliciously as her thighs clench more tightly around my middle, trapping me to her. *Don't worry, my vivacious temptress, I'm not going anywhere.*

The head of my cock is pulsing because it needs to be buried deep in one of her tight, silky, soaked holes. I wonder if her body aches for me as much as I ache for her. I wanted to take things slowly our first time, but I can't help myself. She makes me lose my damn mind!

She leans forward and places her hands on my shoulders to brace herself. Her hair brushes my chest, and it tickles me in a sensual way that has goose pimples breaking out on my arms. Her touch sends shockwaves up and down my body. Then she lowers her face to mine and kisses the hell out of me. I slide one of my hands in her hair to anchor her. With the other arm, I hold her tightly by pulling her in at the shoulders.

This hypnotic dance we're doing with our tongues is probably among the sexiest things I've ever done. Hell, anything we do ranks up there as the sexiest thing I've ever done! I can't wait to take her from behind—now I'm probably getting ahead of myself.

For the record, of course I like to look at the woman during sex, and it's not a control thing that my favorite position is from behind. As a man, I'm like most of my peers and consider myself mostly a visual creature, so the front of a woman is the preferred view. But there's something about bending a woman over the bed, a couch, or any surface for that matter. It unleashes my inner animal. My lion can certainly spar with her cougar, especially since he needs to be let out of his cage.

We finally come up for air, sucking in what feels like endless gulps of breath. My lungs are burning and starved, but the burn in my heart for her takes precedence. She sits back again on my thighs and hooks her thumbs into her lacy black panties. I'm drooling at the sight as she slowly exposes inch by inch of her delectable skin to me.

I start to see her neatly trimmed pubic hair come into view, and it's a shade darker than the blonde on her head. I can't tear my gaze away. She's about to pull them completely down so I can finally see her pussy lips and taste and touch the inside of her. But she stops right before the final unveiling.

"Is everything okay?" I ask with great concern, thinking I did something wrong.

"No, sorry it's not you. It's just…I don't like William watching," she explains.

I'm so confused at first. The hair on the back of my neck stands on end, and that's when I feel like we're not alone. I turn my head to the left, and right there in the doorway stands her ex.

*What the fuck?*

***

I wake with the biggest jolt of my life. I sit up so fast on my bed that I practically fly out of my skin. That was the craziest, most fucked up, creepiest dream I've ever experienced. It was fucking glorious at first and then at the end turned to shit.

I never even met the man and yet I had a vivid picture of him in my mind. I'm sweaty and breathing heavily, almost like I've run a marathon. I don't know where that nightmare came from. One minute I'm in paradise, and the next minute I'm in Hades.

*Very bizarre. And it has me wondering if something is looming….* I shake my head to clear the cobwebs.

I thought after seeing my horoscope today, it was going to be a turning point. Thinking back to reading the words on the damn screen this morning, I was supposed to "dream up new opportunities." *So what the fuck was that, then?*

I throw the covers off me and get up from my bed, heading into the kitchen to get a drink of water. Sitting on my counter, wrapped up, are the last two cookies from the batch we made last night. I wonder if those damn cookies can chase the darkness away, so I pull them out of the cellophane. I glance at the clock on my stove, realizing it's nearing midnight. I've only been asleep for less than two hours, so it must have been a deep sleep up until the nightmare occurred. I don't want to think too much into what I dreamt about, but on some level I feel I have to analyze it.

I can't decide if her ex is a threat to me because she can't let go of him, or if the threat is more to *her* because she wants to let go of him. The mind is a funny thing, and I don't want to discount what my brain was trying to assemble even in my sleep.

I don't want his presence—or, rather, death—to always be hanging over us somehow. Liz deserves a fresh start.

*It makes me wonder if she's haunted by something other than her ex. Perhaps a secret of some sort?*

I hope as I get to know her better, she'll open up to me more. It feels like this dream was a warning of sorts. I certainly can't fix her past, but I'll do my best to mend the current situation, and ensure the future has the best chance of never coming unraveled.

I eat the two cookies, which bring me some comfort; they infuse me with a taste of her. I get a quick drink of water to wash it down, then I place my cup in the sink. I walk back into my room and lie down in the bed once more. My eyes have easily adjusted to the dark, so I stare at the painting on my wall. I focus on it until my eyes become heavy and sleep begins to take me again. I tell myself, *I'm not going to have any more crazy-ass dreams tonight.*

I wish Liz were here so I could hold her. I'm man enough to admit that sometimes it's nice to have that reciprocal comfort from a woman. I want her in my bed every night where we can watch over each other—she'd be my dreamcatcher.

"Goodnight, sweetness," I say to my empty room. And for good measure I tack on, "Sweet dreams."

Yeah, first horoscopes, now superstitions, ha! Don't worry, I realize I'm a unique breed all on my own, but hey, that's the Caleb Daniels way.

# Chapter 11: Make the Call

*Liezel*

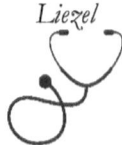

It's been three days since I replied to his text. He hasn't made any attempt to reach out to me. I don't know if that's a good or bad sign. I clearly left it with him that *I'd* let him know when we'd get together next, so it's really my move to make.

I just got home from work and from picking up Leah at basketball practice. I love that she's girly when she wants to be, and she's also very athletic. She'll be a force to be reckoned with as she gets older. I expect boys will be beating down my door, and I'll gladly chase them away. *I'll show the boys one of my needles I use on patients, and I bet they'll run for the hills*, I laugh out loud as I think about the possibilities—come on people, it's no different than a daddy threatening male suitors with a shotgun!

I walk into my bedroom and set my phone down on my dresser as I'm stripping out of my scrubs. It's the first thing I do when I get in from work. I hate bringing germs home to my family, plus I need to rip off my bra and let the girls be free. There's nothing more amazing than that feeling of letting them loose. I swear as soon as that damn contraption comes off, I can hear "Roar," by Katy Perry playing in the background like it's my anthem.

That bra bitch gets tossed in the corner of my room like I loathe it, and I slip on comfy sweatpants and a T-shirt. As I'm throwing my hair up in a messy bun, my phone rings. Hoping it's from Caleb, I go to answer it, nearly lunging at my cell. When I look at the screen, I see it's Caylan calling. I'm smiling as I swipe to take her call—I love this girl.

Before I can even say *hello*, she jumps in and starts on me. But let me tell you, she is the sweetest thing, so even her mean side is like a puppy barking. The girl can't do mean.

"You're driving that poor man crazy, you know that?" She scolds, and I think it's a rhetorical question.

"Well, hello to you too," I laugh.

"Sorry, but that poor man has got it bad, and I hate to see one of my dear friends in distress, knowing full well I can do something to fix it," she explains and sighs in a cute way into the phone.

"Okay, what's the issue, and who are we talking about here?" I ask, half-laughing at her display of pouting that I can practically see through the phone.

She scoffs and says, "Caleb, of course! Please put him out of his misery and call him. He keeps calling and texting Alexi to see how you're doing. I think Alexi has talked to him more than he's talked to me in the last few days."

I don't even know how to respond. I'm shocked and almost drop my cell from my shaking hand. I had no idea I had this level of an impact on *him*. The fact that our little thing we have going on is now trickling over to our friends makes me feel guilty. I bite my lower lip in shame.

"Caylan…I had no idea. I'm so sorry. I just thought I'd give it a few days because I don't want to start something when I don't have my crap together. He deserves someone who's going to fully commit to him. It's intense when I'm with him, and I don't want to string him along when I keep doubting myself," I try to convey, but I'm probably failing miserably because it sounds stupid now that I'm saying it out loud.

"Oh, sweetie, you deserve him, and he deserves you! It's one thing if you're not into him, but it's another thing if you are and don't take a chance. I've never seen him like this over a woman. He's so caring and so attentive. He's the perfect catch! I know he'll treat you like a queen. Let me just ask you flat out, do you like him or not?" She asks, and I picture her batting her eyelashes at me.

"Yes, I do, but it's not that simple," I whisper.

"Oh, yes, it is, if I have anything to say about it." She tries to be stern, but it's so innocent-sounding.

"I think I'm too old for him," I admit, and I'm immediately embarrassed and slap my forehead; yup, I totally face-palmed on that one.

"You're not too old for him! First of all, you're hot. Own it! Second, oh goodness gracious, I'm going to get myself in a pickle by saying this, but, oh well. Alexi can spank me later for revealing this," she giggles.

I roll my eyes because those two make you sick. It's no secret they're too hot to handle in the bedroom. Caylan comes off as this shy, doe-eyed little thing, but I know better than that when it comes to their sex life.

She goes on to say, "Caleb's into cougars. Not that I'm calling you one; I'm just saying that's like his *thing*. I'm surprised you've never noticed.

Anyway, I hope it's a good thing in your case. Believe me, he's all kinds of twisted over you."

I am by no means offended, just genuinely surprised. I had no idea. I never really noticed. Whenever we've been at the same functions, he's always so friendly and personable. I've always seen him talk to women of all ages. I usually think I'm observant, so how did I miss this?

"Sweetie, you still there?" She asks in a panic.

"Oh, yeah, sorry. I was just thinking. No, I've never noticed this detail. I wouldn't consider it a bad thing, I suppose. I mean, I guess I'm technically a cougar. I only thought a hot, young man like him would want someone like you," I admit.

"You mean knocked up and crabby?" She questions in laughter.

I chuckle back at her statement because I guess I walked into that one. She's so adorable. With her being so young and gorgeous, I consider her the stereotypical girl most men Caleb's age—or any age, for that matter—would go for.

When I left Rhode Island all those years ago, I told myself not to revisit the past. Ever since William's funeral and his parents' visit, I feel like there's something impending. I can't tell anyone there's something haunting me…like unfinished business. Caylan is my friend—hell, she's my family now—but I don't want anyone thinking differently about me.

*I don't know if I'll ever be able to share that part of myself—that history— with anyone.*

And I know I can't worry about what people think, yet I do, mainly because I don't want my kids to be subjected to ridicule.

"Don't you think Caleb and I are moving too fast? Nothing's happened between us, but don't you think I'm being selfish?" I practically whine at her.

She gasps, "Selfish? Is that what you think? Liz, you couldn't be selfish if you tried. Besides, why does there have to be a timeline put on this thing between you two? Who's making the rules? If it's outsiders, then to heck with them!" She hits me with rapid-fire questions I can't answer.

"I'm being silly, aren't I?" I ask more to myself than to her. I'm pacing my bedroom like a dog at the pound, not sure what my head and heart want.

"Do ya really want me to answer that? Because you know me and my happy endings. I'm totally going to make this happen, woman! I helped Brent, and I'm sure as heck going to help you. Plus, I must confess that, selfishly, I want my husband back," she explains, then goes off into a fit of giggles.

"That's understandable. I'm sorry for all this. I promise to call Caleb. I can't promise that we'll have a future together, but I will keep an open mind and see where this goes. I have so many things to factor in between William's passing, the kids, my reservations about jumping into a relationship. Ya know, the important shit!" I clarify while shrugging a shoulder I know she can't see.

"I understand. I know I may not *know*, but I do get it. Take all the time you need to heal, but try to keep yourself open to possibilities. Caleb's a good listener and the greatest friend. They don't make'em like they used to. I know no matter what happens, you've got a lifer with him in whatever capacity that'll be," she relays in a sincere tone.

"Thank you. I appreciate it. I know you're trying to help. You and Alexi have been in my corner through everything, and that means more than you'll ever realize," I respond with the beginning stage of waterworks forming in my eyes. I won't let them fall, though.

"Okay, now that the heavy stuff is outta the way, have you given any more thought to my suggestion of writing? I know journaling and poetry helped me in my darkest times. Maybe it will be therapeutic for you," she suggests.

"Yes, I have thought about it, but I haven't done it. Tonight may be the night. Thanks for reminding me," I reply.

"Anytime, lovely! Well, I'll let you go. I can hear Em running around downstairs. That kid just learned how to walk—basically overnight, no less—and suddenly she's an expert at it. How will I survive having another one?" She partly groans, amused by her own insight.

"You'll manage. My three were close in age, and it's a lot of work, but I know you'll tackle it like you do anything else. Give a kiss to Em for me, and we'll make plans to get together soon for lunch," I offer.

"Oh, that would be perfect," she squeals.

I laugh and say, "All righty, I'll talk to you later and…I'll call Caleb soon."

"You better!" She threatens in the sugary way only she can deliver.

We both say our final goodbyes and end the call. I pull out the front drawer of my nightstand, and tucked inside is a notebook. I grab it from its hiding place, deciding at this moment I will heed Caylan's advice and write a little. It may be good to get my feelings out.

I start jotting words down on the paper, but then scribble them out because I deem that they suck. Nothing I write down sounds like I'm even trying. I need to properly articulate my feelings by expressing my emotions. I guess I've been lying to myself in thinking I've been handling this whole William situation well.

And then it hits me! I need lies more than I need the truth when it comes to him—not so much a denial thing, more like a realization of sorts. My hand starts flying across the page, and before I know it, I've written out a poem. *Is this how Caylan does it?* I decide to read it back.

*Title: Love Lies*
*Lie to me,*
*I'm begging please,*
*Lie to me, lie.*
*Cause the truth, it hurts,*
*It's so much worse,*
*Lie to me, lie.*
*I need the words,*
*Just stay the course,*
*Lie to me, lie.*
*My heart is there,*
*It's just not fair,*
*Lie to me, lie.*
*I run from truth,*
*I promise you,*
*Lie to me, lie.*
*I just can't hear,*
*My biggest fear,*
*Lie to me, lie.*
*So just lie to me, lie...please lie to me, lie.*

The words hurt too much as they hit me square in the face. I start to cry. Maybe this writing thing wasn't such a good idea.

***

I finally collect myself after a good cry. Thank God the kids didn't come in search of me. The boys usually get rides home from school from friends and then go to their houses to hang out and do homework; I don't think they're home yet, only Leah. I'm lucky that I never have to worry about my kids getting into trouble. They have wonderful friends who are like-minded, with parents possessing good morals and values.

The boys don't have girlfriends yet, but I know they're interested, and that day will soon come. I have no problem with that notion. High school is a tricky thing and can be a bitch to navigate. I certainly can't imagine what it's like nowadays. All three of my kids do their homework with no complaint and keep up with their studies. They each earn solid As and Bs. Leah, thankfully, isn't boy-crazy—I have a little more time before that kicks in. She has a good head on her shoulders, so I doubt I'll have any issues in that regard anyway.

I already had *the talk* with each of them a few years ago. They know they can come to me with anything, and they certainly know they can call upon Alexi or any one of the guys or gals. An image of Caleb enters my head, and in my mind I picture him sitting with the kids and giving them fatherly advice. I shake my head to clear it away—*nope, not going there.*

I've been holed up in my room long enough. I have to get dinner going. Plus, I promised Caylan that I'd get in touch with Caleb—I keep my promises. I exit my room and head downstairs. Leah is on the couch reading *Twilight* again. I smile to myself thinking what an incredible girl I have. That book is well-worn on the cover, and the pages inside reveal wear from lots of love and attention, but she'll read it to her heart's content.

There's no point in asking if she wants anything because once she's in the reading zone, there's no getting her out of it. When she finally smells dinner later and the boys come home, then she'll snap out of the book-spell she's under.

I decide to make something simple. A stir fry will do. I put fresh veggies in a pan and slice up some chicken. I usually do a stir fry on our designated family movie nights when we watch one of the *Star Wars*, or one of the *Harry Potters*.

While I have everything cooking in the pan, I finally make the call to *him*. My fingers are trembling as I go through my contacts to locate his name—I didn't put him under "favorites" yet because I didn't want to get carried away. It rings one time, and he picks up.

"Sweetness…," he breathes out in the sexiest manner.

I tighten the grip around my cell hearing his soothing voice. There's that hint of desperation and longing hanging there in the one word he says. Immediately, I think of my conversation with Caylan and how she described Caleb's behavior. I truly didn't think I could do this to a man—it's a heady thing, but not one I relish because this isn't some game for me. I don't think I realized until this second, hearing that one word, what he and I are coming to mean to each other in such a short time.

My knees go weak, and I close my eyes, savoring his tone and tucking it away for later when I'll think about him when I'm alone.

"Hi," is what I'm able to squeak out. I know my voice betrays me as it's telling him I'm nervous, unsure, and also laced with guilt for keeping him on the hook—dangling there without offering him a reprieve.

"I've missed talking to you. I'm so glad you called. I would've even settled for a text…anything. I just wanted to know you're okay," he rasps back.

"I've missed talking to you too. I'm sorry I didn't call or text sooner. I just…needed time," I state.

He sighs in an understanding way. "I know. I'm trying to be patient, but you're killing me over here. This must be so confusing for you, and I know you're trying to deal with everything, but can I ask one favor?" He begs.

"What's that?" I ask, not knowing where he's going with this.

"Let me help you deal with it all. Don't shut me out. I'll be a friend, whatever you need. Please let me help you through it?" He conveys, and I can tell he's choosing his words carefully—almost as if he's holding something back.

I crumble at his words and need a minute. I swallow back tears and all the feelings swirling inside me. That poem I wrote earlier took a lot out of me. I wanted William to lie to me when he was alive, and I've needed to lie to myself all these years and even up until now. But I don't want Caleb to lie! The fact that he isn't, and probably never will, says it all.

This beautiful man is showing his vulnerable side, and if I wanted confirmation that he would be there, well, I have it. He's right here, and all I have to do is reach out and grab on to him. I just have to pull him off that proverbial dangling hook.

"Okay," is my response.

I hear him expel the breath he probably was holding while waiting for me to answer him. I may not know exactly where we're going from here, but I said I'd let him in. That's more complicated than it seems, but I will have to take my chances. After all, Caleb may be *the one,* and I owe it to both of us to find out.

*Live, Live, Live….* My daughter planted that seed in my head— enough so that it may have taken root.

# Chapter 12: I'm Owl About You

*Caleb*

March 6, 2018

It's now been a week since Liz's phone call that set my world right again. Before she reached out to me, I was in agony. One call changed everything as if the stars aligned. I don't know what made her finally call, but whatever it was, I'm grateful. We've texted each day since; those texts are my lifeline in this bleak world. As long as she's communicating with me, then I can make it through.

Brent and Everly's wedding is a week and a half away. There's no time like the present than to ask Liz to be my date—it's a *now or never* or *do or die* situation at this point. She at least invited me over for dinner this Friday night to join her and the kids...*as friends*, of course. That's fine by me as long as I stand a chance to be *more*.

So, yesterday I hatched a plan, and today I'm executing said plan that should go off any minute. As I'm sitting at my desk at work—piled high with client folders and documents carted in by my paralegal Melanie—I'm waiting to see if my plan goes as expected.

I went to *Budding Romance Flower & Gift Shop* yesterday after work and arranged for a delivery to Liz's office today. Alexi already knew it was coming as I clued him in last night. He made sure her lunch break would be at the time of the delivery. He said she always eats in the breakroom area for employees, so I knew she'd be there. I owe him and Caylan a great deal for putting up with my shit lately. I've probably been driving them nuts—I'll have to do something extravagant for them when all is said and done.

Thinking back to my visit to the shop, the florist had all kinds of questions from what size of bouquet, what type of flower, what type of arrangement, to the color preference of the bow, color and type of vase, and what sentiment for the card. I was so confused and scratching my head the whole time because I wanted to get everything perfect.

After relaying the details of my hopes and dreams for Liz's and my blossoming relationship—which was weird to tell a complete stranger, but also felt kind of nice discussing with an objective third party—she suggested a bouquet of daffodils. I went with forty-four of them for every beautiful year Liz has been on this earth and because she's made it that much of a better place.

The florist, Kate, as was written on her embossed nametag, was very helpful and knowledgeable. She donned one of those *let me speak to the manager* haircuts, but her bubbly personality didn't match her standoffish appearance. She took the time to explain that daffodils symbolize a new beginning. Their stark, bright white petals with a yellow center are a special representation of what I'm feeling for my woman. To me, the white conveys Liz's gracefulness and loveliness, and the yellow hues kissing the middle of the flower are that of her heart trying to capture the warmth of a true partner in life—and that partner needs to be me.

Kate had set down a blue vase that reminded me of Liz's eyes, I remember staring at the flowers in admiration. It looked like the rising sun in the middle of the daffodils, and I hoped they'd shine upon her and brighten her day when she received them. Kate tied orange ribbon around the vase, and all the colors somehow worked together, making the arrangement stand out wonderfully.

I didn't include candy or any confectionary gifts because Liz can bake goodies better than anything I could have bought. I did, however, enhance the delivery by including an adorable gray owl holding a pink heart suspended on a string from its beak. I had to have every detail exact. Even if she didn't notice the little things like the number of stems, it didn't matter because *I* knew they were there.

I picked a small card with colorful little owls on the front in each corner, and in the center of the blank folding card it said, "I'm Owl About You." I thought she'd adore it. I'm completely content with going the whimsical or corny route in all this. Sometimes you have to pull out all the stops.

On the inside of the card, well, I had to mull over the inscription for a good ten minutes. I'm certainly no Nicholas Sparks, but I did my best. I wrote:

> *Liz,*
> *I hope you enjoy the flowers. I know since I've met you, I've learned to stop and smell them in life.*
> *So, here's to new beginnings and my hope that*

*things will continue to blossom between us. I'm so
lucky to have you in my life.
I would like to ask for you to please accompany
me to Brenneth and Everly's wedding next week,
as friends, of course—no pressure. I can't
imagine having any other woman on my arm. No
one compares to you.
I look forward to dinner Friday night. Have a
lovely day, my sweetness.
Yours,
Caleb xoxo*

I'm quite proud of what I penned.

I glance at my wristwatch, and the delivery should have been dropped off a few minutes ago if Kate stuck to her word of her courier being punctual. I smile, hoping I hear from Liz. I pray for a *yes* in answer to being my date, but I will understand if it's a *no*. I'm the one who mentioned *friends* in my note, so I will in no way make her feel it has to be anything different.

There's a knock on my office door, and I acknowledge the visitor, inviting them to come in. It's Melanie. She approaches my desk cheerfully and hands me yet another stack of files. This time it's for the high-profile case I've been working on. Melanie has been amazing gathering previous court rulings in other cases that could help me with this one. Mrs. Price expects—no, rather, demands—results, and I don't like losing.

Because Liz and I are communicating regularly now, my focus has put my car back in the right lane; if I had continued to keep exiting the off-ramp much longer, I know my superiors would have noticed. Let's put it this way, I almost *stepped on my own dick with track shoes* when I got sloppy with my duties. You like that expression? That was one of my dad's old sayings from his uncles who lived the piney life in the woods of New Jersey. But I'm back on track!

I thank Melanie profusely for being so efficient. That girl has saved me more times than I can count. I make a mental note to send her a gift basket as a show of thanks; more than anything she deserves a raise. She has earned every penny, all the praise, and all my respect. There have been a few of my associates who have wanted to squirrel her away, but thankfully she's loyal to me. I may be ruthless in the bedroom and courtroom, but I think I'm a great guy to be alongside in the workroom.

I'm still hoping for a text or call any minute from Liz as I become increasingly antsy. Melanie leaves my office, and I start drumming my fingers on my desk. God, I must have the patience of a saint. Yeah, Saint Caleb…that's me!

***

*Liezel*

We have a small breakroom area that is quaint, calm and relaxing. It's that way because Alexi let me decorate it. I opted for soft lighting that does not affect your eyes or make you sleepy; I hate fluorescent lights for that reason.

I had the design consultant outfit the room with a couch, reading chair, and small round table with padded chairs for dining. We have all the appliances a normal kitchen would, but on a small scale. None of us cook gourmet meals in here, of course, but we have the gadgets to get by. Alexi always wants us performing our best for our patients, so I love that he treats us well.

The walls are a light tan color, and I chose retro geometric paintings for the room. I actually don't have any owl items in here except the small figurine on top of the microwave. On my breaks and lunch, I either read a romance or mystery novel, or catch up on one of my favorite shows on Netflix. The best part about our office is that Alexi installed a small gym in the back for employees, so I try to take advantage of that after work when I don't have to transport the kids to and from activities.

I just heated up the casserole I brought from home; yup, I still have food in the freezer from all the neighbors and friends. *I'll eventually work through it all sometime this year,* I think sarcastically. I sit down at the table, and I'm about to take a bite when Alexi enters the room.

"Hey, Liz. Sorry to interrupt your lunch, but you have a delivery out front at reception," he explains.

"Oh, no problem. Do you know what it is?" I ask, wondering what on earth it could be.

He licks his lips and chuckles. "Let's just say you have to see for yourself."

Now I'm really curious. His eyes do that sexy smolder thing, combined with a layer of mischief. If I didn't view him as a brother, that look would totally work on me. Well, that is, if he wasn't madly in love with his wife. Thank God neither one of us ever went *there;* given that I'm like twenty years older than his wife, well, I imagine I wouldn't have been his type anyway. I often wonder if he can help himself. I mean, surely he's aware of his appeal to women. He places his hands in his physician's coat and grins at me with that *I've got a secret* look.

I walk down the hall and turn to go to reception. When I round the corner, I see a delivery man in khaki pants and a green shirt embroidered with white thread that says *Budding Romance Flower & Gift Shop*. He's holding a clipboard, and to his right on the counter is the biggest bouquet of flowers I've ever laid eyes on.

My mouth is hanging open. These can't possibly be for me. Then I groan, thinking, *oh God, these are more condolence flowers, aren't they?* I asked everyone who knew William to please donate to The Woodward Center in lieu of flowers; it's a local treatment facility specializing in helping alcoholics and drug addicts recover. I guess someone didn't get the memo. But then I'm confused because William's funeral was a few weeks ago, so this can't be for that, can it?

"Ma'am, can I please get your signature right here?" The delivery guy asks as he points to the designated line.

He passes the clipboard and pen to me, and I'm still standing there with my mouth hanging open, looking at the flowers like they're a mirage. I quickly scrawl my name on the line and pass it back. He mumbles "thanks," and Alexi hands the young man a tip.

*What an idiot I am!* I don't even have money on me. I didn't even know Alexi followed me out. I squeak out a "thanks" to Alexi for saving my ass. And I finally accept that the arrangement is for *me*.

The blue vase is gorgeous with an ornate orange ribbon tied into an elaborate bow. The flowers are the freshest daffodils and couldn't look any better even if they were still firmly planted in the ground. There are so many of them, at least a few dozen or so. Next to the vase is the cutest stuffed animal owl. I tuck in my lips and clamp down on them with my teeth to keep from crying.

I know immediately who this is from. The heart on the string hanging from the beak totally gives it away, and I should have realized sooner. I said previously that I kept thinking how I was dangling Caleb on a hook—*he must view it as dangling on a string.*

I reach out and grab the stuffed animal, hugging it to my chest. We're closed for lunch to patients, so thankfully there's no one around to witness my state of weakness and vulnerability. Alexi must have retreated to his office because I'm left standing there alone. I clutch that poor little owl for dear life. I hold the hanging heart in my hand and regard it. Streaks of happy tears are trailing down my face.

*How does this man do it? How does he surprise me at every turn? Why does he want me?*

I see the card nestled in the flowers, and before I pluck it from the card holder, I stick my face right in the arrangement to inhale the fabulous scent of spring. It's still cold outside, and I expect winter will hang on a little longer. This gift sure brightens my day; heck, it brightens my whole year.

I run my fingers across the front of the card, which contains an adorable sentiment and cute owls. His sweet and charming thoughtfulness has me laughing out loud.

"Oh, my sexy man. I'm 'owl about you' too, Caleb," I whisper to the empty room.

I read the card, even through the tears clinging to my lashes and face, impairing my vision. God, he sure has a way with words. Of course I'll be his date to the wedding. It doesn't even have to be as *friends*, but I'm not going to tell him that. I can finally admit that I have fallen completely in love with him. Somehow he slipped right on through and nestled right in my heart.

At the risk of ruining the moment switching from thoughts of romance to thoughts of desire, I'm going to say what my mom told me growing up: "You have to take the car for a test drive before you buy it."

Hopefully you get my drift. I know Caleb and I will be dynamite in bed, but there's only one way to find out. After all, my mom was a wise woman, and she was forward-thinking when she was alive. So, I intend on following her advice. Caleb will find out at the upcoming wedding how serious I am about going for a *test drive* with his shifter—I can't imagine we won't be compatible in that department.

# Chapter 13: Something Old, Something New

*Caleb*

March 17, 2018

I still can't believe Liz is my date. The fact that she said *yes* to me is a victory. I've enjoyed dinner with her and the kids twice since my flower delivery. The kids seem receptive toward me, and I feel like Leah knows I'm in love with her mother. She's an angel for not saying anything—well, at least she hasn't outed me in front of everyone, but I'm not sure what is said when I'm not around. That young girl is quite perceptive, and I'll do well to remember that. She looks and acts like her mother; it's uncanny.

God, I love the kids already too. It seems overnight I've become super protective of them; I live for hearing all about those three. Liz has said she thought she was boring me when she speaks about them, but it's quite the opposite. I know no matter what happens between Liz and me, I want to remain in their lives—all of their lives.

We are heading over to the reception. The wedding ceremony was exceptional. I found myself a little pea-green with envy, though, watching Ev walk down the aisle to Brent. But hopefully one day I'll get my turn. I'm so damn happy for them.

It was fucking awesome that Brent wore his dress blues uniform. And I like the gray suit I'm wearing; I don't think black would have worked. I feel fortunate to be one of his groomsmen. And the way we were all paired up couldn't have worked out better.

Caylan and Alexi are the matron of honor and best man, followed by the remaining groomsmen and bridesmaids. The pairs flowed out from the church earlier as follows: Anthony and Shanna, Gil and Addison, Liz and me, and Meg and Technical Sergeant Harold Jefferson. Our wedding party fucking rocks!

I was happy to finally meet Harold. He took leave from the base and flew in from North Carolina for the occasion. He is also dressed in his blues. I don't know the whole backstory and his involvement in the handsome couple getting their happily ever after, but somehow he was part of the reason Brent and Ev ended up together. It was something about a letter, but I've never been given all the details. Maybe one day Brent will tell me the story over a beer or something.

The weather cooperated today. It stayed in the forties until the sun set. At least it didn't rain or snow, so I considered it a win for them. Their wedding was held at a church near Everly's work. Brent apparently was insistent that he do things *the right way* for them and out of respect for his mom and dad. Caylan and Brent are very lucky to have Milly and Fred as parents; they are the epitome of what a family should be.

The reception is being held at the building where Everly works as an editor. Ev's boss owns the building, and as a wedding present, he offered to host it there. It's the perfect venue considering her life revolves around the news; I imagine throwing the party at the same place where the publication is housed is a dream come true for her.

Brent once told me that Everly's boss, Stuart, "is a real fucker"— his words, not mine. But he seems like a nice enough guy. I guess at one time there was a misunderstanding, but it appears that everything's all cleared up now.

The girls all wanted to ride together in one limo, and we guys are all in another—except for the newlyweds since they're in their own limo, probably having wild sex, knowing them. I would have loved to have been in my own wheels with Liz, but hopefully there will be time later to be one-on-one with her. Even holding her hand will thrill me.

I've barely paid attention to all the guys as they've been drinking and cutting up during the trip from the church to the reception. I've been too lost in thought. Finally, Alexi elbows me, and I snap out of it. We've arrived at Stuart's building.

I can't wait to see Liz again—pathetic because it's only been like thirty minutes since we left the church after posing for the mandatory pictures. She looks breathtaking in her bridesmaid dress. Each of the women are in sleeveless aqua-colored dresses that flare out at the waist. The hemline hits them right above the knee. Sexy, yet tasteful and playful. They all have banging bodies, so it was a beautiful sight with them in a row. I'm assuming the extra room in the waist is for Caylan and Shanna's benefit since they're both pregnant. Caylan is the only one with a difference in her dress as the matron of honor. She has a pink bow tied around her waist— that woman and her pink, we always get a kick out of it.

Caylan apparently talked Everly into going with tiger lilies as the wedding flower. I know Everly is not really girly, and she doesn't give a shit about details like that. I imagine Caylan was heavily involved in planning the wedding.

I have to admit the orange flowers looked incredible against the dresses and for the groomsmen's boutonnieres. *Who knew I'd enjoy flowers so much?* I guess one trip to the florist and I'm an expert, as well as a professional cookie baker thanks to my lessons with Liz. Yup, I talked her into another round of baking, and this time we made classic chocolate chip.

Fuck, thinking about her has my cock aching badly. I wish tonight was the night I'd finally have her. I told myself I wouldn't drink, but maybe I'll have to throw a few back to loosen up. Ya know, weddings are all about something old, something new, something borrowed, something blue. Well, I've definitely got the blue part covered with my poor balls.

***

*Liezel*

We just pulled up to the reception. *Lord give me strength not to attack Caleb when I exit the limo.*

I think back to the church and how he looked so damn amazing in his gray suit standing opposite me. I'm surprised no one noticed me drooling during the ceremony. I tried to discreetly wipe my mouth with the back of my hand, but I'm sure I gave myself away if I smeared my lipstick. I couldn't take my eyes off him. I was probably acting like a twit when we strolled to the front of the church two by two. I was giddy just being by his side. When I was sashaying down the aisle, I could pretend all sorts of things and get lost in a fantasy.

At one point, I got misty-eyed for the newlyweds when they exchanged vows, and I was fanning my face so my traitorous tears wouldn't fall. As I stood rooted to my spot, dutifully holding my flowers, I wished it was me up there saying the words…with Caleb. *Is that messed up?*

I didn't even think back to my wedding day with William in that moment, and I sure as hell don't want to even now. I'd like to think as each day passes, I can turn more and more pages—and not just close that chapter—but close the book that was my life with William.

Tonight, I'm going to give Caleb a taste of what we could be like together. I'm not nervous. I'm surprised I'm not shaking with fear. Oh, I'm shaking with something all right, but it's anticipation. I don't know how long I'll be able to hold out now that my mind is made up. We may have to leave the party early if my body keeps quaking with need and want.

I'm incredibly hot, despite wearing a cream-colored fur shawl that Everly gave to all the girls as our bridesmaid's gifts. They look perfect with our dresses and are appropriate given the current temperature. We're each wearing strappy kitten heel sandals in a silver shade. Caylan said she could do a higher heel, but for her and Shanna's safety, we completely disagreed. I'm sure she'll thank us later when her feet aren't screaming in agony.

God, she and Shanna are both glowing with that pregnancy look, and I'm so happy for them. Shanna will make an excellent first-time mother, and Caylan will dominate it all over again this second time around. I sigh wistfully...*I sure do love that look and feeling. It almost makes me miss those days....*

Addison and I got to talking on the way over in the limo. She and Gil's story of how they came to be reminds me of a Cinderella fairytale. I adore the girl as much as I do the others, and since she's in the medical field too, she always loves asking me questions, which I happily oblige. She keeps telling me I need to read a poem that Caylan wrote—it had something to do with fate, apparently. So, I tell her to give it to me the next time we're all together.

Before we finally exit the vehicle, I smile at Meg and remind myself I need to visit with her more often. I know she's quite busy these days with assignments. She has blown me away lately. Since she graduated in May last year with a degree in photography, she has completely transformed, not that she was an ugly duckling by any means. I find the beauty in everyone, and I'm not snobbish like that, but let's just say she didn't bring all the boys to the yard. This will probably sound crappy, but she was more like a cute duck when I first met her. Now...oh my God, now she's a captivating swan!

The girl who once upon a time wore purple-rimmed glasses—was actually brazen, although she lived vicariously through others and was on the husky side—is now a stone-cold fox. I don't know how she did it. Gone are the glasses, and she shed the pounds. When I met her a few years ago, even with shoulder-length hair, I thought she looked like a tomboy. Today, however, her long brown hair comes halfway down her back and is styled in beautiful waves like her cousin's. She and Caylan have the most amazing bond, and you'd think the two are more like sisters—now they practically look like they are, and there is no tomboy in sight. Meg's weight loss makes her figure out of this world.

I noticed Harold was all smiles as he walked her down the aisle. So,

I wonder if the two will hit it off. It seems to me that Meg is completely unaware of her newfound sexiness. That girl needs to learn to work it and own it. I'm sure Caylan is on the case, though. And I've been told many times I should heed my own advice.

We finally step out of the limo as we offer the driver our hands, and he assists us out one by one. I assume Brent and Ev's limo is the one idling in front of ours; makes sense if they're going to be announced to the gathered crowd for the first time as *Mr. and Mrs. Peters*. If I look hard enough, I'm sure I can see steam on the windows—those two!

The guys are all lined up on the sidewalk anxiously waiting for each of us to make our appearance. Anthony and Alexi fuss over their women right away as if they haven't seen them in forever. Gil does too, but not in the same way, and I think it's because Addison's not with child. Harold stands there nervously, unsure if he should approach Meg or not, but it appears he finally has some guts and makes his move to intercept her. I think to myself, *good going, Tech Sergeant!*

We're all standing about. We should be trying to get into some sort of formation to enter the building. I'm not sure where the wedding planner is, but surely she'll be whipping us into shape any minute.

And then suddenly…I feel *his* eyes upon me and turn around slowly. *How the heck did he manage to get behind me?* I had only taken a few steps out of the limo, but there Caleb is. Our chauffeur is driving away, and the breeze as the vehicle passes ruffles Caleb's hair slightly and sends my dress flying up a little. A chill runs up and down my spine as the wind rushes in between my legs. But it's quickly replaced with heat. Lots and lots of heat.

Caleb's fiery gaze raises my body temperature, and the chill recedes faster than it came. Somehow his irises take on a smoky hue, and I gulp loudly—I'm sure people down the block heard that noise as well as the guests inside.

Now don't get me wrong. I'm not nervous, so don't go getting your panties twisted. It's more like I'm excited, turned on, and lost to him. Speaking of panties, mine are soaked through just with his stare. I might have to go check myself in the restroom to make sure I don't have evidence of my arousal running down my leg—surely I'd feel it, but this man makes me forget about all sense of time and place.

I am fully aware of every little movement he makes. I notice him swallow. I notice his nostrils flare as he inhales. He seems content standing here looking at me. I faintly hear someone calling our names, but it's fuzzy-sounding in my head. Internally, I'm abuzz with the butterfly sensations that can only come from being so enamored with another person. I've never felt this way before about anyone—not even William. Of course, I was attracted to my late husband back in the day, but not on this scale.

Caleb is off the charts!

I dart my tongue out, rubbing it across my plump upper lip in a naughty manner. I'm calling attention to that area because I want his eyes and focus to be right there—right there, thinking of what I will do with my mouth if given the opportunity. I swear I'm trying not to be rude and ignore those calling our names, but I'm so lost in this moment...I'm lost to this stunning man. He smiles, and my heart melts. My eyes flutter closed as if he's caressing me, and I'm feeling every touch and sensation without him even being physical.

When I open my eyes, he's a breath away. I think he's going to kiss me, but he doesn't. His mouth is hovering near mine. Maybe I should be embarrassed or worried that our friends are bearing witness to something that's still in its infancy; however, I can't worry about that. This is private and intimate, and I'm tuning everything else out. And thank God the kids are already inside and not seeing this display; they rode in with Fred and Milly.

A small puff of breath blows out from my lips, and Caleb licks his lips in response. I don't want our first real kiss to be on this sidewalk, regardless of what my body is screaming at me. If he does move in for it, well, it's not like I'll deny him.

"Sweetness...," is what he murmurs in that velvety voice that makes love to my ears like no other sound can.

My eardrums are doing a salsa to the timbre in that one word. *Mmm*, his voice is dipped in honey, coated with chocolate, and sprinkled on top are these decadent pieces of toffee. *Whew*, I feel light-headed like I might faint. He may notice me swaying because he grabs both my forearms to steady me. *Now I'm the one finding myself grateful to have the kitten heels.*

Once it looks like he's satisfied that I'm not going to topple over, he lets me go. I see a flicker of disappointment in his eyes. *Believe me, sexy, I want you to hold me too.*

We finally come out of the horny haze we've been suspended in. We turn to look at our group, and there are eight pairs of eyes with knowing looks smirking at us.

He offers me his arm and asks, "Shall we?"

I see the wedding planner come out the front entrance, and she's motioning to us to line up. The limo driver for Brent and Everly comes around the car and opens the door for the newlyweds to exit. It's show time!

I loop my arm with Caleb's. I'm so ready to go inside for what is sure to be a life-changing evening.

# Chapter 14: Per*fuck*tion

*Liezel*

After the introductions, eating, and toasts, the dance floor finally opens up. I'm thinking about how we're so lucky we can enjoy the evening well into the wee hours of the morning…if we want; it's not quite that late yet. With Stuart owning the building, there's no fixed time we have to vacate by. The best part is that Brent and Everly reserved a block of hotel suites within walking distance, which is convenient and appreciated—I will probably still opt for driving to the hotel, though.

The kids are going to stay in an adjoining room to mine. The room across from me houses Caleb, and the one next to him is where Alexi's parents will be. I'm not quite sure about the rest of the wedding party, but I know we're all on the same floor. I'm grateful we're all in such close proximity because I don't have to worry about the kids. Milly and Fred will certainly keep an eye on them. They told me earlier to have fun tonight. It's almost as if they know something is going on between Caleb and me. *Am I really the last one to figure this out?*

I don't ponder that notion long, and instead, my eye catches a blue suit. My God, the handsome hero in uniform is sweeping his bride across the floor. Brent deserves the biggest kudos for the honeymoon he's about to pull off. It's a surprise for Everly; Alexi told me all about it.

Brent and Ev are staying at the hotel tonight, and then tomorrow they're flying out to California to visit all the touristy places *Top Gun* was filmed at—it's their favorite movie and was a major part of the proposal. For goodness sake, we've practically heard the whole soundtrack played this evening! But, of course, I'm not annoyed; I find it endearing.

Fred and Milly will be pet-sitting starting tomorrow since Maverick and Pussy—Brent and Ev's dog and cat respectively—will need to be cared for in their absence. They had to kennel the poor things for tonight, so I'm sure they'll be anxious to be sprung from the facility. The cat had a litter of kittens back in January, so Ev wants her white fluff-ball supervised until she gets fixed. I can't say it enough how amazing Caylan and Brent's parents are; I've never met two people like them and probably never will.

I've watched all of our friends swirl and twirl across the floor during the slow songs, then shake their *thang* during the fast ones. I haven't danced with Caleb…yet. I think it's intentional, and mutual, because one thing may lead to another, and I don't trust myself to keep my hands from misbehaving. So, we've been conducting ourselves appropriately for the sake of everyone.

I distract myself every so often by admiring the building. I had never been to Everly's work before tonight, but I imagine a lot of planning went into converting the huge lobby area into an elegant party room. Stuart certainly outdid himself with allowing the wedding planner to make it look so chic. The lights strewn about are magical. And that's how this whole day has been…magical. *God, I want the magic to continue the rest of the night.*

Leah, Tyler, and Kurt are all having fun playing with Emeline and chasing her around. That adorable little girl has everyone wrapped tightly around her little princess finger. Even with her doting nanny, Granny Lil, to tend to her every need, she still succeeds in tiring everyone out. It's really sweet that Granny Lil was Alexi's nanny as a boy, and later her role transitioned to a cook when she was no longer needed in that capacity. Alexi lovingly stole her away from his parents when he found out he was going to be a father, and now the kind, elderly woman lives with them. Please don't think Caylan shirks her duties. Oh no, that girl is a very hands-on mom, but I'm sure she's happy to have the help, especially with the second one coming.

Kurt runs up to me out of breath, and I'm chuckling because he looks exhausted from entertaining Emeline.

"Hey, sweetheart! Em's got you tuckered out, huh?" I smile affectionately at my middle child.

"Nah. If I wanna be in the military, I can't sit around and do nothing," he explains while wiping his brow.

I hand him a glass of water, and he gratefully gulps it down. I tell him how proud I am of him; his dazzling return smile fills my soul—*God, he looks like his father.* When William was younger, he was so handsome. The drinking took its toll even in his late twenties, and when his forties hit, he looked like an old man. I shake my head to forget, reminding myself that William did give me the greatest gift by helping to create this beautiful young man.

Another thought assails me. It will be difficult for me to send Kurt off into the military—if it's his dream, I'll find a way to do it, though. At least Brent has a couple more years to help Kurt prepare if this is what he wants to do.

I remind my son to talk to Tech Sergeant Jefferson tonight to get another enlisted member's perspective, and he agrees with my suggestion. And I make a mental note to finally explore getting him into ROTC or Civil Air Patrol—Brent had mentioned to me not too long ago that these programs are great for grooming potential armed forces members. We had so much going on with the funeral at the time, but now I will make it a priority.

"You look happy, Mom. I think Caleb's an okay dude," he says, half-grinning at me.

"Is that so? He's just *okay?*" I tease.

"Yeah, he's cool. Well, I better get back to it. We requested the chicken dance…again. Em seems to like it." He laughs and puts the glass down. I get a quick "bye," and he races off.

The kids haven't said much about Caleb, and I'm not pushing them. I'm procrastinating on broaching the subject on my end, putting off the inevitable conversation. It's cowardly, but I'm hoping the more time they spend with Caleb, and the more they see us together, they'll see what a developing relationship looks like. William and I were not good role models for what love and happiness between a couple should represent. I have to fix that.

*There will be time later…much later, to have that talk with my kiddos.*

I look at how Brent and Everly are in their little happy, blissful bubble, staring at one another in the center of the dance floor. They're not really even dancing, just holding one another tenderly. I immediately seek Caleb out. I scan the room but don't see him anywhere.

As I'm sitting in my chair at the head table, I sense someone standing behind me off to my left. A finger then lightly trails across my shoulders. Then that same finger makes a swirling pattern on the nape of my neck. I roll my head to the side, savoring the sensations. Of course, I can't rightly say I'm acquainted with Caleb's touch because we haven't ventured down that path, but I *know* it's him doing this to me. It's one of those things you *know* in your marrow. It's your lover's—or in my case, soon-to-be lover's—touch. It's much like how I felt him behind me earlier when we were outside. We're equally drawn to one another.

It's getting easier to admit things to myself. Our passion is like that of a good book. The beginning pulls you right in and holds you hostage. The middle keeps you wanting more as each new twist and turn unfolds. Hell, I'll dog-ear or bookmark my favorite parts along the way too…but that would mean the whole book would be marked-up, because each page of our passion is too incredible not to be considered my favorite. And the end…well, there's no end in sight because this is something infinite.

I feel his breath on my ear as he leans in, and it sends tingles everywhere. Goose pimples line my body, and I shiver. He whispers that one word I have come to love so much.

"Sweetness," he groans.

That word is not a question, it's an answer. It's also a solution. I know what he wants and needs. I know he won't ask or take; he's too respectful and too afraid to hurt me. He rests his hands lightly on each of my shoulders now, and I cross my right arm over my chest to pat the hand on my left shoulder.

"Dance with me?" I plead.

I say it so quietly, I'm not even sure he can hear me. He must, though, because his hand clutches mine and helps me up from my chair. We're about to make what is going on between us public. My kids are about to witness two people falling for each other so completely and deeply right before their very eyes. I shouldn't be naïve because I'm sure they already *know,* but it's nice to live in a little world of naivety—it's a safe world to be in. All three of my kids are very intuitive. Leah knows me like I know myself. I have to ask them how they feel about all this. And I'll be sure to do that well before Caleb and I ever become something official.

He gently pulls me along to the dance floor, and my heart is pounding in my chest. Our clasped-together hands are so sweaty, I'm surprised we have a grip on one another. This is it! It's the culmination of all my hopes and dreams. They will be on display for everyone to see. I'm sure you can witness in my eyes and see it written on my face how I feel about this man.

*Does he know, though? Does he realize what he means to me?*

He guides me at the small of my back until we reach the middle of the floor, then poses my body so I'm standing before him. I look down and gulp because of my jitters. With his pointer finger in a hook position, he uses the knuckle part of his finger to lift my chin so I can meet his gaze. *Mmm,* he has the most dazzling smile. It's one of those mega-watt grins that could blind you because it's too beautiful to even look at.

I feel so small standing in front of him, like he towers over me in the most delicious way. A big, strong, commanding, and drop-dead gorgeous man is so hard to come by. And he manages to make me feel so delicate, feminine, sexy, and wanted when he looks at me the way he does. I crave his scent as much as I crave his touch. I bite my lip because I want to taste every part of him. If I move my hand from his chest and work my way down, I can try to discreetly cup him through his slacks—that's too soon and too naughty, however. Instead, I curl my hands up and tell myself *no!* I will do my best to save that maneuver for when we're in private.

I always melt at the sight of his features. To think a man like him could want a woman like me sends my heart and body into overdrive. He helps me wrap one arm around his neck. Then, he grabs my waist with his one hand and holds our other free hands to his chest, as we move back and forth in a sensual embrace to the slow song. The tune playing is one I will remember forever.

I recognize her sultry style from one of the seasons of *American Idol*. And who could forget that delightful gum commercial in which her rendition of the song was featured? I adore Haley Reinhart. As Caleb and I sway to "Can't Helping Falling in Love," I can't think of a more fitting song for us.

I can picture a wedding in my future. I can picture our friends and family gathered around us like we are right now. I can picture these very things because they can be a reality. Caleb and the kids and I can be a family…one day. I hear him softly clear his throat as if he's caught up by the emotions as much as I am.

"Liz, I…," he starts, then pauses a moment, not finishing the sentence or completing the words I didn't want to hear before today. But now, well, now I so desperately want them, I could cry.

He tries again, "Liz, I'm crazy about you. You must know that by now. Each second we spend together is like magic. You're perfection."

My throat catches, and I can't find my voice. See, this is where I'm conflicted. The part about *perfection* scares me. He has me on a pedestal. This isn't a confidence issue; it's more of an issue pertaining to him not realizing there's no such thing as *perfect*—no one gets that distinction. *God, I'm fearful I can't live up to this image he built of me in his head.*

I'm holding on to his back and grip the fabric harshly, trying to get his attention. I need for him to really hear me and understand the place where I'm coming from.

"Caleb, no one is *perfect*. I'm certainly not anywhere close to that. I think you've misconstrued your feelings if you think that; I'm sorry to say," I produce a whimper as thick tears are forming—my thoughts centering on the prospect that I may lose him.

I feel like I'm being a silly bitch. I'm probably insulting him and making an ass of myself, but this needs to be said. I have to set the record straight before we get any deeper in the waters.

"I haven't misconstrued the situation or my feelings. And I have no misconceptions as to who you are. And who you are is exquisite! Liz, I realize perfection doesn't exist, but it does exist for me. Sweetness, you don't have to be perfect to the world; just be you, and that's the *perfect* for me. You. Are. My. Perfection," he explains and stops us from moving so I'm forced to look at him.

*How does he allay my worries and fears so quickly?*

It's like he has a power over me that I cannot understand. He soothes me unlike any person has ever done before.

I breathe out, "You're my perfection too!"

And then I realize this is the moment. This will be our first official kiss. Everything is moving in slow motion. As the song comes to an end, our lips meet. It's the lightest touch, and if I wasn't so hyperaware, I'd miss it if my eyes were closed. But they're wide open and taking in everything going on around me. It's a sweet and tender kiss. Closed-mouthed and perfect—*there ya go, I'll use his word.*

And then suddenly, it transforms. In an instant, it becomes frenzied and explosive as his tongue slides inside. Thank God he moved his hands to cradle me to him because I go weak in the knees for this man once again. My hands go into his hair. If there are onlookers, I don't care. If my kids are watching, well, I can't dwell on it. I have to seize the moment and do what feels right. I've always put everyone before myself and my needs. And to me, what I'm doing right now isn't even considered selfish. I owe it to myself and Caleb to let myself go.

I could kiss this man all night. Hell, I don't ever want to not be kissing him. Maybe we can be permanently locked together—I'll find an iron worker to solder us. Nothing has ever felt so good and so right. His tongue is silky and warm. He kisses like a dream. I ache so badly for him. I may end up throwing him down to the floor and having my way with him, and that uninhibited and inappropriate behavior is so not me. I'm desperate to climb on top of him and sink down upon every hard inch of male flesh. He has to know what he does to me. I have to tell him.

I reluctantly pull away, but it's necessary. I need to breathe, or I'll pass out. As we break apart, we're gasping for breath. He moves his lips to my neck and plants soft kisses below my ear. I tug him down to me so I can say something seductive in his ear.

"Let's make perfection together," I purr in a tempting tone.

I was aiming for something a little more scandalous—*maybe I should've said "perfucktion" instead.*

Well, whatever, I figured he'd get my meaning either way. His nostrils flare, and his eyes widen. I hear his intake of breath and the agonized sound that escapes him. He doesn't reply, though. He grabs my hand, and whereas before he led me slowly to the dance floor, now he's pulling me along like a balloon on a string.

Apparently his patience has snapped. I'm trailing behind and trying to keep up. I'm sure he looks like a barbarian moving through the crowd. To outsiders, this looks wrong. But to close friends, surely they know what it is: a man on a mission to claim what is his. And tonight I will be claimed!

# Chapter 15: Table the Idea

*Liezel*

I can't imagine Caleb has ever been here to visit Ev's workplace either. So, for someone unfamiliar with his surroundings, it sure seems like he has a clear direction in mind despite the condition he's in. I swear, it's like men are outfitted with an internal compass of some sort, or at least they act confident about it until they figure it out—I've always considered it an inborn kind of thing.

Caleb finally brings me to a bank of elevators and pushes the up arrow button. The elevator car must have already been on our floor because it chimes and opens immediately. I'm thrust inside and before the doors can even close, he's on me. I can't think. I can't speak. I only feel. I slightly register the fact that he hit a button for a random floor.

A part of me is realizing it's slightly wrong to take advantage of Stuart's generosity by using his building for some debauchery, but I shove those qualms out of my mind. Caleb has me pinned to the wall. The metal railing is in my lower back, and I grip each side of the bar with my hands, causing my pelvis to angle forward—right where our bodies line up with our most intimate parts.

His hands are in my hair, pulling my head to him so he can delve into my mouth like a starved man. We're fused together. I'm drenched between my legs and needy. He's grinding against me so roughly, but not in a painful way. Let's just say I won't be surprised if he wears a hole through his clothing to get to me. He finally releases my mouth and moves down to my neck to suck at the soft skin near my collarbone.

My breasts are begging for attention. I need him to suck and bite my nipples, or I'll explode with frustration. His cock is rock hard against my pubic bone, and I want to jump in his arms and wrap my legs around his waist. However, I don't do any of these things because the elevator chimes too quickly, stopping at whatever floor he picked.

When the doors open again, I'm being rushed down the hall into some type of conference room in the left corridor. The lights are off, but the glass panels in the hallway illuminate the area. The table in the center of the meeting room is huge and can accommodate at least twenty people given the chairs all around. The enormous shiny brown desk is like an altar. *Will there be a virginal sacrifice tonight?* It sure feels like it since it's been so damn long since I've done anything with a partner.

Caleb shuts the door without locking it. He doesn't draw the blinds to the hallway—if he did, there'd be no light unless he actually flicked the switch. I have to admit there's a certain level of excitement knowing someone could stumble upon us. Granted, I imagine no one should be up here—or would have a need to come up here—but ya never know. It's thrilling being with this man. The spontaneity of the situation heightens my excitement.

He takes off his suit jacket and lays it on the table. I'm standing a few inches from the closed door, unable to move until he instructs me. It's unnerving that he still hasn't said anything. I'm breathing deeply, trying to calm myself and mentally prepare for what we're about to do.

"How long's it been, sweetness?" He asks.

At first I'm kind of confused and contort my face to match my state of bewilderment. Then it dawns on me. Now I'm mortified!

\*\*\*

*Caleb*

*Ah shit!*

I didn't mean to embarrass her. Well, now I've gone and fucked myself—and that may very well be my fate after what I just asked her. But I have to know the answer. If it's been years—which I suspect to be the case—then I can't be a prick and storm the gates. Instead, I have to ride up to the gate, let the drawbridge down, and proceed at a trot with my valiant steed.

She's wringing her hands in front of her, toiling over how to answer me. I see her swallow hard and can practically feel that lump hit her stomach.

"It's been...," she begins, then looks away.

I will give her time to think, but I need to know. She shouldn't be embarrassed around me, but I can appreciate her reluctance to respond. I don't want her to ever feel an ounce of discomfort or uneasiness around me. *There will be no secrets between us.* I will know *everything.* Or we simply can't work!

"It's been about twelve years," she admits ashamedly and proceeds to look at the floor.

"Fuck!" I exclaim.

I immediately regret saying that word. I realize she's going to misunderstand. It's not that I can't be patient or go slow. And it's not that I'm disappointed. If anything, I'm ironically relieved. That asshole never knew how to treat her. It's like I get to introduce her to everything as if it's the first time.

"I'm sorry. This is so awkward. I should've told you, I guess. It's so humiliating knowing I was married for as long as I was and never had *that* kind of a relationship after the kids were born. He was more interested in the bottle than in me. That was truly his first and only love in life. I wouldn't even say I was secondary," she groans and seems disgusted with herself.

After a beat, she picks up by saying, "I'm sure you're used to more experienced women. William was my first and only since we dated for years before getting pregnant and then married. Jesus, I practically feel like a virgin again," she admits.

Then, she puts her hands to her cheeks and closes her eyes. I can see that a red hue has kissed her skin because of her shame. She shouldn't feel ashamed. *Am I a sick bastard that I'm more turned on than I've ever been? Probably!*

I can't let her stand there and be overwhelmed by guilt, or embarrassment, or whatever is bothering her. I move in and lift her up. She yelps in surprise. I set her down on the table by placing her ass right where I put my jacket so she won't be cold—I knew when her naked flesh touched the surface it would be a jolt. *I try to think of everything.*

She goes to speak, and I hold up my finger to her mouth, successfully shushing her. I kiss her plump lips to take the sting away of me silencing her. Oh, she can be as noisy as she wants, but there will be no more talk about worries or fears in this room.

"I told you, you're perfect. You're still perfect. I only asked because I don't want to hurt you…emotionally or physically. It's like you've been waiting for me. That probably sounds cheesy, but hey, I'm a cheesy guy. And now, thanks to you, I consider myself more of a cookie guy," I try and add a little humor to lighten the mood, grinning at her mischievously.

She smiles brightly, and it's what I wanted to see. She balances my world with one look. *God, how I love her!* I cup her face with my big hands and run the pads of my thumbs in soothing circles on her cheeks.

Her soft-scented lilac fragrance fills my soul as I breathe her in. I finally determined exactly what her floral scent is. When I was at the florist shop, I honed in on that amazing smell. Kate then imparted her extensive knowledge on the purple flower. I have to agree that the blooms are breathtaking in person, smell divine, and immediately elicit a sense of calm and splendor—that's my sweetness to a T! I now have vases full of lilacs sitting in my office and in my apartment. I need to be surrounded by a substitute until I have the real thing with me all the time.

I gently push her down at the shoulders so she's forced to lie back on the surface. With my jacket stretched out, it's enough to accommodate her body. She looks so hot lying there waiting for me to take control. My erection is so painful that it's hard to move. Adjusting myself won't help either because the crotch area is too tight. I'm probably suffocating my poor dick; my big buddy needs rescuing—maybe some mouth-to-mouth resuscitation will do the trick! *No…not yet.* Her first…always her first.

"We're not going to make love. You're not ready. Maybe later tonight when we're back at the hotel and in a bed. But right now, I will give you the best fucking orgasm of your life! I need to taste you and pleasure you. You need to feel what it'll be like between us. And I need you to understand the depths of my feelings and the lengths to which I'll go to make you mine in every way possible. I'll eat at your pussy until they send a search party for us, sweetness," I threaten.

There's no room for joking. There's no room for lightening the mood this time. I'm deadly serious. I meant every word. I need this woman more than I need to eat, sleep, or breathe. I said a while back that I'd hunt her down with my scope, and that's what I'm going to do. I have her in my sights. Her defenses are down. She's not a wounded animal, though. She's merely becoming tamed.

Her respirations have increased, and I watch as she inhales and exhales harshly. Her tits are rising and falling with each expansion and collapse of her chest. I'll have to go to town on those supple mounds later because they're mesmerizing. I grab one of the leather rolling chairs that I had wheeled out of the way when I laid her on the table. I sit in the chair right in between her legs and place my hands on her knees. She's startled by my touch, but it's a natural response because of her nerves.

I effectively pull her body closer to me so my face is properly positioned close enough to her beautiful cunt when I'm ready to chow down. I remove each one of her shoes and place them under my chair. She's like a hawk, watching every move. I love that she has no idea what my moves are. I thrive on keeping her on her toes. And speaking of toes, I grab her naked feet and place each one on the arms of the chair. I'm sure she feels exposed and uncomfortable. I bet, to her, this probably looks more like a gyno exam than a dabble in cunnilingus—believe me, I'm not sheltered and know what goes on at *those* kinds of appointments. Anyway, I can assure you the view before me is sexy as fuck.

I reach up under her dress and remove her panties. She shivers as I brush against tender, wet, warm flesh in my goal to remove the material. I lift each foot to slide them off and then place her satiny purple panties in my pants pocket—*hey, I don't want them to get lost, so sue me...I know a good lawyer!*

Now it's time to play and feast. I inch her dress up her thighs and finally stop at her torso where the material is bunched up. She's completely naked from the waist down. I groan in utter euphoria at what my eyes are taking in.

However, her hands that had been resting flat against the table at her sides move to cover herself—or I'm assuming to pull down her dress. I stand up and halt her actions by grabbing her wrists and locking her hands into one of mine, trapping her. It's necessary so she comprehends the situation and what's about to go down. And how it's going to go down my way!

"Don't hide from me. I want to see you...all of you. I'm sure in a lot of ways this is all new to you. You're rediscovering a part of yourself that was lost years ago. But I want you to go on this journey with me. I want to be the man who makes you smile, makes you laugh, makes you cry tears of joy. And hopefully some tears of ecstasy in there," I convey, laying my metaphorical cards on the table.

We're both baring parts of ourselves to one another tonight. I'm ready. I'm ready for it all. I want to take this next step, and I welcome everything that comes with it.

I place soft kisses to her forehead and then to her cheeks. I give a peck to the tip of her nose and then suck at her juicy, pink-stained lips. She's starting to relax again, but I still keep my grip firm on her wrists. Now that she's a little more pliable, I can continue to work my way down.

I plant kisses on her belly. She should never be embarrassed about her body. Maybe I'm not like most guys, but I find an older woman's body sexy. I can appreciate it. Each curve and mark holds a story. The silvery stretch marks, which are barely visible because of how toned she is, make me admire her strength and beauty all the more. She's had three kids, yet you wouldn't know it. She must've delivered naturally each time because there are no scars to be seen suggesting a previous C-section. If only she knew the ages of the women I've been with, then she wouldn't feel so self-conscious—I'll tell her about it one day.

"You're so beautiful. Your skin's so soft. Your body's fucking amazing. God, you drive me crazy," I murmur against her skin.

The dirty blonde hair covering her pubic bone is so damn hot—I should say it's more of a dark blonde shade. I hate saying *dirty blonde* as it implies a negative connotation, unless we're talking about *dirty* in the sexy, wicked sense. Nevertheless, it's neatly trimmed. I don't like bare pussies— for fuck's sake, they're meant to have hair! Her beautiful femininity pleases me immensely.

I lower my head to her intoxicating cunt and flick my tongue at her clit. Oh yeah, I go right for the gold from the start. She moans, and I can already smell and see some of her juices coat her pussy lips. I'm sure it doesn't take much to get her going because not only is this our first time doing anything sexual together, but also her lack of experience over the years will work to my advantage.

I have her full attention, and she's completely aroused. I let go of her wrists that are still pinned above her head. She leaves her arms there anyway, even after I release them. She's writhing, and her body is arching off the table—I've hardly done anything. She's so responsive and receptive to my touch. It's even more of a turn on for me that I can bring her to such heights so quickly.

I lick my way around her opening and tunnel deeply into her channel with my tongue in the next instant. I palm her left breast with my one hand and alternate sides by pinching her nipples. She keeps creaming my mouth with the most decadent of honeyed flavors. I eat at her like I've never had pussy before. Nothing could be sweeter. Nothing could satisfy me more. Nothing will ever do again!

After lavishing exceptional care to her most intimate parts with my mouth, I then finger-fuck her for a good while. First, I start with one finger, and her hands are no longer above her head. Now they're in my hair, gripping me fiercely as she's deep into this passionate state—I'm not complaining, though. Even if she draws blood, it will be well worth it. I insert the next finger, then rub the anterior wall of her pussy until she becomes even more vocal. *Bingo!* I have located her G-spot. I told you I'm an expert on all things pussy-related—*maybe I missed my calling as an OBGYN or some shit with knowing all these terms.*

I don't want to push her too much with four fingers, so I settle for three because she should be good and stretched. Later tonight when I tunnel into her taut body, I'll revel in the fact that I can stretch her to her fullest with my massive cock. I want her pussy to avoid as much pain as possible, but I'm also a selfish prick and want it nice and tight for me.

I couldn't help myself earlier today and packed condoms—just in case—when I prepared my overnight bag for this shindig. I hope we'll get to use the whole damn box at some point, but maybe I shouldn't put the cart before the horse—or the cock before the condom in this instance.

Fuck, thank God we're alone on this floor because it sounds like I'm murdering her with the flow of screams and moans she's letting loose. I can't make out much of what she's saying, but at some points I hear my name escape from her mouth. That makes me work her even harder, faster, and with more gusto than ever. I'm sucking at her clit and giving it gentle bites. My technique involves the expert combination of suction and laving.

This is by far my favorite part of discovering what she likes…and what she loves. So, I employ my triple threat. I pinch her nipple, softly nibble at her clit, and rub at her G-spot all at the same time. And voila! She loses it for me in the most divine fashion. She screams and creams. Her heavenly nectar flows into my hand. And I pre-cum in my pants but don't give a fuck because I'll clean myself up later.

I let her come down from the mountain as I continue stroking her flesh. She's sensitive, but I feel it's necessary to stroke her further so it's not such an abrupt ceasing of all touching and tasting. God, I felt her cries of passion deep in my bones, and the way she makes me feel is what will propel me forward in this life. I'll continue to reaffirm she's my reason to *eat, sleep, breathe, repeat.*

In my line of work, I advise clients of the risks when entering into an agreement, whether verbal or contractual. An indemnity clause is not often one I have to apply to domestic law, or even in a personal sense. Yet, I can't help but wonder what type of clause I should've put in place for my brain and heart. Because if Liz ever decides I'm not what she wants…it will break me—I'll respect her decision. Okay, I'm partly lying because I won't be *okay* with it. *I guess I should've drafted an affidavit for myself while I was at it.*

This relationship we're forging—in an unspoken sense for the moment—is all I can focus on. Now that I have her, I can't lose her. I look down at her beautiful face, and her eyes are closed, no doubt still hovering in a blissful cloud.

*I love you.…*

It's right there on my tongue, but I don't say it. I'm a coward. *Why do I feel like there's this constant push and pull of sorts between us?*

And I can't shake the feeling that she's hiding something from me, and that's why she can't completely let go. Call it intuition; call it me being Mr. Sensitive—call it whatever, but some things you just *know.*

I do love her, but the question is, does she—or will she—love me back?

# Chapter 16: The Waiting Game

*Liezel*

We found restrooms near the conference room, so I'm putting myself back together. Of course, I have that telltale look where my hair is mussed, and I need to smooth out my dress and whatnot. My tissues are sensitive, and it still tingles from all the attention he bestowed upon me. It took forever for me to get up off the table. My legs were jelly. Even now as I stand at the sink continuing to freshen up, I still feel weak. The man is a dream. He's a god. He's a legend.

I should have told him *I love you.* I was going to say it, but then I thought better of it because I didn't want him to think it was because of how grateful I was for his oral treatment. It would have been on the heels of an orgasm, and that doesn't make for a first-time-I-love-you moment.

*When I say it, I want it to be right and I want it to be an intimate moment.*

I don't drink, for obvious reasons thanks to our family history, but I need something tonight. Maybe a glass of champagne will do. However, it does tend to make me horny on the rare occasions that I've imbibed.

I hope we haven't been gone too long and our absence wasn't noticeable. All that was really left to do wedding-wise was to cut the cake and say goodbye to the couple as they're whisked away to their hotel room for the night before their trip.

I run my fingers across my lips and can still feel his kisses. I wanted so badly to reciprocate with my mouth on him, and I hope I get the chance later. The poor guy was sporting one of the biggest hard-ons I've ever seen. I should have given him a hand job or something to help take the edge off. I feel like a jerk for not giving him relief. I'm not a selfish person. I want to make it up to him.

I take one last look in the mirror and smooth back my hair. I don't have my clutch on me, so there's no way to reapply my lipstick. What I have to work with will have to do. Thank God Caleb gave my panties back to me. Not that I thought he'd keep them as a souvenir or trophy of some sort, but still. It's nice to have coverage and protection.

I exit the restroom, and Caleb is patiently waiting for me, leaning against the wall and looking so yummy. *How jealous must everyone around him be of his physique, personality, and brains?* I'm rethinking the whole rejoining-the-party thing downstairs, and instead opting for going round two on the table. On still semi-shaky legs, I walk in his direction.

He groans sexily. I wish I could saunter up to him, but it's not possible in my condition. I can't manage a sinful sway of my hips for anything. I probably look like a newborn baby deer trying to walk for the first time.

"Mmm, you know, you're good for my ego, sweetness," he waggles his eyebrows at me.

And, of course, I'm coy and have to ask, "Hmm, and why's that?"

"Because the way you're walking tells me I did my job thoroughly," he conveys with a lot of yearning as he stares into my eyes.

"Oh," I reply in a breathy way.

He offers me a chaste kiss with his soft lips, and we break apart all too quickly.

"Come on, we better get back down there," he suggests.

*Yes, down there…*I sigh dreamily in my mind. I know he's actually referring to going back downstairs.

I bite my lip and respond haughtily, "I thought you were waiting until they issue a search party?"

He narrows his brown eyes and smirks at me. Clearly, I'm taunting him and loving every minute of it.

He playfully slaps my ass and whispers in my ear, "That one's gonna cost you…later."

I shiver at his words, and after a few more minutes and a few more kisses, we finally rejoin the reception. The party is still in full swing when we enter. No one really seemed to miss us, thankfully. I grab a flute of champagne from a nearby server, as does Caleb.

We end up dancing and hanging out with the kids and the rest of our wedding party until Ev and Brent cut the cake. After that, the newlyweds take their leave, and Fred and Milly recommend getting all the youngsters down for the night. They take all the kids back to the hotel along with Granny Lil.

I was already feeling a little tipsy from the one glass, so I knew I had reached my limit. Caleb told me he was ready to go, and my stomach bottomed out. *Ding, ding, ding…I'm being ridiculous, sound the alarms!* After the otherworldly orgasm of a lifetime, you'd think it would have calmed me and prepared me for the after-party in my hotel room.

The limo drivers are kindly shuttling guests from the reception to the hotel, and we behave ourselves on the short ride. I'm sure all the couples in our group are going to have a wild time tonight, and I won't be the exception. My heart hasn't stopped jackhammering. Caleb is one of those guys who leaves a mark on you. He's like a fingerprint leaving behind trace evidence showing he's been there; you can't always see it, but it's definitely there—that latent print is on my heart. Okay, maybe I've been watching a little too many *CSI* reruns lately.

As we pull into the entranceway to the hotel, Caleb turns to me and asks, "Your room or mine, sweetness?"

All I can do is gulp.

*\*\*\**

*Caleb*

My girl is nervous, but those butterflies will soon turn to pleasurable flutters. I consider myself like a cupid of sorts. Instead of delivering hearts by way of arrow, I deliver orgasms from my rod. I'll have her flat on her back and panting in no time, and she'll forget she was ever this frazzled.

I'll make the decision easy for her. "We'll go to my room."

I tug at her hand and help her out of the car. I lead her through the lobby and head up to our floor. My room is across the hall from hers. I hold the keycard up to the reader, and we enter. I put the "do not disturb" sign on the handle and shut us in. As I'm still facing the door, I hear her intake of breath as the locks click. *Oh yes, I have you trapped well and good now.*

The suite has a decent-size living room, a guest room to the right and a master bed and bath to the left. I think my room is bigger than Liz's since she has an adjoining one, so I'm glad we're in mine so we have lots of space for…activities. I walk up behind her and kiss her shoulder.

In a shaky voice she asks, "Can I have a minute alone to myself?"

I give a smooch to her shoulder again, rubbing up and down her arms a few times to reassure her. "Of course. Take all the time you need. I'll find some way to occupy myself."

I chuckle softly at my innuendo, but I will not be doing *that* by myself since I finally have her. I think she's still too nervous to respond verbally. She nods but doesn't look my way as she turns to head into the master bedroom, and I hear her shut the door to the ensuite bathroom. Unperturbed, I head to the living room area and remove my suit coat. I look around, admiring the digs, and think it's ideal for a special night such as this. I didn't get to appreciate its beauty earlier today upon check-in because there was so much to do before the wedding.

I undo my silver monogrammed cufflinks—groomsmen's gifts from Brent—and place them on the coffee table. I take out my wallet and cell from my pants pocket, then divest of my tie, belt, shoes, and socks. Gone are the days of wearing cummerbunds, thank fuck for that! Brent didn't want vests or pocket squares, so the simple but elegant suits did nicely today.

I sit back and make myself comfortable with my hands behind my head, fingers laced together, just chillaxing. I shut my eyes and breathe deeply. I'm anxious and beyond ready to make love to her. I'm summoning the strength for patience. She needs time to sort out her feelings; this will be another big moment for her.

At least a few minutes go by before I hear my phone buzz on the table. I open my eyes and realize I should have put it to silent instead of vibrate. I switch the mode so it doesn't disturb us later. I glance at the screen to make sure it's not some emergency.

It's not a damn emergency. It's from Mrs. Price.

> *Caleb, I'm rethinking the Tuscan villa. I don't believe I want Darron to have it after all. When can we get together to discuss this pressing matter?*

I groan because this will be yet another setback in the divorce proceedings. Every time I think we have everything settled, she seems to come up with a new way to fuck up the deal. Now I'm beginning to think she's dragging this out intentionally, but I haven't quite figured out yet what the goal is. Darron will pay dearly, there's no doubt about that, yet her torturing him in this way really doesn't gain her anything; it certainly doesn't bode well with me. I know how the partners will feel about it, and they'll want me to do whatever it takes to *keep her happy*—they're salivating over the potential gains. Her demands and contingencies have become more frequent as of late, so it begs the question, *what is she really after?*

I type out a quick reply, letting her know when I'm back in the office on Monday I'll have Melanie contact her to set up a meeting to draft yet another amendment. Darron will surely have heads rolling on his end over this latest modification. This villa is the *one thing* Mrs. Price has made abundantly clear from the start she wasn't interested in. She hates the property because its less-than-stellar location makes her "look like a pauper"—in fucking Tuscany of all places!

Yeah, that woman is a piece of work. I refuse to even call her by her first name because we're not on friendly terms. It's strictly a client-attorney relationship all the way. I can only wonder if she now wants the property because I bet Darron has been taking his lover there. Eh, doesn't matter the reason; I guess I'll find out Monday.

I also shoot off a text to Melanie regarding setting up the appointment with my vile client. I'm one of those people who, if I don't set a reminder, get my paralegal to do it, or write it down, then I'll forget. You don't get to be successful unless you're organized, that's for sure!

I put my phone back down on the table in disgust. All the people who really matter know where to find me if something comes up. And I'd already briefed Melanie on my whereabouts for the weekend, so she can certainly put out any fires in my absence. No more shop-talk. It's time to solely focus my attention and talents on one very fine woman.

I'm just getting comfortable again when I hear a door open from what I'm assuming is the master bathroom. My hands are starting to sweat. Normally I'm as cool as a cucumber, and I've been under lots of pressure and grueling situations at work. In the bedroom, I'm even more controlled—call me a thermostat because I can dial it up or down as needed. But Liz so easily causes my control to slip.

I'm staring at the entryway to the bedroom without even blinking for fear of missing any little thing. I'm tracking her like I'm on high-alert, waiting for any sign of movement. My heart is pounding out like a war cry. This is it!

# Chapter 17: Not Pre*dick*table

*Liezel*

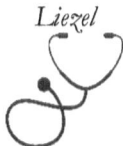

*Oh my God, this is it!*

I can't believe we're finally going to be together. I took my time in the bathroom to fluff my hair, strip out of my dress, empty my bladder, and brush my teeth—I used his toothbrush and I don't care if that's gross because he'll thank me later. The champagne still lingers in my system, which is good because, like I said, it makes me horny—even one glass does the trick.

I'm about to walk into the living room area where I assume Caleb will be. I take a deep breath to steady myself and look down at my purple bra and panties—the very same panties the man took off me earlier. I don't know why I'm nervous; he's already seen me *down there,* for God's sake! He's already seen my stretch marks too. The only thing he hasn't seen are my naked breasts, but I think they're a good pair.

I have to remember that guys really don't care about the little stuff women obsess over—like stretch marks. Put a naked woman in front of them, and all is forgotten. Alexi has told me enough times that men are visual creatures and need *tits and pussy to play with*, and they don't notice every bump or wrinkle because their attention is focused on the *fun parts*. I'm feeling marginally better now and decide to make my appearance.

I step into the living room, and Caleb is sitting on the couch with just his dress shirt and pants on. His feet are bare, and he's leaning forward with his arms resting on his thighs like he's waiting for something…waiting for someone. And thank God I'm that lucky someone.

"Fuuuccckkk!" He says, enunciating each letter and deliciously dragging it out with what I imagine is his sex-roughened voice.

A current of electricity runs through me at his clear appreciation for my state of dress. I can't help but surge with pride at knowing he wants me. I see him make fists with his hands, and as I move closer to him by the couch, I feel wetness forming once again between my legs.

"You look unbelievable. God, you make me so damn hard. I can't believe I get to make love to your sweet, tight little body all night long. I hope you're prepared to pull an all-nighter, nurse, because I need some medical assistance in the lower quadrant," he deadpans.

*Mmm*, his filthy mouth makes me so hot. I never knew I'd be into his dirty language, but anything he says makes me swoon. I don't know if I can quite reciprocate with wicked wording, but I'll sure try.

"Well, in that case, I wouldn't want my patient to suffer any unnecessary discomfort. So, I'll be sure to issue one-hundred cc's of saliva to the affected area…stat!" I cheekily reply.

His nostrils flare; his eyes smolder and turn to molten chocolate, and his loud intake of breath through his nose gives away how deeply I've hit the mark. He quickly gets up from the couch and stalks me like I'm some kind of prey. I quiver with anticipation and think I should be the one pouncing on him since I'm the dang cougar—no such luck.

I find myself in his arms again as he passionately kisses me and lifts me from the floor as my feet are dangling. He's so big and strong and walks with me in his arms until we're in the master bedroom. I feel the back of my legs hit the bed, then he lowers me to my feet.

I think my worries have finally subsided, and all that's left is desire and hunger for this man. He moves my hair off the one shoulder and sweeps it to the other side, but not before running his fingers through it and stroking it almost reverently, as if he's been wanting to do it for a long time. Then, he starts nuzzling and sucking my neck and collarbone. He smells so good being this close to me. It's like a woodsy, mouthwatering musk. My eyes flutter closed. I brace myself by gripping his forearms because that naughty tongue of his has a way with words and actions that can destroy me so easily.

He's like the *Terminator*, a cyborg from the future sent back in time to annihilate my pussy from this planet by screwing me into oblivion. *Okay, I've gone off the rails now!* Why I think of that movie, I don't know; it happened to be the most popular movie when I was a preteen, but clearly that has nothing to do with what's about to happen in this bedroom.

"Undress me," he commands.

My eyes shut, I'm overcome in the moment, but now they pop open when my ears register the firm order he just gave. Boy oh boy, this alpha male snaps to it when he wants to. It's sexy as hell. I don't want him to be super sweet, soft, and gentle in every aspect. I want him to be bossy and domineering because I've never experienced this, and I had no clue this would push all the hot buttons on my sex panel—*good Lord, maybe I'm the cyborg!*

With trembling hands and unsteady fingers, I unbutton his crisp, white shirt. I push the two sides apart and bare a marble slab of chest with delectable pecs and six-pack abs. Now I feel like a female cat of sorts. I'm sure I'm purring and licking my chops. I'm sure my eyes are glimmering like a feline's as I sigh loudly at his beauty.

He doesn't give me too much time to stare and admire before he delivers his next command, "Now my pants."

I go from gazing at his chest to looking him square in the eyes. I keep yo-yoing from the huntress to the hunted every few minutes. It's dizzying. Of course, I damn well love it; it's all so new. It was never like this with William. He never made me feel so consumed with love and lust. I never felt so overwhelmed in the best possible sense; I want to orgasm one instant and the next instant cuddle with Caleb because of how thoughtful he is. I don't know how he manages to pull off the duality of personality traits. The *sweet* and the *alpha* are not something I would've thought went together—on him, though, they do marry well. He's not predictable.

"I'm still waiting," he affirms.

*Oops!* I'd gone off in my head again on a tangent. So, I move my hands from his shirt, placing my palms flat against his chest. He swallows, and I bite the inside of my cheek, knowing I can celebrate that little victory of getting to him. I inch my hands down his front until I reach his waist. Instead of unbuttoning and unzipping, I become brazen and work my fingers past his underwear until I feel his pubic hair tickle my hand.

*Oh my God, I'm about to grab his dick!*

I am no longer looking in his eyes but down at what I'm doing so I can enjoy the experience more. My fingers are moving so slowly until I finally feel warm, velvety flesh. Lower still I go until my fingers curl around his cock, and I close my hand to grip it. Steel. God, it's magnificent! I chance a peek at his face, and the expression he's wearing is one of agony.

"Motherfucking hell!" He hisses through gritted teeth.

"Mmm," is my only reply.

At my response, he wrenches my hand away and tosses me onto the powder-blue duvet-covered bed. I don't even have time to process his rebuff because the next second, I realize it's not a rebuff. He's just lost control of whatever patience he had up until that point.

He's practically clawing at his pants, trying to undo the button and unzip the fly. He angrily pulls the slacks down his thick, muscled thighs and yanks off his dress shirt, which goes on the floor to make a messy pile. His underwear will be the death of me when they come off. I want to look, but don't want to look, if that makes any sense. I think I'll pass out once I get a load of what he's packing. It felt so good in my grasp, but touching and seeing are two different things.

He doesn't mess around, and pulls the briefs down his legs until he's standing there in all his glory. And God bless him for raising the flag! *Holy shit!* I know my mouth is hanging open in a large "O." I'm gaping at the huge cock that sits atop his massive balls.

*There's no way he's going to fit!*

\*\*\*

*Caleb*

"Oh, it'll fit all right," I assure her.

She didn't have to voice that concern. It was written on her face. I'm not cocky; I just happen to have a lot of cock and know it. This is usually the general reaction to my well-endowed feature. But since this reaction is coming from her, it's the best of my life. I've said it before, and I'll say it again, she's become my mantra as I *eat, sleep, and breathe her.*

I can't wait any longer. I amble over to my suitcase by the dresser and pull out a condom. I tear the packet and expertly roll it down the length of my shaft. I can feel her gaze burn into me as she's watching everything I do. I kneel on the bed and position myself to crawl up her body. I hook my fingers in her tiny panties and pull them down her silky legs.

"I love this color on you, Liz. Fuck, it reminds me of lilacs, which in turn, reminds me of you," I rasp out.

I toss her panties over my head. She's squirming all over the place at my touch. I move up her body, and my dick brushes her skin. We both shudder. I slide my hands under her back and unhook her pretty bra. I pull the straps from her shoulders and remove the cups from her front. That thing gets tossed over my head as well.

I'm now face-to-tit with two gorgeous mounds of creamy splendor topped with puckered nipples that are berry-dipped in the most luscious pink color. *Fuck me!* God, she's magnificent. I can't stop using the word *perfect* to describe her. Every time I unearth something new about her, I fall more madly and deeply in love. It's not in lust; it's fucking in love!

I lower my head to her right breast and flick the peak with my tongue. Her legs are thrashing, and her hands go right into my hair. *God, I love when she does that!* She's moans, and I can smell her gorgeous cunt as it's surely overflowing right now in anticipation of receiving my huge cock. My dick is impossibly hard, and I'm afraid I might bust the condom before I even get inside her.

I move my one hand down to her entrance and rub around her pussy lips. Her juices are definitely flowing, and I coat her tissues thoroughly with her liquid. And because I'm a selfish bastard, I rub her juices on my sheathed cock for good measure. Fuck, it feels so good knowing that a part of her is touching me, and I'll have the real thing soon enough.

I place my middle digit inside her hole to test the waters. Her slick walls welcome me and clamp down on my finger. I immediately insert the second finger and work it in and out. She says my name over and over in a raspy whisper, spurring me on all the more. I work in the third finger, and I know she's stretched enough again—my cock will have to stretch her the rest of the way. That tight passage has never received anything like this, but it's about to get it and get it good. I avoid her clit because I want her to come with me when it's time. The orgasm I gave her earlier will have to sustain her until it's time for the final liftoff.

"Okay, sweetness, it's time," I begin, then take a moment to pause in my speech so I can make sure she's paying attention.

I still my fingers inside her. I can hear her heavy breathing, but she stopped saying my name, so I know she's with me.

I continue, "If I do anything you don't like or doesn't feel right, or if you need to stop at any point, promise me you'll tell me. Know that it won't change anything between us in a negative sense and that I'll completely understand. If you're not ready, it's okay; it doesn't have to be tonight. Promise me, Liz."

"I promise," is her quiet two-word answer.

It's enough to reassure me. I rest my forehead against hers in worship—I don't deserve her. She's been through so much, and tonight I don't want there to be any secrets or ghosts between us. There's no room for anything or anyone else to be here in this room and in this loving space we're creating.

I reluctantly remove my fingers from her slick channel so I can replace them with my prized possession. I position myself above her and line my cock up to her opening. I look into her eyes to ensure she's okay. She bites her lip and gives a slight nod, knowing I'm silently asking for permission to enter her.

I move the head of my dick in, and she immediately tenses. Her eyes squeeze shut, and her expression is one of discomfort and not pleasure—that will soon change once she's used to the invasion. I ease in a little more. I keep going at a slow rate until finally I push through to the hilt and my balls are resting against her skin. We both groan—I can't tell yet what hers signifies, but mine sure means pure fucking ecstasy.

I kiss her lips while I'm still buried deep. I can feel her loosen up a bit and relax. Her pussy is still gripping my dick with an unrelenting hold, and I know there's got to be pre-cum in the damn rubber already. I finally pull out so the barest inch of my shaft is still inside, then ram back into her.

"Caleb…oh my God, you feel soooooo good," she cries out.

It's music to my ears, and confirmation the initial discomfort has faded away—thank God because I need to move and rut into her like my life depends on it. I keep up an in-and-out motion for a good while. Sweat coats my skin, and hers is slick with a thin sheen of sweat as well. We're panting and grunting like feral beings, and it's the best sex of my life, even just being in the missionary position. But, I also want to do more.

"Ride me, sweetness," I tell her.

I want her tits in my face bouncing away, and I want to watch her raise and lower herself on me while my dick impales her. She complies immediately—ever the good girl she is—and straddles my hips. She gives my dick a few pumps with her hand. *Fuck! I love it when she fists it!* When she grabbed my dick the first time, I was about to fall to the floor and convulse. It's so intense and hot as fuck watching her face alight with wonder at holding me in her hand.

She then guides it to her sex and puts it inside her pussy. She sits down on me, and my balls painfully tighten to the point I'm so afraid I'll blow my load. I reach out to tweak her nipples, and she throws her head back as the blonde tresses tumble down her shoulders. She licks her lips, then braces herself by putting her hands on my chest for leverage.

I have come to discover that she loves when I talk dirty to her. Not everyone is into it, but Liz definitely gets hornier and hotter the filthier my mouth becomes. I suspect neither of us will last much longer, so I have to make this first encounter set the bar. It will be epic, and I'll never let her forget what it's like between us.

"Sweetness…choke my cock with your pussy. Squeeze it tight with your dripping lips. I want you to suck my dick back into your body each time you move on top of me," I explain in an intense rush.

"Ahh!" She yells as I thrust up into her more forcefully.

She definitely liked what I had to say because her cunt does in fact choke my cock like a clamp, and her creaminess coats our sexes even further. As she rides, the slurping sounds of her channel sucking my dick back in has me wanting to shout from the rooftops. *Yup, any second now, and I'm a goner.* I quicken my pace, and I feel like my dick, mind, and heart will explode as all the sensations are mounting and culminating right where she and I are joined.

"I want to come together. You're going to smother my dick with all your honey and show me how much you love me fucking you," I dare.

I move my hand between our bodies and rub at her clit furiously. Then, I give her nub a pinch, and she loses it. She screams. Her cries of pure pleasure cause me to grunt. I shoot my cum with a loud growl and arch my hips up into her one last time.

I empty into that fucking annoying condom and wish I could feel her without it—*hopefully one day soon I'll get that chance.* My dick finally stops twitching and begins to soften. She collapses on top of me, landing on my chest. Her hair falls in my face, which I love. I'm still wedged inside her, and I let her rest for a few minutes. It smells like sweat and sex swirling in the air, and it's intoxicating—*I want to lick the air and catch it on my tongue as if I'm catching snowflakes with my mouth. Is that fucked up or what?*

It's difficult to extricate myself, but I need to remove the rubber, and I should clean us up. I'm not nearly done with her, but I also don't want to exhaust her too much since this is her second orgasm of the night. There will be plenty more times in our future to fuck like rabbits.

I shake her lightly, and she mumbles something, making me chuckle. God, she really is good for my ego like I told her earlier. She makes me feel like the king of the damn jungle. I begin to move, and she grumbles something else about being too tired. I let her settle back down as I get out of the bed. I walk into the bathroom to remove the condom, tie it off, and throw it in the wastebasket.

Before heading back into the bedroom to collect her, I turn the knob on in the shower stall. I lift her from the bed, and she doesn't protest as I carry her into the hot spray. After placing her feet to the tiled floor, she slides down my body, making me want to fuck her all over again. Once I'm satisfied that she'll stand and support her own weight, I let go of her to grab the shampoo. I quickly do my hair and then suds hers up. She moans as I massage her scalp and work my fingers through the strands.

I switch to lathering our bodies with the perfumed soap, taking great care when I get to her pussy. She winces, and I know she's sore. I decide right then I'll let her sleep for a bit after our shower, then take her at least one more time in the early morning before she returns to her room—I know she wants to be in her room in case anyone needs her.

After we're as clean as we're going to get, I turn the water off and towel us dry. I wrap her up then help her step out of the stall. I reach for my toothbrush and can tell it's still damp, so I realize she used it, which is fine and gives me a thrill—I thought I tasted the mint toothpaste in her kisses. I brush my teeth and guide her out to lie down.

She faceplants on the bed, and I proceed to cover her. Her wet hair will have to air dry; she's obviously too tired to care. Within minutes, she's gently snoozing. I pull her body to mine so she's positioned with her back to my front, and we're effectively spooning like the lovers we are.

I kiss the back of her wet head, letting my lips linger there for a minute while I breathe her in. This is where she belongs, and this is where she'll always be from now on.

"Goodnight, sweetness," I say to the room since she doesn't appear to be conscious.

She, of course, doesn't answer back, and that's quite all right. I'm too keyed up to sleep; I'll wake her in a few hours. For right now, I'm content to just lie here and hold her. In my arms is the most important human being nestled against me, and when I was a boy I never dreamed I'd find my *unicorn* in life…yet here she is!

# Chapter 18: Water You Waiting for?

*Liezel*

I wake and do a little stretch. I feel deliciously exhausted in all the right ways and all the right places. I'm sore, but it's a welcomed sensation because it's a reminder of what we did last night. I move my hand to reach for him, and then I remember I'm back in my own room.

I sit up and glance around, and sure enough, that's where I am. I look at the clock on the bedside table, and it's after ten in the morning. I feel awful for missing breakfast with my kids, even though they're self-sufficient—it's still no excuse. As much as I need to learn to cut myself a break sometimes, I still don't ever want my three to feel like I cast them aside.

I know at some point Caleb brought me back here, yet I'm having a hard time piecing that room-change scenario together. We were both sad to part, but I needed sleep, and it didn't seem like either of us would get any if we stayed together. I had drifted off after the first time we made love. So, I'm not sure how long he let me doze exactly, but he woke me up by sucking on my nipples and sliding his fingers inside me—that got my attention. I even got to put the condom on his beautiful cock. What a ridiculous fiasco that was. I might as well have been blindfolded—it was like trying to play pin the tail on the donkey. Obviously, I'm not experienced with prophylactics.

That second time we made love, he took me from behind. William and I never really did a doggy-style position, so it was all new to me. It was so weird being face down on the bed and having my ass in the air exposed to him—once he entered me, well, you didn't hear any complaints from me and certainly none from my man. He moaned, groaned, grunted and screwed me like it was the end of the world. I'm looking forward to trying many more positions.

I still haven't been able to go down on him with my mouth, but that's coming soon—*ha ha, I didn't even mean to insert the pun, but I nailed it!*

I finally get my lazy bones out of bed and take a long, hot shower to relax my muscles and mitigate some of the sting from the way my body is smarting. After I dress, I pack up my things because check-out is at noon. I knock on the door adjoining my room, and the kids don't answer. I ring Fred and Milly's room, and they tell me my kiddos are down at the indoor pool. Alexi and Caylan already left with Em and Granny Lil, and Fred and Milly said they're now leaving too; I'm officially back on mom duty.

I glance at my watch, and it's 11:10 A.M., so my three should be back soon to get ready to leave, I imagine. I decide I'll go down in search of them, but first I'll stop at Caleb's room to see if he wants to join me for a quick bite to eat down in their in-house restaurant. I'm famished from all the sex last night and during the early morning hours. My body needs nourishment.

I'm surprised I'm handling everything so well. For some reason, I thought I'd somehow fall apart after spending the night with another man. I was being an idiot in this line of thinking, but, truthfully, I didn't know what to expect. I should've realized sooner that with the *right man,* things would be different.

I knock on Caleb's door, and it opens. I suck in my breath at the bright-eyed, bushy-tailed sex god standing before me. He manages to look like a man who can walk the runway and not one who spent a night of unbridled passion. He's wearing his glasses and I'm swooning.

He grins at my staring and says, "Good morning, sweetness. Am I still the patient, or do I need to be the one to doctor you up now?"

He waggles his brows at me, and I swat at his chest playfully. God, he's such a bad boy, and I damn well love it. The kicker is he damn well knows it!

"I'm good. I'm starving, but I can't imagine why that is," I say sarcastically.

He rubs at his stubbled chin, pretending to be deep in thought as if he's really contemplating my words. I swat at him again but he catches my hand mid-air and nips at my fingers lightly as I try to pull it back. Then, he smacks my ass and holds on to my left butt cheek as I yelp in surprise.

"I missed you. I wanted to wake up next to you this morning and hold you. Now, let's go eat before I pull you back in this room and fuck you long past the time we're supposed to check-out," he threatens, then quickly kisses my lips as he removes his hand from my ass.

I take a deep breath and steady myself. I was not expecting him to admit all that, but it's exactly how I felt when I woke up and wasn't in his bed...in his arms. Thinking about the possibilities has my breasts swelling and my nipples getting all tingly. My pussy clenches, and I'm going to end up walking all wonky down the corridor trying to hide the way I need to rub my legs together. *Damn the man!*

He asks for a minute to switch out of his spectacles into contacts. I wait out in the hallway because I don't trust myself going into his room. *Those glasses are his superpower or something because they sure cripple me.*

We make it down to the restaurant and are immediately seated at a quaint little table in the corner that affords us privacy from prying eyes—not sure who would pry, but I still appreciate the privacy. Besides, I want him all to myself. I'm not ready to share this thing between us with the world—last night on the dance floor was enough of a preview. I feel like once the world is let in, it will take on a life of its own, and it will no longer be our relationship. Relationship...*God, aren't I rushing things here?*

I realize there's still so much to learn and know about one another. We still have to have the talk about what will happen with us. We never said we'd converse about it, but it's a necessary means to an end...or hopefully a beginning.

*Am I crazy for wanting this?* My husband has been dead for only eight weeks—it's a sobering thought.

The waiter comes just then, and we proceed to order our meals. Caleb is being merciful and letting me be lost in my thoughts after we rattle off what we'll each have to eat. I suspect he knows I've got this inner battle going on with myself. Maybe he does know me better than I think he does—but he doesn't know *everything,* and I don't want him to know everything. I'm afraid if he does, then he won't want me. William knew my past, but look how that turned out!

I sip at my drink and wonder if he feels a phantom distance growing between us, and that's not what I want. I'm being paranoid! See, this is what happens. When I'm left to my thoughts, I start thinking these things. After last night, I'm left worried I'm messing this up.

I feel someone grab my hand, and of course it's Caleb. I jump at his touch, then look in his eyes.

"It's going to be okay, Liz," he assures me.

I sigh, realizing I needed to hear it. *Is that pathetic?* On some level I know I'm being ridiculous. So, I'm going to try to refrain from torturing or criticizing myself further because it's not healthy. I smile at him as our food arrives. We eat in companionable silence, yet glance at each other over our bites. I don't even know what I'm eating, but I shovel it in because my body is starved. I can't even tell you if it tastes good or not.

After our plates are clean, he settles the bill, and we start to head to the pool area. However, Caleb grabs my hand and steers me to the front desk in the lobby instead. I look at him inquisitively, and he gives me one of his signature winks. He proceeds to explain to the attendant that he wants our rooms to have a late check-out, so the kids can swim longer, and so we don't have to rush. God, he thinks of everything. My chest constricts as I'm overwhelmed by his caring and nurturing ways.

After he once again takes care of yet another thing for me, which I'll have to argue with him later about because he's being way too over-the-top generous, we walk hand in hand to the pool. We find the kids having a blast. One thing I adore about my boys is that they're never *too cool* or *too old* to hang out with their sister, or to do adolescent things. I'm the luckiest mother, of that I'm certain.

Leah blows me a kiss, and my boys smile my way. Like the loving, doting mom I am, I wave like a lunatic at them.

"Hey guys," I say as we enter the room.

*Wow, it's like a sauna in here.* I grab a poolside chair, as does Caleb, and we hang out near where they're swimming. There's only a few other people in the pool, so they practically have the place to themselves.

"Mom, I promise we'll be out in a minute. I know it's late and we have to leave," Leah says sadly.

"Well, you're in luck because this guy right here got us a late check-out, so you have a few more hours," I say, grinning.

Leah squeals and goes back to splashing, then she alerts her brothers of the extension they've been given. I hear her yell her thanks to Caleb from the deep end. I turn my head, and he's all lit up, knowing he made my girl smile. This is how I wish it was for the kids with their father, doing dad things and having someone give a shit about them.

"You want to go in?" I ask Caleb.

"I thought you'd never ask," he replies.

I stand up, about to tell him we should go back to our rooms to change, when he throws me over his shoulder and jumps in the pool at the shallow end. I didn't even have time to stop him or react. Instead, I find myself soaked. Clothes, shoes, and all! I'm sputtering and coughing from the water attack. Despite my initial shock, I'm laughing at the situation. The kids are hooting and hollering and cracking up.

I turn to Caleb and dunk him easily; he knew I'd retaliate and is letting me win in doing so. Once he surfaces, he picks me up and throws me in the air, and I hit the water ass first. Oh my God, we're going to get kicked out because of this horseplay—forget the late check-out, we won't need it if we get the boot—surely they have cameras somewhere. But I'm having too much fun to stop him.

He's so adorable and spontaneous and playful. I deeply love this man. I'm wet, and not in a good way—it's fun, though. He brings out a side of me I didn't know I could embrace. Caleb then moves through the water and holds me to him, kissing me thoroughly.

My reservations about being this affectionate in front of my kids have momentarily gone out the window. Obviously, my kids know something is going on between us because of the time we've been spending together—it doesn't take a rocket scientist to know what we were up to last night. The dancing at the wedding gave it away if nothing else did.

*I think I'm scared to talk to them about what's going on because I don't want to hurt them—it makes me feel like a shit mom, though, for not opening that line of communication.*

I want to shelter them from this in the event Caleb and I don't work out. I don't want to see them suffer any more unnecessary pain if they get attached—this again is where the denial comes in: *if I don't talk to them about it, then they can't get hurt.*

I know I can't hide or shield them from everything, though. My poor babies have the misfortune of knowing what it's like to lose someone, and it claws at my insides to think about what they've endured.

I'm lost in thought, so I startle when Caleb wraps his arms around me from behind. Leave it to him to pull me back from wherever my mind travels off to.

*Make me forget about my guilt and fears Caleb....*

"You look good wet," he whispers in my ear, then bites my earlobe sensually. I shiver, but it's not because I'm cold.

"Mmm, you do too. I'm ready to get in the shower. So, I guess I'm willing to get wet again, just under different circumstances. Take me back to your room and get me dirty, then clean me up," I beg as I breathe in his ear and return the favor by nibbling his earlobe.

He moans as I rub my cheek against his stubble. I can't wait to have whisker burn on my sensitive flesh when he's in between my legs again. We're sure going to make the most of this late check-out.

We leave the pool area, head back to his room, and do everything I said we'd do when I begged him. *Ahh, I never want this feeling to end!*

***

Four weeks later I find myself smiling from ear to ear over the way things are in my life. The kids are doing great—still no conversation, though, as I continue to let things progress naturally.

All of us girls got together for lunch last week to catch up with one another, and I got to hear all about Everly's honeymoon—even the steamy bits I didn't ask for. My goodness Brent sounds like a beast in bed, and I love that Ev doesn't sugarcoat things; it's refreshing. She's so different from the other gals in our group. I'm not jealous by any means because Caleb and I are explosive in our own way; *not too bad for someone my age.*

We also had a double baby shower in celebration for Shanna and Caylan. It was absolutely adorable. We had it at Everly's house and played all the fun baby games like *guess which candy bar is in the diaper* and *guess which mystery meat baby food you're eating.* What a hoot—see, told you I like owls, ha ha!

I groan as I think about the fact that I still have William stashed in the closet. His parents recently called and asked what I'm going to do with his ashes because they'd like to have them. I explained that it's best they remain here at my home until I figure out what to do with them and that I didn't want to upset the kids or make any rash decisions. Of course, they hung up on me. I wouldn't be surprised if they file a court order to get possession, but I'll cross that bridge if it ever comes to it. Thankfully, I have the best attorney in my corner.

Now, you may wonder why I'm still holding on to the ashes, and I promise it's not a morbid thing. I'm learning to let go of the need to remind myself of my failures; eventually I'll let my late husband go completely. I'm holding them because it will be therapeutic for me and help us all heal if I find a way to honor his memory somehow, a way for us to remember him in a positive light. It will be difficult, but not impossible. I won't be doing it for William; I'll be doing it for his children.

My birthday is in two days, but Caleb insists we all go out tonight to dinner as a big group to *Tai-Phoon.* Then, tomorrow, he's taking me out with just the kids to celebrate. The man is spoiling me rotten, and I'm trying to let him do it. After taking care of myself and everyone else for so long, this is such a foreign concept.

I don't feel like I'm about to turn forty-five, but it's coming whether I like it or not. I feel younger than I am in some ways, and in other ways much older. I know my mind and body are not that of my true age, but sometimes my heart and spirit feel like I've lived a lifetime already. Caleb has done his best to chip away at those thoughts, though. The more time we spend together, the closer we get to professing our love, it seems.

I haven't let him stay overnight at the house yet, but I can tell he's itching for an invitation. I don't think it's appropriate at this juncture. I hope tomorrow at my birthday dinner with the kids, we can sit down and finally talk to them about our *potential relationship.* I don't want things moving too fast for them.

My handy man has helped me around the house with a few more projects—I swear he's purposely finding stuff just so he can help me fix it. And we've enjoyed watching reruns of his guilty pleasure—*The Golden Girls*; I can learn a lot from each of their characters.

This is surely going to be an exciting month within our group because Shanna is due at the end of the month; Tyler's junior prom is in a week; Caleb said his one case is finally settling; and, camping season is starting. We're avid campers, so this is another thing I hope to share with Caleb.

Caylan won't be too far behind Shanna since she's due mid-May, but that poor girl has already run out of room in her ever-growing belly. Shanna isn't carrying as much—the lucky duck. Call it mom*tuition*, but I think Caylan is having a boy and Shanna a girl; I guess we'll have to wait and see!

I'm so excited for my son because he has a prom date. In his inclusion classroom, which is comprised of both gen-ed and special-ed students, there's a girl named Ellie who asked him out. She's used to his sensory issues and tics, and I had the chance to meet her when they recently went to the movies. She's a lovely girl, and I'm ecstatic she'll be his date.

I'm so grateful she doesn't treat him like he's different—to me, he's not different. He just happens to have autism. And while some may feel that's a handicap, affliction, or the kiss of death, I don't view it like that. I think it makes him the most incredible person I know. Throughout elementary school, I had to take him to a number of specialists, and he was in various therapies such as OT, ABA, and CBT. Eventually, in middle school, he became more mainstreamed in his classes, and his education plan changed drastically. I have high hopes for him for the future now that he'll be finishing high school next year.

Tyler's so smart and super talented. He's a whiz with computers, so maybe he'll explore that in college if he decides to go. Caleb loves to talk computers with him since he grew up working on them.

Speaking of Caleb, I don't know much about this *big case* that's finally settling, but what I do know is he's been preoccupied with it; which is understandable. Ever since the wedding, he's had to throw himself into work more so than usual—you won't hear me complaining. He's very dedicated to his job, and obviously I value and admire that quality. He's certainly proving to be a role model for my kids.

So, that's been me in a nutshell lately. Oh, and most importantly, I decided I'm not going to wait for the other shoe to drop. For once I'll be happy…with a man, no less, and there's so much to look forward to!

# Chapter 19: Has a Nice Ring to it

*Caleb*

Tonight is Liz's birthday celebration with all of our friends. I couldn't very well let her birthday pass and not do something extravagant. I'm excited because I have two presents: one for tonight and one for tomorrow. I only hope the surprise tonight will solidify our relationship. No one knows about my plan; Alexi only knows part of it, the part where he lets me borrow his lake house for next weekend.

I'm sitting in my kitchen, eating away from the plastic container with a new batch of Liz's cookies. She even took the time to put hearts on the top in purple royal icing; see, I'm learning some more baking shit. I'm vaping too—this time it's a peanut butter flavor. I'm trying to shake the feelings of being nervous, anxious, and overwhelmed; they're coming at me all at once. Tonight is an important night—one of the biggest of my life. I take off my glasses and rub at my eyes. I need to go put my contacts in before it's time to pick up my woman.

As I place my glasses back on my face, and her gifts sitting on the counter come into focus, I smile to myself. *I love this woman, and I'm finally going to make it official.*

\*\*\*

We arrive at *Tai-Phoon,* and everyone is already here: Shanna and Anthony, Brent and Ev, Addison and Gil, and Caylan and Alexi. I wanted to make a grand entrance with the birthday girl, so we arrive fashionably late. The table has a beautiful decorative birthday centerpiece in the middle thanks to Caylan. Everything is perfect!

We all exchange hugs, claps on the back, or kisses on the cheek. Liz rubs at Shanna's and Caylan's bellies affectionately, and I swell with pride knowing how loving, caring, and nurturing she is and that she's all mine. The women immediately begin to chatter, and I'm sitting next to Alexi watching everyone and thinking about how damn lucky I am.

Alexi nudges me and asks, "What's got you so fucking smirky tonight?"

"Dude, is that even a damn word?" I challenge him.

"Fuck you! It's a word if I want it to be. You look happy, though, I must say," he remarks.

"Well, you of all people should know what the right woman does for you. And I'm not smirky...I'm 'twitterpated,'" I correct his mistake.

"What kind of hokey shit is that you're spouting? Man, you've lost your fucking mind," he chastises.

We're still trying to keep our voices as low as possible. I know Alexi is kidding around, and even if he wasn't, I don't care. It doesn't bother me in the slightest when my friends give me shit because I'm the one who used to get the ladies with my sweet demeanor. Now, I just need and want one lady.

"You'll see." I punch Alexi in the upper arm, and he sits there brooding away.

The girls all squeal and start pulling out their phones to take selfies, and we guys grumble. Women and their selfies, I've never understood it.

Liz laughs as she says to the group, "Umm, I'm not a big selfie person. I guess you can say I have low 'selfie-esteem.'"

All the girls laugh at her joke, and I chuckle. God, she's so damn charming—my mystical unicorn.

The waiter arrives, and I explain that I've already taken the liberty of ordering for our party ahead of time. The waiter disappears to go round up my requests. They're supposed to bring out platters of various dishes so we can all eat family-style.

Our server returns with our drink orders, and I'm having champagne brought by for toasting purposes; the two preggos will get water, of course.

Our once-upon-a-time former waitress Courtney doesn't tend to us anymore. She had her heart set on Alexi and messed around with some of the guys in our group of friends. She spread her legs for anyone, and I don't like devaluing women like that, but in her case, it's the truth. We never even had to ask her to stop serving us; thankfully, she decided on her own after Alexi married Caylan—it finally shut her up. She cornered Caylan one night in the bathroom a few years ago, and she should've been fired. I'm certain she performed a sexual favor or two to keep her job.

Speaking of that evil woman, I just saw Courtney staring daggers in our direction before she scampered off somewhere—jealous twat, if you ask me!

Our food and champagne arrive, and I let everyone pile their plates high. I notice Liz isn't drinking the bubbly alcohol, and I laugh because I remember how it affected her at the wedding. I want nothing more than to find a dark corner or a restroom to ram into her delicious body, but I suppose she wants a clear head. That's probably good considering what I have planned for this evening.

We all enjoy eating, and I keep the drinks and food coming until everyone is stuffed and satisfied looks grace their faces.

I'm confident in my plan, having worked out all the details with expert coordination. I arranged for the kids to stay next weekend with Alexi and Caylan, while I whisk Liz away to Alexi's lake house in the Poconos for a lover's getaway; that's part two of said plan. Part one is to give her the gift I have in my suit jacket pocket, and part three is having dinner with the kids tomorrow night. I'll give her my other present then.

My moment is upon us. I pick up my knife and lightly tap my champagne flute so it makes a clinking sound, effectively getting everyone's attention at our massive round table. Our group quiets down, and all eyes are on me. I'm grinning and can't contain my jubilance.

I clear my throat and begin my long-winded speech, "As you all know, we're here to celebrate a very special woman's birthday."

I turn to Liz, staring at her tenderly. She smiles, and my eyes smolder knowing I'll make love to her right after dinner when we get near a bed.

I continue speaking as I turn back to our group, "Liz is the kind of woman every man prays, wishes and hopes for. She's an incredible friend, stellar mother, outstanding nurse, and dream-worthy companion. I never thought I'd find someone like her. Since she's come into my life…she's made my world perfect. She. Is. Everything. And so, I want to give her everything."

I glance her way again as she's seated to my left. Tears shimmer in her eyes and the eyes of the other women. I take a deep breath and…here goes.

"Liz, I love you more than I ever thought was possible to love another person. I love your kids. I want you four in my life each and every day. You'll never want for anything. You'll never be without my love, devotion, support, friendship, and heart. I'll love the kids like they're my own," I express with tears of my own starting to form.

I hear some gasps from the table as I reach into my suit jacket and pull out the ring box. I go down on my knee in front of Liz. I grab her hand, squeezing it, and smile as I try to put everything into my next set of words.

"Liz, will you do me the honor of marrying me and making me the luckiest guy ever?" I ask with my heart and future in her hands.

As I look at her face, though, expecting to see a *yes* forming on her lips, instead, my stomach drops out. The look she's wearing is not one of happiness and acceptance. It's one of confusion. The grooves in her forehead are deep-set as she continues to process my words. She's shaking her head in what appears to be disbelief.

*What's going on?*

\*\*\*

*Liezel*

So many thoughts are running through my head as Caleb kneels at my feet while I sit rigidly in my chair.

First, I can't believe he said he loves me. I've been wanting to hear the words for so long, but I thought we'd do that type of thing in private. Second, what he said is what every woman wants to hear—I'm no exception, but…is he nuts? The timing is so far off, I'm still trying to figure out if this is some kind of joke.

Third, I haven't even discussed *us* with my kids yet. However, I take full responsibility for that one and never should have waited this long.

We haven't even said we're officially an item to each other. How the hell can he have us already walking down the aisle in his mind? Now I'm a little pissed off. I love him, but this is moving too fast!

*I'm second-guessing everything!* Old habits die hard as the self-deprecation creeps in once more in my vulnerable state.

It's so unfair to my kids. How could he not include my kids on this? I mean, thank God he didn't have them here because I wouldn't want them to witness this. They're my priority; their thoughts and feelings come first, and I'd want to make sure they're comfortable with everything before Caleb and I even explore the possibility of getting married.

My marriage to William was an absolute nightmare. How do I know this potential one with Caleb would last? *What am I saying?* There is no potential—that's not in my realm of thinking or vocabulary right now. Sure, I've fantasized about it, but it's just that…a fantasy. Ugh, we're so at opposite ends of the field on this, I don't even know where to begin to explain myself to him.

Lastly, to put me on the spot like this in front of my boss and our closest friends is absurd. I'm flawed—doesn't he get that? I can't be anyone's wife right now; I'm barely over being William's wife. Hasn't he noticed how I wince every time he says I'm *perfect*? That's why I really question if he knows me at all.

*Is he in love with me or the idea of me?* Because this spectacle he just put on is only showing me that he lives in a different kind of fantasy world.

I frantically dart my eyes around at our friends, and I must look like I'm about to throw up. Shit, that's exactly what I want to do! I yank my hand out of Caleb's, severing him from me. I move my chair back, and it screeches across the floor as I make a run for the restrooms. I don't care how or what I look like. I'm sure I'm a blur practically sprinting through the mass of tables, people, and servers. Making it into the first empty stall of the restroom, I upchuck my dinner into the toilet.

I'm crying and throwing up at the same time. This is miserable and awful. I feel someone rub my back, and it's Addison—she's such a dear. With her medical background, she's very much used to bodily fluids. Bless her heart for trying to soothe me. Someone must have handed her a wet paper towel because she places it on the back of my neck and continues to let me heave.

I hear Everly, Caylan, and Shanna talking in hushed tones outside the stall. I'm so embarrassed, hurt, upset, and crushed. I can't believe Caleb put me in this position. I slink back from the toilet and take the paper towel from my neck to wipe down my face, then I sit on the cold, tiled floor.

"It's going to be okay, Liz," Addison coos.

I'm sniffling, trying to find the words to argue with her, but I don't.

After a few minutes, Addison helps me up from the floor, and we exit the stall. I look at my girlfriends and begin to cry all over again. Each one passes me to the next for a hug, letting me wet their outfits with my unstoppable flow of tears.

Everly, being the outspoken one she is, asks, "You want me to kick him in the balls for you, or would you like to do the honors? Some birthday, huh, girl?"

I swallow and nod. I don't want anyone to kick my man in the balls. *God, is he even my man anymore?* He may not be now that I clearly refused his proposal. That's why I've been saying all along he needed to move on to find someone his own age, and this is niggling at me more than ever, no matter what Caylan said about him being into older women. I know I'm in a vulnerable mindset.

I'm grateful we're the only patrons in this restroom. I'd hate for more people to observe my suffering and humiliation. I shake my head, still in denial and disbelief. I don't even think I cried like this after William died. In fact, I know I didn't. I'm already mourning the loss of a relationship—for him to propose would mean he considered us in a relationship. *Well, that was news to me, buddy,* I huff in my mind. Step one, share that tidbit of information with your damn girlfriend before you try and give her a ring!

Caylan strokes her rounded belly and bites her lip. "None of us knew this is what he had planned. I mean, I knew there was a surprise, but not this. I don't like spoiling things, but if I had an inkling, I might've tried to give you a heads up of some sort. We're just as shocked as you that he popped the question. I thought the big surprise he teased us with was him wanting to take you away to our lake house next weekend. We were supposed to watch the kids for you."

I laugh bitterly at the mention of the lake house. It's a beautiful place—romantic—and already holds memories for me since it's where Alexi and Caylan got married. It's also where I really noticed Caleb for the first time as a groomsman while I was a bridesmaid.

"I can't believe him. We've never even said 'I love you' to each other," I say to no one in particular.

"Well…do you love him?" I hear Shanna softly ask.

"I do, but I don't know if he really loves me or just the idea of me. We still have so much to learn about each other. This is so bizarre and much too soon," I reveal to my girlfriends, publicly unearthing the main crux of my problem in this makeshift confessional.

"I'm sorry, sweetie," Caylan says with sympathy and great concern.

"Well, I suppose I can't hide in here all night. Time to face the music. I'm sorry if I ruined everyone's evening and made it uncomfortable," I explain as I wipe my face again.

I get a chorus of "Don't be sorry," "Our night isn't ruined," "We're on your side," "We love you," responses all at once. I love them dearly for being here for me and not judging. There's no sides in this, though. There's only right and wrong, and the proposal is so wrong.

"We'll let you have a few moments alone to collect yourself. It's gonna be okay," Addison tries to assure me.

I nod my thanks, and my girlfriends exit the bathroom. I swish some water in my mouth and splash my face with the cool liquid. Screw the ruined makeup, I look my two-days-shy-of-forty-five self anyway.

I'm smoothing some fly-aways in my hair when a svelte blonde with big boobs and a tiny waist walks in sporting the uniform for this place, indicating she works here. Her nametag says *Courtney*.

I don't pay her much attention, but she's standing there staring at me. *Do I know her?* I don't believe I do. She looks familiar because I've probably seen her working here the times we've come in, but she's never waited on our group that I can recall.

"Since you said *no* to Caleb's proposal, thanks for putting him back on the market, hun. I think you've got at least twenty years on me in age, so it was smart to give someone else a go at him. He's better off with someone his own age," she throws my way.

I'm frozen in place. Unable to speak, move or formulate a comeback. She tore me down in an instant. All my insecurities cave in on me at once—there's an avalanche occurring, and I'll be buried alive. This is what I feared everyone would think. I'm certainly not old enough to be his mother, but is that what others see?

Courtney—the bitch—fluffs her high pony tail and flicks it over her shoulder. Then she gives me a serpent's smile and disappears out the door. I'm left tattered, battered, and bruised with her sickly-sweet, cheap perfume hanging in the air. I reach out to the counter for support and decide I need to throw up again.

*Happy birthday to this old fart*, I think as I run for the stall.

# Chapter 20: *Horror*scope

*Liezel*

My stomach finally settles from flip-flopping and retching. I emerge from the bathroom after another ten minutes, and Caleb is standing outside the alcove to the restrooms with his arms crossed, leaning against the wall. He has a very defeated look on his face. I want to comfort him, but I can't—hell, I can't even console myself. I know his distress is my doing, but he caused me pain too.

Then my blood pressure rises thinking about that awful woman. He must know Courtney, and I wonder if she already made a play for him. Obviously, she's on a first name basis with him—*maybe even an intimate one?* It doesn't matter anyway!

His normally warm, inviting brown eyes search my face, and I can't tell what his emotions are. Regret? Sympathy? Disappointment? Love? Hatred? Longing? I don't know what to think. Maybe a combination of all of them?

"Can we talk about what happened for a minute in private?" He questions softly.

"Well, there's really no place to talk, so go ahead and say what you have to say right here," I suggest because I'm not going home with him—I'll let him know that in a minute.

"I don't know what to say, Liz. I don't know what happened back there. I thought things were great between us, and then you blindsided me with your reaction. Clearly, I was wrong about us. I had this whole thing planned. I wanted to go away to Alexi's lake house next weekend. I was going to talk to the kids tomorrow night and do a second proposal in front of them too. I thought it's what you wanted," he comments, looking disgusted as if I'm a villain.

"Are you serious right now with this? What did you expect? What, that I'd go along with this? I don't think you know me at all, Caleb. I think you want so badly to find your other half that you don't care who it is. Maybe I'm too flawed for you. Maybe you should find someone your own age. I've lived my life with marriage and kids. Don't let me deprive you of doing the same. You can't just have an instant family by butting your way into mine," I acerbically deliver my blows.

He rears back like I sucker-punched him in the face, and I guess I did with the words I lobbed at him.

"Is that what you think of me?" He asks as I see him stuff the ring box he was clutching in his right hand roughly into his pants pocket.

Then, he finishes by saying, "I guess you don't know me either, Liz."

I deserve that, and it's probably true. We're not getting anywhere with this little chat of ours. I think we should call it a night, so I tell him as much. He offers to drive me home, but I respectfully decline, and we walk back out to join our friends.

"Can someone please drive me home if it's not too much of an imposition? If not, I'll gladly call a cab." I find myself having a hard time getting the words out.

"We'll take her! Won't we, Gil?" Addison says as she turns to Gil, who's nodding.

I'm borderline having a breakdown as I give my thanks. I'm such a shit friend, though, because I can't even muster the strength or ability to thank everyone for coming. I already said my apologies to the girls about the fiasco, but I don't feel like repeating it, even though I should for the guys' benefit.

I wave goodbye to everyone, and Addison and Gil lead me out of the restaurant to their vehicle. As soon as I'm situated in the back seat, I begin to ugly cry. I'm winning in one way because I manage to breathe through my nose and out my mouth, successfully warding off more vomiting episodes.

I continue to lose it in the back, and I'm grateful they leave me to my own devices. I lay my head against the headrest and close my eyes, trying to get a hold of myself. I feel so broken. After driving for a little bit, my exhaustion takes over, and I end up dozing off.

I awake once we arrive back at my house. I'm apologetic to them both, but of course they understand given the circumstances surrounding the evening. I'm really lucky to have such caring friends. Gil comes around to open my door, and I'm about to cry all over again at his kindness. It's so chivalrous, thoughtful, and sweet. It's something Caleb would do and has done—my heart breaks a little more thinking about how we crash-landed before we barely got the tires off the runway.

Addison holds me in a warm hug and kisses my cheek. She's like the little sister I never had and always wanted. I mumble my sincere "thanks." Gil says "goodbye" and goes around to his side to get back in the car. Addison shuts her car door, and we're left standing there for a moment. I assume she wanted to say something to me without an audience.

"Listen, I'm the worst at probably giving advice, and I'm not trying to stick my nose in where it doesn't belong" she begins.

And I can hear her winding up for a big *but*.

"But…I think you need to let the dust settle and see what things look like in a few days. Sometimes guys can be stupid and say and do stupid things. I hate dogging on them, but they're *guys*. I think sometimes we gotta cut them some slack for their stupidity. I know you were married, so I'm sure I'm not telling you anything you don't already know. I'm sorry, I'm probably not being helpful, am I?" She panics, looking so worried she's upset me.

I squeeze her hand reassuringly and tell her what she said means a lot. She breathes out a sigh of relief and turns to get back in the car. I start heading up my walkway to my front entrance when she yells for me to wait. She jogs up to me, clutching her purse, then starts digging frantically inside it, looking for something. After rummaging for a little bit, she finally pulls out a folded piece of white paper. She doesn't smooth it out, and instead tucks it into my palm and folds my fingers over it almost reverently. *I wonder what it could be?*

"Remember that poem of Caylan's I mentioned?" She looks to me for my response, so I nod, and she goes on.

"Well, this is the one. It seemed to fit what was going on between me and Gil. I think you'll find it helpful when you're ready to read it. Take a bath, or get a massage. Pamper yourself. Please promise me you'll do something girly and relaxing," she begs.

I appease her by confirming I will do just that. She gives me one more hug and runs back to the car. I trudge to my door and go inside to shut myself in. I don't want to come out until I absolutely have to.

*** 

*Caleb*

It's been a little over two weeks since Liz's disaster of a birthday party. I've been ignoring my friends. They've been blowing up my phone with texts and calls, but I'm not having it. I think at one point someone tried to stop by my place—I didn't even bother answering the door or attempt to see who it was. I've been going to work and coming home, and that's it!

I think back to the day after the restaurant scene, and how I was trying to distract myself that morning. I ended up reading the newspaper and immediately regretted it. Want to know what my horoscope said for that day? Well, I'll tell you, and it cut me to the core. It read as follows:

*Sunday, April 15, 2018*
*Virgo*
*A vacation with your romantic interest is in the works. You're also finding yourself making a life-changing commitment at work or in your personal life, so embrace all that is in store. Forge those bonds you've been contemplating and find an outlet for channeling excess energy.*
*Your lucky number is 2.*

I'm sure you can figure out that I ended up throwing my phone across the room. Thank God for screen protectors because that screen would've shattered without one. I was even contemplating pissing on it like a dog, but thought better of it.

Despite that shitty horoscope, I still went ahead and made one last attempt to reach out to her. I ended up sending her second birthday gift that Monday on her actual birthday. But there were crickets—no reply came. No text, no call, no nothing from Liz's end. That's when my world upended because I knew it was over.

Melanie has been doing a good job keeping me in line at work, but I fucked up the other day when I snapped at Mrs. Price. I thought she'd fire me as her attorney—I wish she would have. But, instead of being offended by my behavior, I got the feeling she was turned on—I shudder with the willies even now just thinking about it.

It was hard last weekend when I realized I should've been at the lake house with Liz celebrating our engagement. But instead, I spent it drowning my sorrows. I hate myself for doing that because I know what alcohol did to her ex, and I don't want to be anything like him.

Since today is a Tuesday and part of the workweek, I finally decide I can't avoid my friends forever. Shanna's due in the next week or so, and I don't want to miss that. Plus, I owe Alexi a lot for being there for Liz. I know without even having to talk to him that he's been keeping an eye on her.

It's hard not to feel sorry for myself, though. I threw myself a pity party last weekend when I was on my drunken bender. I even crumbled up the rest of her cookies and smeared them all into my floor. I made my very own abstract painting on the tile with the purple icing that used to form hearts. The whole thing was incredibly idiotic considering I'm the moron who had to clean it up. But when you're drunk, you don't think of these things.

Now that I decided I'll finally show my face to someone, I think it's best to start with Alexi. So, I walk into his clinic, and the receptionist tells me he's in his office. I head back that way, hoping I don't run into Liz, but also secretly hoping I do. It's been torturous. At one point, I contemplated rubbing my hands with the lavender flower petals and then masturbating so my dick would smell like her. *I know, I'm a sick fucker!* But these are the kinds of fucked-up things you resort to when you're screwed up in the head from a damn four-letter word that's supposed to make you happy—not a word that destroys you!

I make it into Alexi's office without a sighting of my sweetness. *Pfft, she's not mine anymore,* my snarky side reminds me. I don't even knock; I just walk in. I guess you could say I've become a dick of the highest degree over the last two weeks—yup, add it to the list. Gone is the *sweet one.* There's a new sheriff in town, and he's named Clusterfuck Caleb.

I shut the door behind me. Alexi is sitting at his desk with his fingers steepled and the hardest scowl I've ever seen my friend don.

"What the fuck, man?" Alexi fires at me.

I don't say anything, so he slams his hands on the top of the desk, further demonstrating his annoyance toward me.

"So, you've been ignoring us, and you've got Caylan worried sick about you. Not to mention you never explained yourself for that whole proposal thing. And now you waltz in here, and I get the silent treatment. Why the fuck did you even come here then?" He questions with lightning bolts practically shooting out of his eyes and in my direction looking like a formidable entity.

"I don't understand why you're attacking me. Don't be an ass. I was a shit person for avoiding all of you, but trust me, I was in no condition to be anyone's company. As for the proposal, I see now that wasn't the way to go. I got carried away. I thought we were both ready. She's the one who doesn't want me, though, so I guess she doesn't love me. Maybe I'm better off not being with someone who doesn't return my feelings," I almost whine, trying to explain my perspective.

"You stupid motherfucker!" Alexi says with revulsion.

"I don't get your animosity. What's wrong with you? Shouldn't you feel bad for me? Dude, I'm the one who got filleted that night. She turned me down in front of everyone. How the fuck do you think *I'm* supposed to feel? Then to top it off, she accused me of trying to butt into her family.

God, I thought *we* were going to be a family!" I'm seething now replaying the scene in my mind.

I'm more hurt than anything, but I'm covering that hurt up with anger because that's what guys do.

"I never thought you of all people would be this thick and so obtuse. You're usually so in touch and in tune with this kind of shit. Half the time I think you're part woman because you get chicks better than any guy I know. But right now, you're being selfish and a prick. Do you not realize her side of things?" He chucks the words my way.

I guess I'm stupid and a fool in love—now a fool in pain. I don't get what he's referring to. I never even told anyone this, but I bought the ring right before Brent and Everly's wedding. I've been carrying it around with me. If she went through my suitcase the night of the wedding, she would've found it. Yeah, it's been on my mind for a while to put it rightfully on her finger.

I know I said I'd take things slow, but once we started acting like a family, I naturally thought it was time. I didn't realize there was a protocol for how long I had to wait. Even within my group of friends, they all knew right away that their own partner was *the one* after a short time—I didn't think our relationship was the exception.

"What's there to realize? I love her; she doesn't love me. End of story!" I bark out.

"Okay, I can see I'm going to have to approach this differently," Alexi sighs and switches tactics.

Then he levels with me. "Liz is a mess. I had to give her a leave of absence. Don't you get it? Anyone who's seen you two together knows damn well she loves you. But you proposed to her in front of all of us. You told her you loved her for the first time in front of all of us. You took away a private moment and made it public, and then you put her on the spot so she'd look like the asshole when she turned you down. How'd you expect her to say *yes* when she probably didn't even know you were truly in love with her? Think about it, man. Her husband of eighteen years died two months ago. Don't you think that messes with a person, even in a loveless marriage like they had? And you don't even know her entire past. She has a history—apparently a dark one *I* don't even know about. She's hinted at it, but I never got the story."

He sighs again and obviously isn't done raking me over the coals yet. "And for fuck's sake, the kids don't even know how you feel about them, let alone Liz. You made it seem like just anyone would do for your wife and kids."

I am hit smack-dab in the face with the truth, and it knocks me for a loop. I feel like I'm going to pass out. I stumble backwards and am grateful when my ass lands in a chair. I open my mouth to reply, but only air comes out. It's like speech eludes me right now.

Alexi gives me that *now you're getting it* look. What a dumbass I am. I really thought every woman's dream was to be swept off her feet or rescued like a damsel in distress. Here I've been for the last two weeks feeling sorry for myself, and poor Liz has been in hell. Alexi's right, *how could I be so fucking obtuse?*

Shit, I never dreamed she would be this affected and have to take a leave of absence. I drop my head into my hands and can't even look Alexi in the eye. I'm a damn pussy!

"Liz…," I croak out without looking up.

"She's at my lake house. Fred and Milly have had the kids for the last few days, and they've been getting them to and from school. She got your package on her birthday, and that sent her into a downward spiral. She basically made it through Tyler's prom last week, and then I could see she was falling apart. I made her leave and promise not to return until she was feeling herself again. I've never seen her like that. She wasn't like that even once in all the years I've known her. Not even after that fucker husband of hers died. She's always been so strong. I think there's something else going on with her. I don't know what it is," he says sadly.

Well, now I'm even more concerned and feel like a failure as a man, as her friend, and as the one who loves her. I don't know if she'll want to see me, but I need to at least try.

"Before you go getting any ideas about running up there to be with her, I'll just tell you *no*! If you want to get back in her good graces, or make it up to her, you need to give her time and space. If you go up there and try to worm your way back into her heart, I don't see that working. I think she needs time to heal and figure out things for herself before she can deal with your crap. And that fucking bitch Courtney put some bad shit in her head the night of the party. I've already ensured she was fired. For her to accost Caylan that time and now make Liz think you two have a history, that was the final straw!" He says menacingly.

"Whoa! What did Courtney say to her, exactly?" I demand to know.

"Some bullshit about how since she refused your proposal, now Courtney can make a move on you. And she basically told Liz she's too old for you," he relays, waving his hand and trying to get the words out.

Now I'm on my feet, boiling with anger. Of all the things for Courtney to say, she couldn't be more wrong about me and my taste in women. But, then I think about how I still never told Liz I prefer older women. Another failure on my part for not putting her mind at ease and assuring her the age difference is welcome. *Fuck!* I have a lot of wrongs to

[131]

right.

"Thanks, Alexi. I don't know how to ever repay you for all you've done for her. I'll make this right," I vow.

"Caleb, that's what families do. You've been there for me in my darkest times when I went through what I did to win Caylan back. Have faith and unfuck this situation before I end up losing my best employee and friend!" He threatens.

I hold my hands up to placate him and back out the door slowly. He shoots me the middle finger, and I give him a two-finger salute as I head out of his office.

As I'm walking out of the clinic, I feel a little better having this new information. Don't get me wrong, I still feel like shit because I'm a dumbass. But at least I can try to *unfuck the situation* as Alexi said.

*Liz...I'm sorry. I love you. I'll fix this...somehow.*

# Chapter 21: Oh So Charming

*Liezel*

It's Tuesday afternoon, and I've been at Alexi's lake house for a few days now. It's almost—and I reiterate *almost*—difficult to be miserable when you're at a place like this, but my misery is warranted.

This two-story, multiple bedroom and bathroom, three-car garage house is like a mansion. I don't even know how many rooms there are in total because I've never taken the time to count during the occasions I've been here; it's probably rude of me to do so anyway. Let's just say it's huge and gorgeous. It's a modern, meets chic, meets *MTV Cribs*-type deal—God, I used to love that show!

I was so embarrassed when Alexi asked me to take a leave of absence, but he was right. I needed a break from everyone and everything—not that I wanted a break from my kids, but they need me at my best, and right now I'm not at my best. Then when he offered me the place to escape and clear my head, I had to take him up on it. I figured sitting on the deck and watching the water would give me solitude and help me sort my crap out.

It gutted me that Caleb and I are over, but some things don't last. I've learned that lesson one too many times.

It was difficult going to work on my birthday after the unbearable weekend I'd experienced. The kids did their best to cheer me up, but I was so broken. When Caleb's delivery arrived, I never expected to get another gift from him. I still remember what the card said.

> *Dear Liz,*
> *You are the rightful owner of this next gift. I was*
> *going to give it to you last night at dinner when*
> *we were accompanied by your three beautiful*
> *children.*

*I still want you to have it, and I only hope you'll accept it. Its place is with you because it represents you.*
*Please know I'll always be here for you and the kids no matter what. Take care of yourself.*
*Your faithful friend,*
*Caleb*
*P.S. – if you flip this card over, I have explained what each item signifies.*

Inside the box, underneath the note, was a velvet case. I wondered if another piece of jewelry was inside. I opened the lid cautiously, and sure enough, nestled in there was a silver charm bracelet. I examined each one of the dangly items, and immediately my eyes were full of moisture. I didn't think it was possible to cry so much given that I'm normally not a crier.

I ran my fingers across the dainty charms; they consisted of a piano, an owl, a stethoscope, a heart, and a unicorn. At first, I maybe understood all but the piano and unicorn. So, I remembered his card said he wrote the meaning on the back. I flipped it over and read it.

*The piano is because I know you love Billy Joel, and hands down "Piano Man" is his best song.*
*The owl is for obvious reasons with your passion for them.*
*The stethoscope of course is for being a nurse.*
*The heart represents you as a mother and working in the field you do.*
*The unicorn is because there's something magical about you, and I couldn't believe a woman like you exists.*
*~ C.*

I accepted the gift but not the man. I know he means well and tries to say and do the right things, but he doesn't get the bigger picture. I don't think I'm ready to let him back into my life even as a friend.

Recalling that day…eh, I'm already tired. I drag my sorry ass over to the bed in the enormous master bedroom and flop down on it. I thought I'd at least go in the hot tub, but I have no desire. Sleep. I need sleep…I need to forget.

***

I wake up a few hours later. I end up running to the drugstore and grab a salad from a nearby restaurant. Yup, I'm even too lazy to cook for myself, so you can imagine baking has been out of the question. It's amazing how things I used to adore no longer hold the same joy.

I've been eating like a bird lately but forcing myself to at least get some nourishment. I finally convinced myself there must be something really wrong with me health-wise since I've been feeling sick. I'm not the type of person, or nurse, who will self-diagnose, though.

My suspicions are finally confirmed!

I'm staring at the two pink lines on the pregnancy test cradled in my hand, indicating a positive result. I've taken five of these damn things because I decided to grab multiple boxes and multiple brands, just to be sure. Obviously, I got pregnant from that first time we slept together. I'm sure it's from when I attempted to put the condom on. I knew I sucked at it; it probably tore or something. I haven't been on birth control since my early thirties because there was no need as the years went by.

I sit on the closed lid of the toilet seat and continue to hold the stick in my hand. For the last few weeks I've been thinking how I'm too old for Caleb. Well, clearly I'm not too old to have his baby. I sigh obnoxiously.

"Well, now you've really done it, Liz, and done it well," I say aloud.

Surprisingly, I'm not upset. And I'm certainly not miserable about the result. If I really analyze this, I'm happy, believe it or not—only the circumstances aren't ideal. Regardless, I love children. Of course, I never expected to give birth at forty-five, but I'm also not ancient. It's perfectly doable nowadays. And it's funny that I've felt so old for the last several weeks, and now all the sudden I'm justifying how young I am—life is ironic that way. I look upward and say to the heavens in my mind, *I guess the joke's on me, isn't it?*

I blow out a long breath as I realize the respectable thing to do is to tell Caleb. I owe it to him. I already know he'll want to be involved in our child's life. I can accept that. We can manage co-parenting. I'm not ready to tell him today. It will not be by phone; it will have to be in person. I might not even be ready to tell him tomorrow. But I will tell him, and I promise it won't be when I'm in the labor and delivery ward!

I'm more afraid to tell my kids than anyone. I don't know how they'll feel. I will hope they'll be accepting and awesome siblings. I will make sure they understand this child will not be their responsibility. If they help out, that's great, but they're not going to be expected to be the babysitters, and I certainly don't want them changing their future plans for me.

I have a great job, great friends, and a wonderful support system. I will make this work. I did it once all those years ago with three little ones, so I can do it again, and this time I'll only have one little one to chase around.

I smile and rub at my non-existent belly. A baby does change everything. I'm okay with that. He or she will be loved and cared for by both parents. *One day at a time*, I tell myself.

\*\*\*

*Caleb*

May 4, 2018

It's been three days since I went to see Alexi. I'm trying desperately to heed his advice to respect Liz's need for time. I have so many things running through my head. All the things I want to say to her—all the different ways I want to say them. I will do my best to get her to understand that not just any woman will do for my wife.

I. Only. Want. Her.

If she'll let me explain, and let me try again, I will do things differently this time. For one thing, I'll make sure she knows how much I love her before I attempt to propose again. And next time, the proposal will go down perfectly. I can't fathom that there won't be a next time because I can't imagine my life without her. She's mine, and I'm hers. And that's all there is to it!

Melanie knocks on my door. I finally gave her a five percent raise. It's not much, and far less than she deserves, but the partners of this firm wouldn't go any higher. When I'm promoted, there will be changes. My paralegal has been an angel in helping me get through my workload lately, and I make it a point to thank her often.

"Excuse me, Mr. Daniels," she begins by addressing me formally, which means there must be someone within earshot.

"Yes, Melanie," I acknowledge her.

"Mrs. Price is here to see you if you have time to meet with her," she clarifies and gives me a sympathetic look because she knows I'm tired of this woman's crap.

I mumble some curse words under my breath and give a wave, gesturing for Melanie to let the despicable woman in.

Mrs. Price breezes through the door, strutting her shit like she owns the place. She has those oversized Jackie O sunglasses on with an elaborate updo hairstyle. She removes the shades, and I don't even want to look into her piercing eyes. I couldn't even tell you the color because I don't like looking at her that long.

The ivory trench coat she's wearing—which is questionable given the current weather—is expensive-looking, and the blue handbag on her arm probably costs more than what most people make in a year. Her designer heels echo in my office, clacking on the floor as she makes her way over to me at my desk.

Normally I'd meet with her in a conference room, but I just want to get this over with as quickly as possible. I'm sure she has yet another issue with the agreement that will ultimately hinder the proceedings. If this is the situation, then I'm probably going to lose my chance of making partner because I'm going to have to drop her as a client.

I'm not willing to sully my reputation because of her. The judge is going to think this is another type of stall tactic, and I don't want to find myself in contempt when we finally go before him because I'll be bitching out my client in open court for all the stunts she's pulled. This has gone too far and gone on too long. We're set to have this all wrapped up in a month's time, and I'll be damned if she fucks this up on me again at the eleventh hour.

"Well, hello there, Caleb," she says as she tries to make her red-stained lips pouty when she's done greeting me.

I tip my head and reply a curt, "Morning, what can I do for you now?"

She smiles, and I feel like she should have flying monkeys and a broom somewhere in sight because surely she played in *The Wizard of Oz*. In my peripheral vision, I see Melanie still lingering in the doorway.

"Melanie, would you be a doll and give us a few minutes alone? I have something pressing to discuss with my attorney that I believe is privileged information," she commands with a voice that sounds like nails on a chalkboard.

It's asinine to have Melanie leave, but I won't argue—my paralegal, by all rights, knows all the ins and outs of all my cases. My interest is piqued by what Mrs. Price said, though, because I'm wondering if she has something on Darron that might be useful when the final judgment is ruled upon. In my mind, I'm rubbing my hands together with a wicked grin, thinking this thing might finally come to an end. Melanie makes her exit.

"Before we begin, do you mind doing something for me? Can you please bring me a sparkling water? I would've asked Melanie, but I need privacy for this delicate matter. I'm sure you understand. By the way, I've been singing your praises to Clyde for weeks on end," she conveys with a devilish grin.

Throwing my boss's name into the mix certainly adds the element of giving her the upper hand. I have to admit, this woman knows what she's doing. That's why it's served her well in her marriage and now impending divorce. She's ruthless, always prepared for battle, and always one step ahead of me.

"Of course, Mrs. Price. Please feel free to sit down. I'll be back momentarily," I respond.

She laughs conceitedly as she sets her purse on the edge of my desk and explains, "Oh Caleb, you must call me Yvette. Surely we're well-acquainted by now."

I don't like the sound of that. Internally, I'm grumbling like a son of a bitch because I'm not an errand boy either, but again I'll kiss her ass…for now. I'm confident she's not delaying anything by being here today, and for that I'm grateful—so grateful I'll do just about anything to keep her happy. Maybe I can still pull off this promotion somehow.

I exit my own office, shutting the door behind me. I certainly don't want any partners to see her and keep her here longer than necessary. They'll expect me to take her out to wine and dine her, all part and parcel of the job. However, I can't fake pleasantries all night with that woman.

I notice out of the corner of my eye that she closes the blinds so you can't see in. *How bizarre,* I think. But I walk off in the direction of our kitchen anyway, which is fully stocked to accommodate our numerous clients—I don't have sparkling water in my office. Thank God I won't have to deal with her much longer!

***

*Liezel*

I returned from the lake house late last night. I will see my kids later today when they get home from school. I decided when I woke up this morning that I'd be brave and go talk to Caleb now that I got some rest and clarity.

It's crazy to think that tomorrow I'll be seven weeks pregnant. I'm in a good place for the most part. I've had a few days to adjust to the idea of the baby, and each day I find myself more and more elated about it. I'm nervous to see him again. I didn't want to have to see him so soon, and I wouldn't if it weren't for the fact that I have to give him the good news.

I probably should have told him I was coming, but I may have chickened out if I heard his voice come across the phone line. I've only met his paralegal once, so I didn't feel comfortable calling her directly either. I dropped off lunch to Caleb one time several weeks ago when I had a school function for Leah. So, on that occasion, I got to see his firm and meet Melanie.

His office building in Center City is beautiful and located in a lovely area. Traffic is a nightmare, but nothing I can't handle. I park my car and finally make it to his floor. The receptionist, whose name I can't for the life of me remember, waves me in. She must have a damn good memory because I've only been here that one time. I feel like a VIP or something as I stroll right into the place.

I walk down the hall to his office and notice Melanie isn't at her desk. Hopefully I'll be able to say hi to her on the way out—she's a wonderful woman. I see Caleb's office door and blinds are closed, which I'm hoping means he doesn't want to be disturbed. I take this as a good sign, though, because he must be doing paperwork. He's told me before that if he's in a meeting, or with a client, he goes to a conference room to conduct business—the research and prep is done in his office.

I rap on the door a few times and hear a female voice say, "It's about time; you've kept me waiting long enough."

It doesn't sound like Melanie, but it must be because who else could be in there? So, I enter anyway. As I swing the door open, I halt in my tracks.

Perched on Caleb's desk is an elegant woman who looks like she's in her forties, but her facelift is aiming for thirties. She's wearing nothing but heels and a matching red lace bra and panty set. She even has garters and stockings on. This is a woman who's here for sex and seduction.

My mouth hangs open in horror. I don't see Caleb anywhere, so I momentarily feel a little better. I close my mouth, swallowing as I try to find my voice. *Am I in the right place?*

I stammer out, "I'm ssssorryyy, I must have the wrong office."

She looks at me like I'm the dirt under her expensive shoes. I lick my suddenly dry lips and feel about two feet tall.

"If you're looking for Caleb Daniels, he'll be right back. He was just running to get me something to quench my thirst. That man is one talented attorney, and I intend to put his other skills to use. So run along now because we have business to tend to," she relays with her tongue practically wagging at all the innuendos she's delivering.

I'm sick to my stomach. Her dark red lipstick is making me dizzy. It's an awful shade, and, despite her clear affluence, it makes her look whorish and cheap. I don't know what to think right now. I'm so confused by everything.

I thought Caleb would go for a younger woman because of Courtney, and now he's with someone my age—I'm puzzled by this scene. I guess Caylan was right about the older woman thing. And to top it off, he's already moved on. I know I said I would accept that we're not together, but deep down I never expected him to move on from me so quickly. This is so painful. I guess I was right when I told him any woman would do for a wife—here's *any woman*.

I can't say anything more to this stranger. I don't even want to know who she is. I know what she wants, and that's obviously Caleb for pleasure. And the fact he's her lawyer disgusts me even more. There are certain lines you don't cross, and this is one of them. I turn on my heel and run out, effectively slamming the door behind me.

I hear a woman in the distance calling my name, but I'm not stopping. It might have been Melanie calling out to me, but I can't say for sure. No one else knows me here, so I suspect it was her. I'm proud I haven't vomited. I make it into the elevator to start my descent to the parking garage, chanting to myself to *breathe deeply*.

I'm alone in the elevator, and I've never been more grateful because I have tears streaming down my face. I look down at my arm, and more tears flow as I examine my wrist. I claw at my hand, trying to get the damn bracelet off that Caleb gave me for my birthday. I was wearing it today as sort of a peace offering. Now I can't even look at it, let alone wear it. I get it off and toss it in my purse as I'm brought to my floor to exit.

I get in my car and drive out of there faster than it took for that brunette in his office to take her clothes off. I leave the vicinity, heading to the on ramp for the bridge. God, I want to go home. I'm lucky I manage to drive through all the tears, but I'm trying for the sake of myself and my little one.

I rub my belly and send my apologies to the baby nestled in my womb. This is not how I expected the day to go. I feel like this is a nightmare I can't wake up from. I never thought I'd feel this much love and hate at the same time. I pray I hold it together until I get home, and then I can thoroughly fall apart.

# Chapter 22: Game On

*Caleb*

I shuffle back to my office. I'm equally torn because I want to know what Mrs. Price has to say, but I also don't feel like entertaining her all day. I'll have to try to get rid of her quickly once she imparts the information.

Shit, I don't know why she rubs me the wrong way. There's something about her that turns me off. It could be her personality, or something else entirely. Even if I wasn't in love with Liz, I still wouldn't find Mrs. Price the least bit attractive—appearance-wise or even personality-wise. I've said it before, I believe she has some hidden agenda.

You'd think she'd be right up my alley being a cougar—and she is what I consider a *classic cougar*—but it's not the case. I don't go for every woman who's over the age of forty. Besides, I'd never sleep with or date a client, and I don't have it in me to view Mrs. Price as anything more than that.

I knock on my door twice so she isn't startled when I enter. As much as I don't give a shit about customs and courtesies with her, I still can't let all my manners go out the window until she's no longer my client or problem. I open the door, walk in, and immediately drop the glass of sparkling water to the floor.

Mrs. Price is standing by my desk with her chest sticking out in her fucking underwear. Her underwear! *What the ever-loving-fuck is going on?*

Melanie yells to me, asking if everything is all right. *Fuck, no! It's not.* But I tell her I'm clumsy and not to worry. I quickly shut the door because I don't need anyone rushing in here and getting the wrong impression about us. I have to get her to clothe herself as soon as humanly possible.

*What the fuck is wrong with her?* And then I realize the answer to my rhetorical question…*I'm the game.* This was what she wanted all along. I don't know the reason, but I know she's probably been planning this thing for a long time.

I have no clue if it's because it's exciting for her—the thrill of it being taboo with the professional relationship we have—if she's trying to get me fired, or if she's starved for attention—hell, it could be all of the above. Another possibility is she could be seeking revenge somehow with regard to Darron. Whatever the reason, it doesn't matter. And it certainly doesn't excuse her behavior—I'm not the least bit flattered.

I never invited this behavior. I don't welcome this now or ever. I can't even recall one time in our various encounters where I've ever given her any indication I was even remotely interested in her.

I gnash my teeth together and roughly spit out, "Mrs. Price, I don't know what you're up to, but I'm about to open the door and blinds in about thirty seconds. So, I suggest you find your clothes. I wouldn't want anyone to get the wrong idea that something's going on between us."

She laughs. She. Fucking. Laughs! And it's that annoying tinkling laughter that grates on my last nerve. She waves her hand as if I'm being silly and this is no big deal.

"Oh, Caleb, that's what I love about you. You're so serious all the time. All work and no play can make you a very dull boy. Don't you want to take a walk on the wild side for once? I've asked around about you. Even Clyde told me you desire older women. I knew there was something about you that spoke to me. I'll show you what the others have lacked," she replies while licking her lips as if she thinks she's going to devour me.

My face must be turning a scary color by now. My blood pressure skyrockets, and I'm furious that she's pulling this shit on me. How dare she!

"Twenty seconds, Mrs. Price," I grit out.

"You're no fun. I suppose Clyde will want to hear about how you're not treating your star client right or tending to my needs," she warns as she starts straightening her garters and stockings.

"And I suggest you be careful how you're treading. I'm not worried about what this firm can say or do to me. I'll start my own damn firm if I have to. If you think for one second I'll be intimidated by your threats, you're sorely mistaken. You certainly don't know me well enough to understand what I'm capable of. I'm the best fucking lawyer around. I'll slap an injunction on you so fast, it will make your head spin. And your little secret you think Darron—and I, for that matter—don't know about…ya know, the one about your little boy toy lawn guy? Yeah, that will become a thing of public record," I threaten menacingly.

She huffs and retorts, "Well, I never!"

"And you never fucking will. Ten seconds!" I almost bellow.

Her olive skin turns pale white, and her eyes go wide. Oh yeah, I hit my mark. She has no idea the dirt I have on her. I make it my mission to thoroughly investigate all my clients. If they don't try and fuck me, then I certainly won't fuck them. I don't consider myself an asshole for doing it; I think of it as an insurance policy. If anything, it's smart business. I didn't see this interesting twist coming because, ironically, I thought she was into guys even younger than me.

She starts scrambling for her coat she laid across my chair. She puts it on and I'm already opening the door so she can't try and corner me or pull some other stunt. I stick my head out and tell Melanie I need help cleaning up the drink after all. Melanie jumps to her feet, and somehow, I know she heard the whole thing, which doesn't bother me. It's best I have a witness, just to be sure.

I move to the windows and open the blinds as well, announcing to my paralegal, "Mrs. Price has decided to seek new counsel. She realized we're not a good fit. Melanie, please see that all my files on her case are transferred to one of our junior partners, and I'll discuss the situation with Clyde."

Mrs. Price is still tightening the belt around her coat when she picks up her handbag from my desk, gives me one last look that is the ugliest glower known to man, and storms out of my office. Hopefully storming out of my life…for good.

I want to sag against the door with relief. My adrenaline is pumping overtime, and I feel so rattled by the whole experience. Melanie puts her hand on my bicep, giving it a squeeze for comfort. She then walks over to the hutch in the corner of my office where I have a beverage station set up, grabs some paper towels, and returns to where I'm standing. We both bend down and start picking up the glass and wiping up the liquid.

If I, for some reason, have to leave this firm because that fucking nuisance of a woman pursues something, I will be bringing Melanie with me. I'll pay whatever she wants. I'm hoping it doesn't come to that because I love working here. My next order of business will be to talk to Clyde as soon as I can to ensure I still have a position. I'm sure Mrs. Price is already beating me to it.

Melanie and I don't comment on what happened, and I don't think there's a need to. She understands me and respects my desire to let things be. I don't feel like rehashing what happened behind that closed door anyway. I want to forget about it and move on. Melanie speaks, though, and what she says couldn't have been more surprising than Mrs. Price's little show—yet it is.

"Liz stopped by. I think she briefly talked to Mrs. Price. I can't be sure, but she was running from your office when I came down the hall from copying some briefs. I tried to stop her, but she kept going. I'm sorry," she says with great remorse in her eyes.

I look at her face and know she's silently telling me that if she was at her desk, this wouldn't have happened. I can't formulate a sentence. All I can do is nod. I'm not mad at Melanie by any means. I'm beyond pissed off at that bitch, and if I ever see her again in my life, well, it would be too soon.

My ass meets the floor because I can no longer support my weight. What must Liz think of me? If she walked in to find that devil in her fucking underwear, well, surely she thinks the worst of me now—more so than she did before.

I'm kicking myself. I should've gone to the lake house. Fuck the strict orders that Alexi gave! I should've made her listen to me. This day has gone from bad to worse. I feel Liz slipping through my fingers now more than ever.

Without me having to ask, Melanie informs me she'll reschedule all my appointments and meetings for today and tells me to go find Liz. I'm already on my feet and in action. I'm typically way too professional at work, but I give Melanie a hug and a kiss on the cheek. Boy, I hit the lottery with this paralegal. I thank her, and she's still cleaning up the mess as I'm flying out of my office.

I'll start with a phone call to Alexi to see if he's heard from Liz, and then I'll head straight to her house. She's going to hear me out. I won't take *no* for an answer. This has gone too far and been blown out of proportion. I will not lose her again! My resolve is unwavering.

*** 

Liezel

Lost. I feel lost.

Lost in a black darkness, and it's not because I have the blackout curtains drawn. I brought William back out of the closet, and I'm looking upon his urn. I know it's sick and twisted. I'm in a dark place. It's reminiscent of the day of his funeral. My life has changed so much since that day, yet it's remained the same somehow.

I'm doing everything I can to prevent images of what I saw in Caleb's office from entering my mind. I don't want to think about him making love to her on his desk. I don't want to think about him kissing her with lips that once touched mine. Hands that once caressed my skin, and a heart that once created a baby with me.

*Why does it have to hurt so much?*

The kids will be home in a few hours, and I hope I can pretend for them. I don't want them to see me like this. It's not healthy for me or the baby. I can't cry anymore. I'm at the point again where I'm all dried up. In my hand, I'm clutching the poem Addison gave me. When I threw it in the closet the night of the dinner party to join the urn, I completely forgot about it. When I grabbed William, I saw the folded paper lying next to it. I'm going to force myself to read the damn thing once and for all.

*I mean, why not punish myself further and put another nail in the coffin, right?*

I unfold the sheet and smooth it out. It's typed in black ink on white copy paper, and there's a URL at the bottom. I guess Addison must've printed it off the internet from Caylan's collection of poems. I take a deep breath and read.

*Title: Trysting the Night Away*
*A tryst, a turn of fate with a burn,*
*The night twisting and winding,*
*The heart wanting and finding.*
*A tryst, a turn of love and the yearn,*
*The sweet gentle binding,*
*The light so blinding.*
*Weaving its way through your soul each day.*
*Consuming and taking, claiming and making.*
*For life isn't living,*
*Without the one giving.*
*Trysting the night away,*
*Until two halves stay.*
*When a whole is finally combined,*
*Until the end of time.*

Yup, it hurts more now. It's killing me reading the words and seeing for myself what I can't and won't have. I know I'm the one who ended things with him, but it doesn't mean I'm over him. I loved him. Correction. I. Still. Love. Him…always.

I hear banging downstairs and some yelling. Then, my doorbell rings a bunch of times. I'm not answering the door. I wouldn't answer it for anyone—even if it's the cops, at this point I don't care. If it's Alexi, I know I owe him so much already that I don't even want to face him. I don't want to tell anyone about the baby. I wanted Caleb to be the first to know, and that dream was shot to shit today. I can't face Alexi because I'll end up blurting it out.

Alexi knows where my house key is hidden. It's tucked away in the old planter on the corner of my porch. So, if he comes in, then so be it—it doesn't mean I have to talk to him. I'll probably be catatonic anyway. I definitely won't make for good company right now or for good conversation. He's better off leaving me alone.

Sure enough, I hear the front door open, and my alarm system—which isn't armed—signals the entry. There are heavy footsteps on the stairs. Then, a soft knock hits my ears, and the door creaks open.

I'm sitting on the edge of my bed with my back to the door. The light streams in from the hall, and I lose my night vision even though it's sunny out.

"Liz…," Caleb croaks.

I stiffen immediately. He's the last person I expected to come here. I thought he'd be pussy-deep in that twatish woman by now. I can't look at him. I can't talk to him. If I sit here long enough, maybe he'll go away.

I hear him move around the room until he's in front of me. He kneels down and grabs my hands. I'm unmoving and unfeeling.

"God, Liz, you're freezing cold. Shit!" He exclaims.

He reaches for an afghan at the end of my bed, wraps it around my shoulders, and starts rubbing my hands together, blowing into them to infuse them with warmth. I still don't budge.

"I'm going to make you some tea to warm you up, sweetness. I'll be right back," he says in a tortured voice, almost as if he's afraid to leave me.

I wait until he steps away to wince at his pet name for me. Now I can't stand the word *sweetness*, so I add it to the list along with *perfect*.

# Chapter 23: Living with Ghosts

*Liezel*

After a little bit of time passes from when he went to get my drink, he dutifully returns with a steaming mug and places it in my hands. It's not scalding hot, and I admit it does feel good against my skin. I didn't realize how cold I was. I probably do need liquids since I threw up when I got home. I'm failing on all accounts right now in taking care of myself, my kids, and my unborn child.

"Please drink it. You have me so worried. I understand if you don't want me here. If you want me to go, I will…eventually. But I hope you'll let me explain a few things first. I'll even call Alexi to come be with you. He's worried sick too. You need someone to take care of you for once, Liz," he gently reprimands me.

It makes me sad that I'm affecting other people's lives. I don't want to worry my friends. Hopefully he hasn't told Caylan because, knowing her, she'll march over here and demand that I resolve the issues at hand. I feel somewhat guilty, but I still can't respond to him. I'll let Caleb do the talking. He can say whatever he wants. It doesn't mean I have to listen.

He sighs heavily, "I don't know what you think you saw today, but please believe me when I say that whatever it was, it's not what you think."

I can feel his gaze boring into me. If he stares long enough, I'll have holes—well, hell, they'll match the gaping holes in my heart. Still no reaction from me, though.

So, he continues, "That woman in my office was a client. And I say *was* because she crossed a line today that can't be uncrossed. She said she was there to meet with me about her divorce, and then ambushed me when I returned with a beverage at her request. While I was in the kitchen, you apparently came by to see me. I had no idea what trap awaited me in my office. Her name is Yvette Price, and normally, she's not a woman to be trifled with. But, I'll make sure her life is a living hell if she starts spouting untrue shit about me. I realized today she's probably been dragging this case out to bait me—this is that *big case* I've been telling you about. However, she didn't count on the fact that I'm so madly in love...with you."

I think he pauses for effect, but I won't be swayed.

He clears his throat, "Anyway, as I said, I didn't see it coming until I walked into my office and was surprise attacked. I immediately terminated our professional relationship, and I'm going to my boss about her so there isn't any unnecessary backlash. She has some skeletons in her closet that will be devastating if they're ever uncovered. I'm not a man who stoops to blackmail, but in this instance, it's tit for tat if she tries to go toe to toe with me."

I see him half-smile and I know he's trying to lighten the mood. It's not going to work.

In a deep voice he mocks, "May her name be stricken from the record! ...Sorry, bad lawyer joke. I'm just trying to assure you that I have no intention of ever seeing her again professionally or otherwise."

He takes a deep breath and continues to forge ahead yet again, despite my disinterest. "Melanie said she saw you and called to you. You must've not heard her as you were taking off. I get why you ran, sweetness, but I wish you would've talked to me. The fact that I wasn't even in my office should've had you come in search of me. Although, I get why you didn't. It must've been a shock. I would never do that to you, Liz. Please know this and believe this. You have nothing to worry about with me. I'll be here waiting for the day you decide to take me back."

He kneels down at my feet again and rubs his cheek across my knee. I looked cute today in a skort with sneakers and a fitted T-shirt—I feel like skorts are making a comeback, so don't judge, please. Now I couldn't care less what I look like—*it's funny, I cared a few short hours ago.*

He runs his cheek along my exposed skin, and I feel the stubble of his five o'clock shadow. It feels good—I don't want it to feel so good. My instinct is to shiver at any touch from him and tremble at his every whim. I'm holding the sensations at bay pretty damn well.

"I want to also tell you something, and I'm afraid you'll think something's wrong with me. I didn't tell you before because I didn't want you to think this was my sole reason for wanting you in the beginning and even now. You see, I have a thing for older women. I don't feel the word *cougar* serves as a proper term, but I use it anyway. That's why when Alexi told me that Courtney insulted you at *Tai-Phoon,* she couldn't have been more wrong about my sexual proclivities and taste in women. Apparently, Mrs. Price found out about my preference and tried to use it to her advantage." He shakes his head as if he's not quite finding the words he wants.

"This is why I'm trying to explain to you that not just *any* woman will do for me," he pleads with me with his eyes as he looks up from my lap.

Call me ridiculous, but it's not that simple. I can't kiss and make up. I can't flip a switch and forgive him. Hurt doesn't immediately go away just because someone says they're sorry. I spent too many years hearing excuses and sorries. I want to believe him about this Yvette chick. Maybe another day I can find it in me to forgive him. Today's not the day!

Of course, it should be a relief that he confirmed he's in love with me for who *I* am. And it's a relief as far as the age thing. *But how can he love me if he still doesn't know me completely?* He needs to love that person too! Will he still love me when he finally knows? This is why I'm driving myself nuts because I'm too unsure.

I finally decide he can witness some life in me since I've remained mute and practically corpse-like. I put the mug of warm tea up to my lips and moan. It tastes so good. He breathes a sigh of relief. I try to drink it slowly and not be piggish. I guess I didn't realize how thirsty I am. After a few more sips, I finally set the mug down next to the urn, and he eyes it. I don't care what he thinks about it—William stays for now.

This is the first time Caleb has been in my room. Actually, it's the first time I've really let him inside my space. Maybe I'm the one who messed this up from the start with trying to be so guarded. So, I'll level with him. I can't help but think *if he understands what a headcase I am, then he won't want me.* Now, that could also work against me—he could want custody of our child. God, I hope not! I'm all for doing the co-parenting thing, but I can't live without my children. *I'm certifiable today!*

I start to try to say something, but my throat is still so raw and dry from vomiting, crying, and dehydration. I pick up my mug to drink some more, and he tells me to take my time. I know he's going to be disappointed when he hears what I have to say. It's because it has nothing to do with me forgiving him, and everything to do with him finally getting to know *the real me*.

I close my eyes and begin my story. "I've been living with a ghost for many years—eons it seems. I've never told anyone my secret. Shit, I should say 'secrets' because it's definitely plural. Not even Alexi knows. William knew, of course, as do his parents, but that's because we grew up together. Sometimes I feel like my past is someone else's life. I almost forget who that girl is. And then I may have a dream, or rather, nightmare, and it all comes flooding back." I'm trying to work up the courage to tell him what I've been holding in for so long.

I open my eyes and I inhale while imparting this next admission. "I was addicted to prescription pain pills when I was sixteen. I tore my quadriceps in my right leg due to a volleyball injury. It took months to heal. I wouldn't stick to the physical therapy, and I found it was easier to medicate. When my doctor refused to give me any more medication…well, I fell into the wrong crowd that would remedy the situation."

He swallows hearing the words coming from my mouth. I shudder at the memories. I need to get this all out, though—it's like trying to suck the venom out of a snake bite.

"Back then I wasn't into boys, or school, or any usual teenage stuff because I was too consumed by the medication. Maybe that's why I coddled William so much, because I could relate to his misery when his condition got so bad. An addiction of any sort is the strongest bond. You think mother and child is strong—which it is—but an addict and their choice of poison is probably more hardcore," I painfully explain.

I hate the analogy I'm using, but I think it's the only way I'll get him to realize what it does to your life. Unless he's personally experienced it or witnessed it, he couldn't know what it's like.

"My parents didn't know what to do with me. It went on for over a year. I was getting terrible grades. I was completely withdrawn from life, and since I didn't have volleyball anymore, I had nothing and no one. So, the pills were my best friend—much like I've always considered the bottle to be William's mistress. One particular night, I was at a party, trying to numb my pain. My dad went out to find me and bring me home. I think he and my mom were finally going to put me into some kind of a treatment facility, even though they couldn't afford it. I know my dad would've broken his back working overtime to get me the help I needed if that's what it took. But it was too late…for him, that is." Now I'm really choked up.

Caleb closes his eyes as if he's reliving the memory with me.

"Once my dad discovered where I was holed up at, he raced over to the house party. Unfortunately, he never made it. A drunk driver hit his car and killed him instantly. It was awful and gruesome, but at least he was taken quickly. God, he was T-boned and never had a chance. The driver walked away with minimal injuries. Subconsciously, I've always wondered if I ended up with an alcoholic husband as some kind of a punishment and retribution for what I did to my family." Now I'm crying uncontrollably.

I take a few minutes to swipe at my tears and still manage to go on, "I cleaned up my act on my own after his death. My leg was already healed, so obviously I didn't need the meds. I quit cold turkey, believe it or not, and haven't touched anything since. My penitence had to be a way to honor my father. That's why I became a nurse. I needed to make amends somehow."

I fidget with my skort and pull at the hemline. He reaches for me, but I hold up my hand, letting him know I still have lots more to say. "I wanted to help people because I couldn't save myself or my dad back then. He died because of me. I was selfish. I lost my dad because I wasn't strong enough, or brave enough, to say *no* to those little white pills. I think being a nurse was therapeutic because I could see all the good those pills *could* do—but God, those things are capable of so much destruction. I needed saving all those years ago. Then when I realized I couldn't save William, well, you can imagine how I view it as one epic failure after another. My kids seem to be the only thing I've done right in my life."

His beautiful brown eyes open and search mine. "Liz…God, I'm so sorry. I had no idea you carried all that pain and suffering around with you. You're the most amazing woman I know. That's not the only thing you've done right, sweetness. I've always seen you as a person who represents nothing but love, strength, caring, and comfort," Caleb says as he kisses my hand, and I feel a tear leak from his eye, which lands on my wrist—the wrist that is no longer wearing his bracelet.

My voice is scratchy, but I'll finish this story no matter what. "I ruined my mother when I killed my dad. She died right after I got married. None of my children ever met those grandparents. They only ever had William's. And I'm sure you've noticed their contempt for me. Not only do they blame me for causing their son's alcoholism, but they also think I enabled it. They've resented me since we started dating. Then once we had Tyler, well, their hatred only intensified. When Tyler was diagnosed at four with being on the spectrum, I was blamed for that too. They didn't want to hear the possibility of genetics. They thought *I* did something in-utero to cause it."

I bite my lip, thinking about the baby I now carry and how I'm sitting here with his or her father, and *he* doesn't even know. Caleb reaches for me, but I don't go willingly into his embrace; he more or less pulls me to him. I'm like a ragdoll, so I go with it. He's rocking me back and forth. I know he'll be a good father when the time comes and do this very thing with our child in a comforting manner.

I'm sure he can put two and two together to realize that William came into my life at a time when I needed a crutch. I thought he was the answer to my prayers. Then, when William started drinking, and it became evident alcohol would consume him, it became a bitter pill—or truth serum, rather—to swallow. It stung like a bitch that it was done at the expense of our kids.

Caleb is still holding me and telling me things—some things I already know, but I need to hear them anyway—other things are new to me. He explains that people all have pasts and family history. His was apparently just as dysfunctional as mine. Learning that he lost his infant brother, then had to deal with his mom's depression and cope with his dad's stress…oh God, it's heartbreaking. I feel selfish once again for not seeing that other people carry pain too. Some of us are better at hiding it than others. And I guess Caleb has been good at hiding it.

It makes me sad that our baby won't have any grandparents, but thankfully he or she will have plenty of doting aunts, uncles, and cousins within our group. Plus, I know it goes without saying that Fred, Milly, and even Granny Lil will be grandparent figures.

He whispers to me over and over that I need to stop punishing myself. I really thought I forgave myself a long time ago, but I guess all this talking reopened the wounds.

He holds me for a bit longer before I finally pull away. He dries the remainder of my tears with his fingers, then wipes the moisture on his suit pants. We've been through a lot in revealing ourselves. The problems are not resolved—they're far from it. I can't do that today. And even if we do fix ourselves, it doesn't mean we'll fix *us*.

"I need to rest, Caleb. I don't feel well. And I don't want the kids to see me like this," I say as my eyelids are already drooping.

Pregnancy takes so much out of you. Between the stress, the not eating well, the lack of sleep, and the vomiting, I'm not able to keep my eyes open. I need to get better.

"Don't worry, sweetness. I'll be here when you wake up. Just rest, and I'll make sure the kids get home from school," he says as he helps me lie down and get situated under the covers.

He kisses my forehead, and I feel his lips linger there. I breathe in his scent, and it's like a shot of melatonin because it lulls me to sleep. I'm wiped out and gone within seconds.

# Chapter 24: The Fourth is Strong in This One

*Caleb*

I made a few phone calls before the kids arrived home. I had a talk with Clyde, and in an interesting turn of events, it seems my promotion is pretty much guaranteed. I wasn't expecting that. I'm not going to question it, but it seems Clyde was relieved when I told him what happened with Mrs. Price.

So, it leads me to wonder if he was the victim of a similar situation of sorts, or one in which she only thought she had Clyde in her back pocket. I'm still contemplating opening my own firm one day, but for now I'm loyal and will stick with the company as long as they stand by me.

My next phone call was to Alexi to give him the update on Liz. I was a mean SOB earlier when I chewed him out. It was unfair of me to do so. I was a jackass for blaming him for what happened at my office. It's not Alexi's fault…it's mine. I apologized to him, and I think he took it in stride. I was angry because she never would have been at my office if I would have gone to see her at the lake house.

I was there for Alexi at a time he needed me most, when Caylan was in trouble. They needed legal counsel, and, of course, I stepped in. He doesn't owe me a damn thing, but I've often pondered over the idea he somehow thinks he has to make it up to me. His friendship—no, brotherhood—is enough.

I'm still reeling from all that Liz revealed in her bedroom. I never would have guessed she struggled with so much in her teens. Our pasts are different but still coincide in some ways. I may not have suffered from an addiction personally, but, similarly, I watched what addiction of another sort did to my mom—my mom's addiction was her grief. Of course, the medication ultimately killed her, but it was the addiction to grief itself that led to her demise. Mom was deeply consumed by it, and it took her from me the day Christopher died.

When the kids got home, I explained that their mom still wasn't feeling well, and they completely understood. Leah started dinner—man, what a great kid she is! The boys got working on their homework. I even helped Kurt with some trigonometry problems, and that shit is hard. Why is today's homework designed to make parents feel so stupid?

I may be a glutton for punishment because I can't stop myself from hoping and wishing this will one day be my family. The kids and I really seem to get along. I would never try to take the place of their father, but obviously they didn't have a relationship with him; I realize it doesn't mean I can automatically be a replacement. Only Liz knew him before the alcohol, and it's sad they never got to experience a warm, nurturing, and caring father figure.

I get how and why she ended up with him. It all makes sense now. It's like the puzzle can finally be glued down because the pieces aren't changing. I didn't even realize I was missing pieces or that they didn't fit before. No wonder why Liz thought I didn't know *the real her.* I can accept her for who she is both then and now. I love all parts, sides, and pieces of her. I can accept her past. *Can she accept me and our future?* That's really what it comes down to.

Leah tells me dinner is ready. She made a pasta dish, and it smells amazing. She said she's going to let her mom know so she can join us. After a few minutes, a very bleary-eyed—but still beautiful—Liz comes ambling down the stairs. She looks so pale and gaunt. I feel the acid churning in my stomach because I contributed to her current condition.

I've never wanted to bring her even an ounce of pain and sadness. I want to be her protector. I've failed her. She thinks she's flawed, well, I'm the flawed one. I will never be able to stop using the word *perfect* to describe her because that's what she is to me and always will be.

I give a tentative "hello" to her and gauge her reaction.

As she comes toward the kitchen table, she gives me a small wave. I'll take that as progress. Then, she kisses each of her kids on the crown of their head and tells Leah how wonderful she is for making the meal.

"Mind if I stay for dinner? I certainly don't want to impose, though," I say with puppy dog eyes and hope in my voice.

I'm going to use everything in my arsenal to convince her to let me back into her world. We're back at the beginning taking baby steps. I will tell you that my face and irresistible eyes can and will be used against you in the court of law—*I know, I'm a dork with my legal jargon!*

"Sure. We'd like that, wouldn't we, kids?" Liz says while looking around at her sons and daughter, seeing if she can read anything contrary in their expressions.

They all chime in that they want me to stay. It's not just for selfish reasons I want to stay, it's also because I want to look after Liz. I really believe she needs me—she just doesn't realize it.

We all sit down, and I heap a big scoop of pasta onto my plate. I give my compliments to the chef, and Leah is adorably smug, as she very well should be; I'm moved each time I can make this young girl smile.

Liz pushes the food around on her plate, and every now and then takes a bite. I whisper to her, "Are you not hungry?"

She sighs and bites her lip. "Not really. I'll force myself to eat because of the...."

She quits mid-sentence. *That's odd,* I think.

"*Because of the*...what, sweetness?" I ask in concern.

"Please don't call me that," she says as quietly as a mouse and looks down at her plate.

It's so natural for me to call her that. But I will do my best to refrain. I will bite my tongue for her. I apologize and tell her I'll stop. She never told me what the *because of the* is, but I don't press her any further.

The kids are chatting away among themselves about some movie, and they let me join in on the conversation. I help everyone clean up, and Leah goes to the freezer to get ice cream for everyone. I have a big sweet tooth, in case you didn't already guess. And they have mint chocolate chip, which is my all-time favorite.

After ice cream and cleaning up the kitchen, I was going to suggest that Liz go lie back down and that I'd stick around for a little while longer. But before I can say as much, my cell rings. I look at the screen, and it's Alexi.

"Hey, man, what's up?" I ask in greeting.

Alexi's voice comes across the line with a bit of excitement to it. "Hey, Anthony called me. It's about Shanna. It's time!"

*** 

*Liezel*

Thankfully, it's a Friday night, so I don't feel bad about keeping the kids out so late. We're all so excited about the baby. Shanna's a week past her due date. Goodness, I remember those days of pleading with God, just wanting the baby out already. Poor girl.

I must have gotten my second wind because I'm a little perkier. Maybe dinner, the nap, or Caleb's nearness has put a little spark back in me. It's hard to believe that in seven months I'll be welcoming another one of my own into the world.

It's nearing midnight. She was in labor for a while before she was brought into the hospital. Anthony did everything by the textbook at home, waiting until her contractions were at the right interval; with him being a pediatrician, well, it's certainly coming in handy. I'm sure he's still a nervous wreck. I know sometimes I forget I'm a nurse because I'm always a mom first. But then your instincts kick in, and you find you can do both jobs when it comes to your children or loved ones.

Alexi, Caleb, Brent, and Gil are drinking coffee and huddled together. We girls are camped out on the chairs—well, me and Addison, that is. Everly is hanging with the guys. She has a mouth like them and can fit in easily with either group; we all adore her for it.

As for Caylan, she's the only one of us who stayed home since she would have been too uncomfortable being this close to the end of her pregnancy. I don't have a belly, and there's no strain on my back yet, so the chairs don't bother me. My kids are playing on their tablets; however, Leah keeps nodding off. I've asked them multiple times if they wanted to go, but they've insisted we stay for the big moment. It gives me hope that they'll gladly welcome a little brother or sister.

Addison sits next to me, and we've been talking about her work. Then, she switches topics. "So, what did you think of the poem?" She hedges.

I knew it was coming. I'm sure she wouldn't have brought it up, but everyone plainly sees Caleb and I are on friendlier terms just not *together*—so, I'm sure to her the subject isn't off limits.

"It was beautiful," is all I say.

She gives me a sympathetic look, then follows it up with a half-hug since we're sitting side by side. I don't want anyone's pity or sympathy. But truthfully, I don't know what I want. Every now and then Caleb glances my way. I'll admit it's sweet that he keeps checking on me and cares so much, but it's getting on my nerves because I need a break from him to think.

Really, I need time to analyze this. I need time to be on my own again and sort this all out. I was fine with him staying for dinner, but this can't be an all-the-time type thing. We need to press the pause button, then rewind, and try to start fresh. I would say we moved too fast, yet there were times I wanted it sped up. Now we're going to have a kid together, so I have to figure out how I want to proceed.

Alexi manages to talk to me one-on-one to check in with me. It works out to my advantage because he gets to go into brother mode, and I squirrel away information from him. I slyly ask him who he and Caylan use for their OBGYN. I prefer to go off referrals from friends and not always the ones insurance recommends. Needless to say, I'll be calling Monday to schedule an appointment with their doctor, who will hopefully take me on as a new patient.

I also tell Alexi that I'm coming back to work on Monday. He can see he won't win the battle of trying to convince me otherwise. I need to get back to a routine. Then I'll feel more like *me*. Alexi starts talking about the latest toy Em is into, and before we know it, Anthony comes out and tells us he's a father.

I guessed right! It's a baby girl for this amazing couple. She's seven pounds, three ounces, and twenty inches long. Both mom and baby are doing well. The newborn has red hair like her mama and light brown eyes like her father. They're naming her Leia Lucky Parker. I adore how they made her middle name Lucky. Shanna's engagement ring is a green diamond four-leaf clover, which is perfect for being an Irish girl. Plus, we all got a kick out of the fact they chose a *Star Wars*-themed first name until we remembered today's date—yes, the *fourth* will be with us!

We all give our round of hugs, congratulations, and some of us shed happy tears. It's a wonderful experience adding to our group. It keeps expanding each year, and it makes my heart so full that we keep growing our family.

We can come back tomorrow to see Shanna and the baby, so we all head out for the evening. Caleb drives the kids and me back to my house, and my kiddos immediately head inside to bed. I'm still in the car with him because I don't want him to follow. We have to do this here in private.

"I don't want you to come in," I say firmly.

A wave of pain and disappointment washes over his face, but he nods his understanding.

"Caleb, it's been a really long day. Too much has happened, and so much has already been talked about. I'm going back to work on Monday, though. I think we need to start over again, in a way, and get back to what we had when we were just friends. I certainly want you in my life, but I need time to figure some things out. I only hope you can respect that," I tack on the request at the end.

"Liz…," he breathes. "I'll be here in whatever capacity you need me to be. Don't shut me out completely, please. I'd love to be your friend. I think you need a friend right now, and I want to be the one who's there for you and the kids. I can do slow, even though my past actions suggest otherwise. Let me know when I can see you again, and I'll be here," he promises.

He takes my left hand that is resting in my lap and kisses it softly across the knuckles. I hear him mumble something about lilacs, then he releases it.

"Goodnight," I tell him.

He tells me "goodnight," and I exit his car.

***

May 15, 2018

My ultrasound is today. I'm sitting in the waiting room ready for them to call me to the back. I told Alexi I had a doctor's appointment, so it wasn't a lie. However, he thinks I'm being seen because I've been so fatigued. Once the bump eventually comes, there will be no hiding it. I hope to share my surprise with everyone well before a baby bump is present.

The OBGYN had me come in last week to do bloodwork, and she confirmed my pregnancy. Due to my maternal age, they wanted me to have an ultrasound done even this early on. I swore to myself that after today I'd tell Caleb.

It may sound awful to some, but I decided the night we went to the hospital for Shanna that I didn't want to tell Caleb until I was sure things are progressing in this pregnancy. I'm considered high-risk because of my age; I find it laughable that somehow my age is always involved—story of my life, it seems. After seeing how excited Caleb was about Shanna's baby, I can't risk breaking his heart if there's already a major complication this early on; especially if I won't make it out of my first trimester.

Once I know today that everything is okay, then I plan to tell him. I'm eight and a half weeks along, so the time seems to be going fast. I've been doing a lot better since we had the major talk. I went to therapy a few times over the years, and before William chose to drink, I even confided in him on several occasions. Despite the times I've talked about my past with a few select others, I guess I never healed from those old wounds. Talking to Caleb about it did help. *It's like the ghosts were finally laid to rest.* I believe I can have a healthy and happy future, and I'm trying to accept that I'm deserving of it. I'd like to think my parents would be proud of the woman I've become.

After another ten minutes of waiting, I'm called back by the tech.

She performs a transvaginal ultrasound on me, and I can't wait to hear the heartbeat; that whooshing sound is the best noise on the planet. However, I can't see the monitor yet since it's facing toward her. She's doing the scan, and I see her face change. It's not a look of panic or alarm, but of surprise.

Immediately, I'm concerned and ask her, "Is everything okay?"

"Oh, yes, everything's fine," she tries to assure me, but I'm not so easily convinced.

I see her tap a button on the wall. We have a similar paging system at Alexi's clinic. That button pages the doctor to come in immediately. Now I'm incredibly concerned and close my eyes. *God, please don't let anything be wrong with my child.* If there's an issue, I will love him or her no matter what, though.

I concentrate on breathing deeply. I know there's no point in asking the tech any more questions because this is a matter for the doctor to tend to. I'm praying with everything I have. Finally, the door opens and in walks Dr. Lisa Miller.

I look at the tech, then to the doctor, back to the tech, and back to my OBGYN. Dr. Miller's face lights up looking at the image of my baby on the screen. She's beaming. I'm so confused. And at this early stage, my poor little peanut doesn't even resemble the classic shape of a baby because he or she is still forming. But so much love fills my chest for the little one. I'm about to explode if someone doesn't tell me what's going on!

"Look at them!" Dr. Miller says with wonder as she turns the screen my way.

Did she just say *them?*

# Chapter 25: Freezing Hot

*Liezel*

The next day I'm still walking around in a stupefied state.

*Twins!*

*I'm having twins!*

To top it off, Caylan is currently in labor, so there's even more excitement going on. We're all once again headed to the hospital, well, minus Shanna, as she's staying home with her newborn daughter. Anthony said he'd be by when he knew for sure she was ready to push. Luckily, none of us live too terribly far from the hospital. Since it's during the workday, Alexi brought in a former colleague of his to cover his clinic for him while on paternity leave, and we have per diem nurses we call in for me.

I don't know how I'm going to tell Caleb that not only is he going to be a father, but he's also going to have two at once! This will be such a shock. Believe me, I never expected to have five kids, but now I'm so in love with the idea. I won't know until the second trimester what the genders are. It doesn't matter if we're having two of the same, or one of each. I'm so excited! I can try and be patient, but I'm anxious to know if they're fraternal or identical. The doctor suspects fraternal because she believes they're di-di twins, meaning diamniotic and dizygotic.

Dr. Miller informed me that the babies—oh my God, it's plural—are developing normally, and from all my bloodwork panels and various testing, everything looks great so far. I have to do some genetic testing because of my age just to be sure, but I'm not concerned. I'm a healthy, fit woman, and I've been taking my prenatal vitamins since the day I saw those two pink lines.

And, boy, do I feel guilty now that Caleb missed the first ultrasound with me. I feel like I deprived him of the most special moment. I'm trying not to beat myself up over it because I could never have predicted we'd have twins—you could have knocked me over with a feather.

But I'll admit, it's still a dick move to have not included him, even if we were only having a singleton. I hope he'll understand my reasoning when he finds out. I really didn't want to get his hopes up if something was wrong. It sounds logical to me, but maybe it won't to him. I sigh aloud, and a headache is forming at my temples just thinking about it.

On a positive note, have I mentioned Caleb has been texting me every day? It's sweet one-liners, but much appreciated. I know he's trying. He's being a good friend. I do respond to him. I haven't worked up the courage to invite him over again, but I suppose I need to do that sooner rather than later. I'll see him at the hospital when we get to welcome Caylan's new baby into the world, but I think it's important he and I have some alone time...as friends.

*** 

Later that night, an eight-pound, one-ounce, twenty-two-inch baby boy comes screaming into the world. We're all shocked Caylan carried him considering how tiny she is. She's lucky this wasn't her first because nothing would've been the same *down there* again, if you know what I'm saying.

The proud parents name him Zane Valentino Graham. I love that Emeline was born on Valentine's Day and her middle name is Valentine. So, they did a variation for his middle name. He's absolutely precious. We got to quickly go back to her room and visit. Caylan looked radiant, and you'd never know she just delivered. Zane's dark hair and blue eyes made him look so striking. For a baby, he sure needs to walk the runway. God, if I was a social media person I would've been tweeting it out to every inhabitant of this planet!

Em was so disinterested in her baby brother, and we all got a kick out of it. Fred and Milly cried, and even Brent was incredibly choked up while holding his new nephew. He doesn't seem to have a phobia anymore like he did when Em was born—thanks to Everly changing him in ways we'll never comprehend.

After our quick visit with everyone at the hospital, Caleb asked if he could take the kids and me out for ice cream. That's harmless and innocent enough, so I agreed. We ended up having a great time. It seemed like how it used to be between Caleb and me in the beginning—joking around non-stop, the laughter so infectious. It felt good to experience these moments again.

This time, I actually do invite him back to the house. We drove in separate cars, so he meets me at my place. The kids retire to their rooms for the evening. We end up hanging out downstairs on the couch and talk. It isn't awkward at all.

"So…any new cookie recipes you're dying to try out on this willing taste-tester?" He asks with the goofiest grin.

I start giggling at his expression. He looks kooky the way his face is contorted.

"Now how can I disappoint that face if I say *no*?" I ask, stifling my laugh.

"My thoughts exactly," he responds while winking at me in an adorable fashion.

We all know I love Caleb. But this playful side of him is so addicting. I thought I'd never have another addiction of any sort, but this one is the healthy kind, I must say. Of course, Alpha Caleb in the bedroom is a whole different addiction, but I can't go *there,* or I'll completely forget about making cookies.

He follows me into the kitchen and sits on the stool. Since we've done this a few times before, we assume our positions to commence with the treat making. I haven't been sick lately, so I hope as I'm about to head into the second trimester, the nausea will once and for all subside. I feel pretty great tonight.

I take out all my ingredients and line them up on the counter. I think I'm going to do mint chocolate chip cookies. He loves that flavor of ice cream, so I might as well spoil him with the cookie version. He's watching me closely as I assemble everything, and then I announce to him what I'm making.

He's like a little kid bouncing on his stool. I love his enthusiasm, but it's only freaking cookies! He cracks me up, though. I let him do the mixing once I measure everything out. I go to preheat the oven and grease a baking sheet. He's having fun turning the batter the precise shade of green with the food coloring.

We finally get them portioned out on the sheet and then place them in the oven. Wow, the smell that wafts out is heavenly as it hits me in the face. My salivary glands are going crazy. He sniffs appreciatively at the air, and we both sigh, waiting for the moment we'll get to devour the ooey, gooey, minty, chocolatey goodness—*ha, ha, try saying that five times fast!*

"Would you like milk with your cookies," I ask sweetly.

"Is there any other way to eat chocolate chip cookies?" He retorts.

"Touché! Well, I have regular milk or soy. You can thank Addison and Gil for turning us on to the soy. Although, I've never tried dipping cookies in it, so that would probably taste weird," I scrunch up my nose, thinking it may be a strange concoction.

"Is there anything else I can dip my cookie in?" He questions with an arched brow, and his voice is all gravelly as it drops low.

My back is to him as I'm staring into the side-by-side refrigerator and freezer unit. He's still seated on the stool, but I suddenly feel him come up behind me. His heat and nearness have my body reacting instantly. God, I've missed him. I can't deny how unbelievably attracted I am to him. That didn't wane in the slightest, no matter how mad I was at him. My head, heart, and body may all be at odds with one another, but as a woman, I still feel and react.

I know my cheeks are suffused with a red tint, and I start feeling warm and tingly all over. My skin comes alive as his body beckons mine, wanting to cradle me in his big frame. If I lean back, I'll be in his embrace. I'll be infused with his strength and warmth. It's so tempting!

I cock my head to the side, and his breath tickles me as he rasps close to my ear, "You have some flour on you."

This is reminiscent of our first time baking.

I suck in a breath and swallow as I ask, "Where?"

"Right…here…," he says as his fingers trail over a small area on my neck.

Then I feel his warm, wet tongue trace the same path his fingers did, and I moan. Now I do fall back against him. My nipples are hard little points since my chest is practically in the freezer, and then I have the heat from behind me. His erection digs into my back, and I gently sway my hips and ass to rub against it, driving him crazy to return the favor. He moves his hands down my sides to rest them on my hips. I want so badly for him to grab my breasts.

"Sweetness…," is what escapes his lips while he's still licking my neck.

This time, I don't balk at the name.

This time, I am his *sweetness*.

***

*Caleb*

*Fuuuuccckkkk!*

I've never been this hard. It seems like I say that every time I'm with her. But it just gets harder each time, as strange as that may sound. My dick has grown infinitely stiffer for her as time has gone by. I slipped just now by saying *sweetness*, but she didn't correct me or stop me; so, I'm going to press my advantage while I'm ahead—*can I fit any more innuendos in there?*

As she keeps rubbing her ass across my groin, I dig my fingers into her hips. I'm so worried I'll leave marks. At least she doesn't seem as delicate as she was the last few weeks. I finally see her color coming back, and she's filling out a little more. She must be doing better with eating or something.

I swipe my tongue at the soft skin right under her ear, and she almost collapses. *Oh yeah, I hit a spot.* I'm there to catch her. I sweep her up into my arms and kick the doors to the fridge closed with my foot.

I walk into the living room, lay her gently on the couch, and come down on top of her. However, I hold my weight off of her as best as I can so as not to crush her delicate frame.

I know what we're doing is wrong because I'm moving too fast…again. I know this is wrong because we're not alone in the house. It's all so wrong, but yet it's all so right.

Our lips connect, and I suck her tongue into my mouth. Her moans caress my ears, and I groan right back as her eyes flutter closed. I palm one of her perfect breasts, rubbing through her shirt as her beautiful rosy nipples stab the fabric. I know if I reach down between her legs, she'll be incredibly wet for me.

I didn't dream of doing anything like this with her tonight, so I don't even have a damn condom on me! *Figures.* I'll have to settle for eating at her sweet cunt for tonight, if she'll let me. Obviously, that's no hardship. I want to be in her in some way—I'll take anything. That's how desperate I am to be with her. This is what we do as human beings; we need this connection.

I need my fill of her. I need a shot of her. I can't keep carrying on for weeks and days without having some kind of relief. I'd never admit to her that I'm a junkie of sorts. It sounds all kinds of fucked up given what she revealed. Yet, that unshakeable, unbreakable bond she was referring to is what I feel for *her*.

"I don't have a condom," I whisper as I kiss my way down her body.

"It's okay. We don't need one anyway," she says, all breathy.

I chuckle because that doesn't make any sense, and she's asking for trouble with forgoing protection. Not that getting her pregnant would be trouble, but considering we're supposed to be taking this slow, it would shoot that plan to shit if I end up putting a bun in the oven tonight.

"Umm, and why wouldn't we need one?" I inquire while I bite her nipple through the fabric.

"Ahhh," is what she says, then follows it up with some garbled sounds as I gently tug at that same nipple that's between my teeth.

"Let me make you feel good sweetness," I tell her.

I get a moan as a form of a response, which is good enough for me. I leave her top and bra on, but remove the leggings and panties she's wearing. I don't hear any movement in the house, so if she's quiet enough, and I'm quick about my work, we'll have an explosion before anyone would be alerted.

I don't waste any time going to town on her pussy. It's wet and ready for me. I stick my tongue in her tight hole and massage her clit with my fingers. She's already losing her mind; she'll come quickly, that's for sure. I don't think I've ever seen her this turned on this fast. I alternate squeezing each tit while I'm at it.

"God, you taste so good. I could eat at you all night. Fuck the cookies, this is better than anything you could serve me," I say in between licks of her pretty, pink, juicy cunt.

"Mmm," is her only reply.

All her sounds drive me wild. Her smell liberates me. Her taste destroys me.

She. Is. Perfect!

And she's almost there! I flick my tongue at her engorged clit a few more times and then blow on it. She arches up off the couch, putting a throw pillow over her face to stifle her cries of passion. I insert two fingers, hooking them to rub at her spot, and she loses it all over my hand.

I keep flicking her clit, though, so she can ride it out and come down from her high. I'll have to adjust myself in a minute because my cock is painfully pressed into my slacks, and my balls are in need of rearranging to alleviate the intensity. But she comes first—*well, you know what I mean, her needs come first*.

She finally stops gyrating her hips, and it looks like she passes out when her arms flop to the sides. She's no longer clutching the pillow to her face—it's more or less sitting atop, freely balancing.

"I don't think I can move," I believe is what she says, but it's difficult to hear with her face covered.

I put her panties and leggings back on. Those leggings are a bitch to maneuver even on her tiny body, but I do it. She hasn't moved or said a word. I think she's asleep. I remove the pillow from her face, and sure enough, I can hear her soft snores.

The timer for the oven goes off, and she flinches and mumbles something. I tell her I'll get it, and she yawns her thanks.

I go into the kitchen to turn off the oven and timer, but not before washing my hands and face in the sink. Then, I remove the cookie sheet and put it on the cooling rack she set out. I return to the couch. I place my hands under her slight frame and lift her, holding her to my chest and nuzzling her head as I carry her up to her room.

I put her to bed, and she doesn't even stir. Once she's tucked in snugly, I kiss her lips. Before I turn off the light on the nightstand, I notice the bracelet I gave her next to the lamp. It delights me to see it there. It must have replaced the urn because that's nowhere in sight now. I hope she'll put my gift back on again soon. It's not an engagement ring, but it's the closest thing I'll get right now.

I turn out the light and exit the room. All the lights are out in the other rooms, so I assume the kids are also asleep. I don't want to make anyone uncomfortable or come off as creepy should anyone happen to wake up, but I feel this fatherly need to check on the kids. I stick my head in to check each of their rooms, and all three are sound asleep.

I head downstairs and proceed to clean up the kitchen by putting the ingredients away. The cookies are still warm, but a handful will be good enough to travel home with me. I wrap them up and head out the front door. I lock up and put the key back where Alexi told me I could find it. I would've broken the damn door down that day to get to Liz if I had to, but I'm glad my friend shared the key's location.

As I walk to my car with my mint chocolate treats, I think I'm ready to finally look at my horoscope again when I get home.

# Chapter 26: Getting Hitched

*Caleb*

June 15, 2018

And so things continued just like that for these last four and a half weeks. I'd go over to Liz's and visit, have dinner, watch movies, basically hang out. She wouldn't come to my place, but it didn't bother me.

Occasionally, we'd perform some oral treatment on one another, but I still didn't push her for sex. I'd eventually work my way up to that, but I was trying to stick to this *friends* thing as best I could. I guess we're in limbo at that *friends with benefits* stage. If she would have told me *no* to doing anything sexual, I would have honored that. The trouble is, I think we both have this unspoken understanding that we can't keep our hands off each other no matter how slow we want to go.

I noticed she did start wearing the bracelet after that night with the mint chocolate chip cookies. I never commented on it when I saw her two days later because I didn't want to scare her and have it result in her removing it again. Knowing it's on her is enough.

I've been reading my horoscope each day now. Today is definitely my favorite.

> *Virgo*
> *Love is in the air. Something you've been putting off is finally ready to be put into action. Don't be afraid to let the stars align in your house. Look to the moon when in doubt, and shift your priorities accordingly. There may be a surprise in store!*
> *Your lucky number is 7.*

So, I'm going to put my plan into action.

*\*\*\**

*Liezel*

"How'd you like to go camping?" Caleb asks.

Well, I'm camped out on my living room couch reading a steamy romance book right now. Or, rather, I was until Caleb called—does that count?

I set my book down, and he has my attention. The kids are out back playing football together. I would join them, but for obvious reasons, I can't tell them why they can't tackle me to the ground.

I laugh and reply, "Umm, okay when and where?"

"How about now, and to Hershey?" He remarks as if it's obvious.

"I'd have to dig our tent out. It's already five o'clock. I don't want to set up a tent in the dark. I'm sorry, maybe some other weekend," I tell him reluctantly.

I'm a little bummed because I would totally go, but it's not ideal tonight to drive two hours. Plus, I seriously have to dig out all my camping gear.

"Sweetness, I want to take you to the saaaaweeeetest city on earth. I'm sure you've been there plenty of times. But you've never been with me! And I'm going to sweeten the deal," he explains.

Okay, now my interest is piqued to full scale.

"Whoa, there. You're sure putting a lot of *sweet* talk into this, aren't you?" I laugh at my own pun since he's overdoing it with that word.

"What if I told you I bought a new truck and a family camper?" He divulges.

"Then I'd say either you're nuts, or that's a lame joke," I convey.

"Well, then I guess I'm nuts because I'm certainly not lame," he comes back with.

"Oh. My. God. You didn't!" I squeal half from excitement, half from bewilderment.

"Oh, I sure did. You all need to pack two days' worth of stuff, and we'll get on the road. We'll worry about groceries when we get there. There's not too much involved with setting up the camper, but I do want enough daylight since I got a crash course only an hour ago at the dealership," he explains with the most elated tone to his voice.

"Okay, I can tell the kids. When will you be here?" I ask as I'm still surprised by all this.

He's spontaneous and adorable and... *this is crazy, right?*

He chuckles once again and replies, "Sweetness, I'm right out front."

***

We made good time getting into Hershey. On the drive up, I was plagued with guilt over still not telling him about the twins—don't hate me for it, I'm definitely telling him.

As unrealistic as it may seem, I'm lucky I don't start showing until I'm well into my second trimester. It's been that way with the previous three pregnancies; every woman certainly carries differently. I'm shocked that these two tiny peanuts haven't given me away. Even the little roundness to my tummy has yet to be revealed since we've been performing oral sex on one another—we've stayed fully clothed for the most part.

He finally pulls us into a well-kept RV campground. His truck is magnificent. It's a midnight-blue color, decked out with all the bells and whistles. Those gadgets came in handy when pulling into the site—the backup camera, towing option, and blind spot sensors made it a breeze. He explained to me that hitching it up can be the trickiest thing because *it's all about precision*, and then unhitching can be difficult if everything's not lined up properly.

He kept talking about the load, leveling the camper, and making sure there's no sway, and blah blah blah. I don't really get it. This is another one of those things that guys seem to automatically know. A tent is good enough for me, but I admit it feels good to go "glamping."

The camper is awesome! It's a gray color with black striped accents. I'll refer to it as a *she* because that's what Caleb keeps saying. So, *she* is thirty-three feet long with two slide-outs. The boys have to share a room in the back that has twin bunks with a seating area under one bunk and storage compartments under the other. Caleb said it's called a bunk-house feature.

Then Leah is going to sleep either on the pull-out couch, or the kitchen table, which turns into a bed. There's a cute little bathroom, a full kitchen with small-scale appliances, and then Caleb and I will be sharing a queen-sized bed in the front bedroom.

I was a little nervous of what the kids would think, but they didn't seem freaked out when they figured out the sleeping arrangements on their own. *I probably don't give them enough credit.*

There's also a big screen TV and electric fireplace to complete the traveling-in-style component. It doesn't even feel like camping in this thing, but Caleb argued, "This is the new way to camp." I rolled my eyes at him when he said that.

My favorite part of the camper has to be the exterior. It has an outdoor grill with a TV inside. And the awning has these amazing multi-colored LED rope lights that give off just enough glow and look dazzling.

He did ask me on the way up if I was mad that he made the purchase. I will confess, I thought it was a little too presumptuous of him to buy this thing. I didn't want to be pressured into something. And then I had to stop myself because I still haven't told him about the babies, so how unfair of me to decide what's *too presumptuous*. Maybe this little trip is what we need, so I can finally tell him this weekend.

Once the camper was unhitched, we went to the nearest grocery store to stock up on essentials. Now, we're sitting down to dinner at the picnic table that came with the campsite, and we're enjoying the steaks Caleb grilled up. We'll get a fire going later.

After dinner, Caleb and I walk hand in hand with the kids down to the campground's little general store. We start browsing around the shop. I let Leah get a pack of marshmallows since we forgot to grab them at the supermarket. The boys don't want anything, so we're moseying around, looking at the merchandise.

Caleb comes up behind me and says, "I'm definitely getting this for the camper!"

It's one of those corny bumper stickers, but I immediately love it as my face splits into a grin. It reads, *My Travel Trailer is Bigger Than Yours!*

I look into his eyes, and he and I both know that if we were alone, he'd make this into some kind of sexual reference. I know exactly what he's packing under those pants, and I know exactly how big it is. I've had it in my mouth several times over the weeks. God, I can't wait to have him in me again one of these days—but wishy-washy me likes that we're not jumping right into bed. It's like rediscovering each other all over again.

"By the way, what should we call *her*?" He asks nonchalantly.

I give him a funny look, not quite getting what he's referring to—somewhat panicked thinking he's talking about these secret babies, but I don't even know their genders. So, I reply, "Huh?"

"The camper. What should we call *her*?" He acts as if it was obvious.

*Whew, okay that HER, I'd already forgotten about the camper's designated gender.* I start laughing, "Oh, hmm. I don't know. It's not like a ship where you have to christen *her,* is it?"

"No, but I thought it'd be fun!" His face beams at his suggestion.

"Well, I'm plum fresh out of ideas." I shrug.

"I was thinking *The Sweetness Express,*" he says and waggles his brows while waving his hand as if he can see it in lights on Broadway or something.

I swat at his arm and roll my eyes as I tease, "How original."

***

It's after ten o'clock. The campfire has to be extinguished by eleven, then quiet hours are from midnight to six in the morning. I would know because I read the brochure for this place from cover to cover.

Caleb and I watch as the last of the embers are starting to flicker and the wood glows red. We're not adding any more logs. The kids have gone to bed. I have a blanket wrapped around my shoulders as I sit in the camping chair and stare at the dying flames.

We're both quiet. It was noisy when we were roasting marshmallows and telling stories. Now, it's silent. Now, it's just us. *Do I tell him right now about this pregnancy?* I probably should because we'll have to keep our voices low, so if there's any yelling involved, then it will be kept to a minimum. I don't know which side of the fence he'll be on—anger or joy, or a combination of both? I want to be able to tell my kids soon and Caleb has a right to know first.

I don't know how you kick off this type of conversation. Should I blurt it out? Should I ask how he feels about being a father? Do I make a joke?

I swallow hard, needing to get this final secret out in the open. Then I can be free once and for all.

***

*Caleb*

This was the best idea I've ever had. We needed this. I needed for her to see us as a family and how it can work with the five of us. I think I'm winning her over each day. All the walls are down. There's nothing left to do but break through to her heart. I think I've punched a hole in it; I just need to get all the way in.

She looks so damn beautiful in the glow of the fire as it's dwindling down. We're sitting on opposite sides, and I can admire her beauty from here. I can't explain it. It's like the last several weeks have put life back into her. Our relationship is blooming the way it should be.

*See, I told you she's my unicorn!*

I know it deep in my bones. I know she'll be my wife someday. I know we'll grow our family one day too.

"You look deep in thought, sweetness," I comment.

Her brows are knit together, and she's chewing on her bottom lip as if she's contemplating something. I'm going to think positive thoughts and not have an irrational fear that she's about to dump me. Well, technically, she can't dump me since we're not officially dating—always these technicalities—but that's not the point. I don't want to be ousted from her life again.

She's nervous when she begins, "I…I…I have to tell you something."

"You can tell me anything." I mean it, and I'm remaining calm, cool, and collected so she's not leery of whatever it is she needs to disclose.

Sure, on one hand I'm terrified there's another secret that could rip her away from me, but on the other hand, I need to know. Nothing, and I mean NOTHING will ever change how and what I feel for her; however, we can't have anything unresolved between us.

She closes her lids and licks her lips. *Fuck!* This must be serious. Now my heart is racing. What can she possibly have to say?

"Remember that day when I told you I had to force myself to eat?" She looks at me pointedly to make sure I'm with her.

I nod to show I'm following. But I'm scared. Jesus Christ, what could this be about? Does she have cancer or something? Am I going to lose her before I even have her?

She licks her lips again and continues, "And remember when I told you that one night that you didn't need to wear a condom? Even though we didn't end up having sex...."

I nod again. Where is this going? I know my eyes are roving as my brain tries to recall these instances and also make sense of this line of questioning.

And then it makes perfect sense. Dare I hope? Dare I put all my eggs in one basket and believe the damn horoscope was right that I have a *surprise* on the horizon? A *surprise little one* on the way perhaps? I can see she's waiting for me to ask. Fuck, I don't want to be wrong!

*Please don't be wrong....*

"Are you...are you pregnant, Liz?" I wait with bated breath.

She looks me right in the eyes, and I try to slow my heart so I can hear—my eardrums feel like they're pumping in time with the organ in my chest making my auditory abilities difficult.

"Yes," she replies.

And it's like my life flashes before my eyes—not one brought on by death, but one brought on by a miracle. In an instant, I see myself running in a huge field with my blonde-headed child as Liz sits on a picnic blanket, smiling away, watching the spectacle before her.

I start to tear up, and I stand so abruptly that my camping chair falls back to the ground. I rush to her side, crouching down so I can place my head in her lap. My face is turned so I can administer a soft kiss to her belly and move my hand, so it's splayed across the area where our child lies. I can't believe there's life in there, life that both she and I created. Amazing!

Then, I raise my head and move my other hand behind her head, pulling her to my lips. I devour her in a frenzied kiss. She has to push me away at one point so she can draw breath. Clearly, I'm a little overzealous.

She's breathy when she jokes, "Obviously, someone's happy...Daddy."

She smiles, and I have to wonder if it's possible to be more in love with her? *Daddy* has the best ring to it. I'm going to be a father!

"I don't know why I was so nervous to tell you. I'm sorry. I've known for a little while now. Of course, we got pregnant the night of the wedding. I thought you'd be so mad at me for not telling you sooner. I shouldn't have kept this from you. I was just scared something would be wrong and you'd be crushed if I miscarried. Still, it's no excuse. You don't know how relieved I am that you're so overjoyed," she says through happy tears.

Her watery smile shows she's not done with the news. "By the way, my due date is December eighth...," she imparts, but trails off.

She takes a deep breath, and I suspect there's still more. And then

[173]

it comes.

"There's one more thing. We may not make it to December eighth," she explains.

I'm confused, so I ask for clarification, "Why's that, sweetness?"

"Because we're having twins, and given my age and the fact that most multiples are born early, well, I have a feeling they'll arrive before they're supposed to," she conveys while putting her hand on top of my hand, which is still resting on her belly.

"Are you shitting me?" I screech rather loudly.

She giggles, "Shh! Keep your voice down. We don't want to wake the kids."

"Holy fuck! Do they know?" I wonder.

"No, I thought we'd tell them together. Maybe in the morning. I mean, this isn't something I feel like sharing over pancakes and eggs, but I can tell my mommy pooch is going to pop out any time now, so I can't very well keep this under wraps for much longer. I'm already thirteen weeks along tomorrow. We're out of the woods as far as the first trimester, which is why I—again selfishly—didn't tell you to begin with. But now that you're the first to know, I feel the kids deserve to be the second." She looks to me for my agreement.

"Absolutely. But I have to ask, where does this leave us?" I'm scared shitless to hear her reply.

"Can we take it one day at a time?" She begs nervously.

It's not what I want to hear, but I'll take it!

"Of course," I respond.

I then pick up the chair that fell over and pull it up next to hers. I sit down and grab her hand, lacing our fingers together. We don't say anything more, just sit and watch the fire go out—it's not a sign of hope being lost. It's a sign of a new beginning being forged from the ashes.

# Chapter 27: Double-Take

*Liezel*

July 21, 2018

It's wedding day...for Shanna and Anthony, that is.

You wouldn't know she had a baby in May because, damn did that girl get her figure back quickly, as did Caylan. And then there's me. I blew up like a tick overnight, it seems.

The bride and groom aren't having a big to-do. It's very low key. It's another wedding being held at Alexi's lake house, and it's stunning. The attendants consist mostly of our gang, as well as Anthony's staff from his clinic, Shanna's girlfriends from art school, and Anthony's parents and siblings. Also, Shanna's dad flew in from Oklahoma.

I'm so happy for the couple. Both Zane and Leia are the ring bearers, and each kiddo is carried down the aisle with a little pillow tied onto their wrist. Zane has Shanna's ring, and Leia has the ring for her daddy. Of course, Emeline is the flower girl, and she toddles down the aisle with Brent's dog Maverick.

*This is how I'd want my own wedding to be.*

We girls are wearing coordinating summer dresses, and the guys are dressed in khaki pants with matching checkered shirts. Shanna tried to get us to wear cowgirl boots, but we vetoed that idea. Instead, we're wearing flip flops. There's a nice breeze in the trees from the lake, so it's not sweltering hot and unbearable. It's simply marvelous! The branches have garden lanterns hanging from them, and the patio has a sophisticated barnyard feel to it.

Shanna is wearing an adorable short white lace dress with fancy white sandals outfitted with rhinestones. She also has a white cowgirl hat on that's stunning against her red hair. Anthony can't stop grinning, and I think his face is going to permanently stay that way. *Gah!* It's all so adorable.

I can't get over how much our lives have all changed the last few years since Caylan entered it. She really was the catalyst to help us all get our compasses to point in the right direction. I feel I owe her so much.

The wildflowers that make up our gorgeous bouquets are wonderfully fragrant, and the reception we'll have after consists of a good ole backyard barbeque feast. My mouth is already watering. When you're pregnant, with twins no less, food is on your mind a lot!

My kids were thrilled for Caleb and me over the baby news, and that camping trip solidified our relationship—it made us whole. After the trip, Leah had another illuminating mother-daughter talk with me about how I'm being stubborn and should've already married Caleb. I adore her, but I explained to her that some things don't work like that.

However, I'm now in a place where I'm finally ready. Once Caleb and I started officially dating, I quickly discovered it wasn't good enough for me. I want more!

*I'm actually going to ask HIM to marry me this time!*

Our circle of friends were quite shocked by our baby news. We all had a get-together at Caylan's and announced it to everyone. Nonetheless, they were over the moon for us. Addison cocked her brow at me as if to say, *see, I knew the poem worked.* And interestingly, Alexi was the most shocked of our friends, yet still happy for us—I appreciate his brotherly ways and will always value that quality in him.

Next week is our big appointment for the anatomy scan and when we finally get to find out the gender of the twins. I'm so excited I may pee! Although, I pee over everything. Even standing up makes me need to run for the potty. It already feels like there's no room. How the hell will I make it until December? Sorry if that's gross, but that's the way things are.

As I reminisce about the weekend after our camping trip, I'll admit that Caleb and I finally made love again. It was out of this world and incredible. I swear these pregnancy hormones are making me horny all the time. He was so worried about hurting me, but he needn't worry because I explained that everything still functions the same—it makes me chuckle at how protective he is.

Caleb has made me feel beautiful and desired every chance he gets. I'll let you in on a surprise: I'm going to remedy the *just dating* part today and make him mine! Ha ha, that sounds so strange, but it's true. All the single genties, put your hands up—I like it, so I'll definitely put a ring on it! Now you're probably singing the real version to yourself—you're welcome; I love that song.

I'm standing here as a bridesmaid thinking all this while the wedding is going on around me. Oh my God, they just exchanged their vows and the rings. Now it's party time and proposal time!

\*\*\*

*Caleb*

So, I've finally cracked.

I'm standing here as a groomsman, and I can't wait any longer for Liz. I'm going to ask her to marry me…tonight. I won't do it in public again—I'm not taking any chances of scaring her off. I'll do it in private. I plan on taking her out on the lake before sunset in a small canoe and asking her there.

I already got permission from the kids, as well as their blessing, so I'm in! Plus, I talked to Anthony and Shanna, and they said my proposal tonight would in no way take away from their wedding.

Everything is set. Now it's barbeque time, and I only have to wait about four more hours until I pop the question and finally have my *goddess among us*.

\*\*\*

*Liezel*

I feel like I'm making a pig of myself, but I can't help it. The food is delicious. Whoever did the catering nailed the menu!

I think I'm nervous-eating too because I'm going to make an ass of myself when I ask for Caleb's hand. He went all out for me on the first proposal and put himself out there, so I'm going to do the same in front of friends and family. I talked to Shanna right before the wedding to see if she wouldn't mind me asking Caleb during the reception. She couldn't stop giggling, as if she knew something I didn't; luckily, she didn't have an issue with it. In fact, she strongly encouraged me.

I talked to my kids before I had to do my bridesmaid duties, and they seemed to find it funny too. Leah threw her arms around me and told me, "It's about time." Shanna also suggested that while the toasts and speeches are going on, I make one, then turn it into the proposal. It's an awesome idea. Now to execute!

The best man is Gil, and the maid of honor is Addison. They recite their speeches and then Addison announces to everyone that I have a toast to make. I take a deep breath and take the plunge.

I stand up next to Caleb, who's seated. He gives me a funny look because clearly everyone is confused as to why I'm speaking, but I'm determined to do this thing.

"Hello, everyone. So, my toast is going to be a little different, if you'll indulge me," I begin as I clear my throat.

I reach for a sip of water, then apologize and tell the crowd I'm nervous. Caleb smiles away at me. He's so unsuspecting of what I'm about to do.

"Anthony and Shanna's love for one another, and their love for their child, is why we're here today. I asked Shanna if I could speak because it's couples like them who we all aspire to emulate." I look at my dear friends seated around the patio area.

"In moments like this, we're reminded that life brings surprises and miracles. Life's all about twists and turns. And in my case, trysts and fate." I wink at Addison for partially quoting Caylan's epic poem—*wow, maybe I can pull off a wink after all.*

I sip my water again, then put the glass back down.

"My children, and my unborn children, are my miracles in life. They're my reason for existing. But I've also found the *sweetest* reason for enjoying life. And that happened when Caleb came into mine." I turn toward my man, staring him down and pouring my heart and soul into my words and to make sure it shows through my eyes.

"Caleb, you are my *perfect* too. I'm also *owl about you.* I never thought I'd find a love that could exist between two people like this. At times, I don't feel I deserve you, but then, when one of the twins karate chops me from the inside, I think it's you who doesn't deserve me." Everyone starts laughing at my joke—*sometimes I can be humorous too!*

"But seriously, it's taken me a long time to feel worthy or deserving of what you've given me. I promise to spend my life making you feel the same…if you'll let me. So, Caleb, will you please complete my life by joining yours with mine?" I ask with tears running down my face.

Of course, I have to make another joke when I explain, "And, just know, I really can't get down on one knee for this."

Everyone chuckles, and I reach into my purse to pull out a ring box, then pop it open. Inside sits a silver band, and he'll find out later it's engraved inside with two kissing owls.

[178]

There's so much emotion surrounding us, and I can feel it spilling out from all who are present. All eyes are on Caleb as he's sitting in his chair with his mouth hanging open.

Finally, he reaches into his pants pocket and pulls out a ring box, the same innocuous ring box that he presented to me all those weeks ago.

"I was going to propose to you tonight," he states while shaking his head, still in an apparent form of shock.

Everyone erupts into laughter and applause, and I hear various voices chanting, "Say yes, say yes!"

"That's a big hell yes!" Caleb confirms, standing up, and he gently dips me back while he takes my lips.

The crowd continues cheering, hooting, and hollering. My happy tears are still flowing, and I think some of Caleb's drip down onto my face. When he repositions me and I'm upright, he kneels down and kisses my belly, then places my sparkling princess-cut diamond engagement ring on my finger—*I'm surprised it's not in the shape of a cookie*, I laugh to myself in my head. I take his band out of the box and place it on his finger.

"You're stuck with me now," I taunt while grinning and hugging him.

He quips back with, "And I have witnesses, so you can't rescind the contractual agreement you're making here today, unless you want to go to court."

"Take it up with my lawyer!" I say sassily.

He gives me one more kiss, and I say in my mind, *yup, we're perfect!*

# Epilogue

*Liezel*

November 17, 2018

No more ghosts.
No more secrets.
Only us.
It's been magical. We wed in September right before Caleb's thirty-fifth birthday. We had a backyard wedding at our new house. Simple, understated, and an utterly perfect ceremony.
The kids were more than happy to leave behind our old house and start fresh with new memories. It's a two-story, six-bedroom home, so the only ones who have to share, of course, are Caleb and I. We're going to put the twins in one room for now, and then they'll have the other as a playroom. As they get older, they'll need to be separated.
It's Tyler's senior year, and he's still hanging out with Ellie; I knew it was only a matter of time before one of the boys got a girlfriend. Kurt joined Civil Air Patrol at the start of the school year and stays busy with that. He uses Skype to contact Tech Sergeant Jefferson now and then—I'm so glad he found another mentor. Leah continues to show her disinterest in boys for the time being, and she's having fun doing my hair just about every morning as it's gotten so long from the months of prenatal vitamins.
The kids still receive therapy at school, but it's more or less a way for the counselors to check up on them—everyone's doing great! As a family, we all share our feelings and continue to have family meals, movie nights, ice cream outings, and game night. It seems like the kids helping us prepare for the twins has been a full-time job—double everything requires all hands on deck. Painting exhausted us, but we managed to get it done. The room is complete!
The nursery is decorated in none other than owls, and Caleb has stocked our house with plenty of lilacs and daffodils even when they're not

in season. Our camper is parked next to our house, and Caleb said he'll upgrade to a fifth wheel travel trailer as the twins grow. The man knows no bounds!

Out of all the things to be excited about with having newborns again, do you believe I'm jumping for joy at getting to carry around a diaper bag? My God, I miss the days of having a diaper bag act as my purse; it's so incredibly convenient with all the stuff you can carry in there. The downside is, I know we won't ever sleep for the first few years of their lives, but I can deal with that. I'll have help this time with a doting husband and father.

Caleb and I agonized over what to name our babies. Did I tell you we're having a boy and girl? Our little boy will be named Cristoff Curtis Daniels. We chose Cristoff to honor Christopher and Curtis to show Kurt some love. Then, our baby girl will be Leanna Tyla Daniels; named after a combination of Leah and Tyler.

I was so overwhelmed when the kids asked if they could take Caleb's last name. He's in the process of adopting them, and my heart about exploded from all the love this family has. And speaking of adopting, Brent and Everly submitted their application to adopt a child. Everly is still interested in having one naturally, but because of her childhood, she wanted to give a home to a little boy or girl in need; it's the most lovely and selfless thing a person can do.

I did something therapeutic at the end of September that I wish I would've done a long time ago. It was Caleb's idea, actually. That man is beyond brilliant and supportive. I wrote a letter to my deceased parents. He even drove me all the way up to Rhode Island to visit their graves. I haven't been back to my hometown since the day I left. It was good to clear the air, so to speak. We ended up taking the camper and making a big trip of it before we winterized it and parked it for the off-season.

It was difficult for me to visit their graves and place the letter atop their joint headstone. Lots of tears. Lots of apologies. But I'm glad I did it. The kids got to see where their grandparents were laid to rest. I also visited William's parents during the trip. We had a heart-to-heart, and they told me they were bitter and angry for many years, but they don't wish me any ill will. I wouldn't say we're going to be friends, but we can at least have a civilized conversation now.

After talking with the kids, we also decided to give the urn to William's parents. Bill and Anna promised me they'd sprinkle his ashes somewhere special. They said maybe by the old fishing spot he used to go to as a kid with his dad. They were incredibly grateful I brought him *home* to them. We all agreed we wanted William to be free of the urn so he'd never be confined or held prisoner to a vessel ever again. Forgiveness does wonders for a person's mind, body, and spirit.

Gil and Addison are planning a springtime wedding for next year, so we all have that to look forward to. They're still not ready for kids, but we all know it will happen eventually. Meg is all set and ready to take pictures of the twins as soon as they're born. She did my maternity shoot, and the pictures turned out amazing. They're on our mantle in our living room, along with our wedding photos, as well as the kids' school photos. Of course, I lovingly framed the latest sonogram image of *Baby A* and *Baby B*. Cristoff is *A*, and *B* is Leanna.

Caleb said a while back that he needed to get a big gift for Caylan and Alexi for everything they did for us. He went all out and got them ballroom dance lessons for a full year. I know Caylan will love it, and Alexi will hate it, yet he'll attend for her. Caleb is eager to give them the gift tonight and rib Alexi about it.

It's exciting that Caleb and I became godparents to Zane. And tonight we'll see our godson because we're going over to Caylan's for a family get-together. It will probably be the last time we're all in one place before the twins arrive, unless I keep them incubating past Thanksgiving; however, I suspect it'll be any day now.

I'm sitting on our bed putting my earrings in place and slipping on my shoes—I can't do anything with laces. My darling husband enters our bedroom to check on me since we're supposed to be leaving in a few minutes to head to Caylan's. He's wearing a very mischievous expression, and I know he's up to something.

"Do I even want to know what *that* look means?" I ask dubiously.

He has his hands behind his back, so it's obvious he has some sort of a surprise.

"You want to do something kinky before we have to leave?" He queries with that goofy grin I adore so much.

"Umm, it depends on what it is," I reply hesitantly.

"Well, it involves an orgasm," he says, trying to sweeten the pot.

"In that case, I'm in. But what's behind your back before I agree to this?" I raise a brow at him in question.

Instead of answering, he pulls out the item that was behind his back. I burst out laughing. It's a vibrator that's rainbow-colored and in the shape of a unicorn's horn.

I'm still laughing as I say, "You're crazy!"

"Nah, sweetness, not crazy. I like to think of myself as being 'twitterpated,'" he smirks as he turns on the vibrator.

### The End

## *Nursing Myself Back*—Playlist

"All of Me" by John Legend
"Can't Help Falling in Love" by Hailey Reinhart
"Die a Happy Man" by Thomas Rhett
"Distance" by Christina Perri ft. Jason Mraz
"Fight Song" by Rachel Platten
"Heavy" by Linkin Park ft. Kiiara
"I Could Use a Love Song" by Maren Morris
"Love on the Brain" by Rihanna
"Love the Way You Lie" Eminem ft. Rihanna
"Perfect" by Ed Sheeran
"Piano Man" by Billy Joel
"Praying" by Kesha
"Roar" by Katy Perry
"Somewhere Over the Rainbow" by Israel Kamakawiwo'ole
"Time After Time" by Cyndi Lauper

# Acknowledgements

It was incredibly difficult for me to let go of this series. This fulfilled a dream I never thought would come true. From my first book-baby with *Playing Heart to Get*, to this one, they have all been my children, in a sense. It's hard to see them grow up and go out there in the publishing world. But I have high hopes for each one of them, and at the end of the day, they still need their mama.

I can't thank each and every reader enough for embracing this series. This five-book adventure has been my heart and soul. Each and every character has a piece of me, and I have a piece of them. Y'all are the reason I write!

I have to thank my friends and family for seeing me through another creation. Their support, love, and encouragement is never taken for granted.

My team is amazing. My proofreaders, betas, editor, tribe, and crew who help promote my books are so valued and appreciated. Hugs and kisses!

A special shout-out to fellow writer Dain for letting me quote his poem at the beginning. *Watching the Fire* is reflective of the tone of this book. What I love most about poetry is the individual interpretation. I love that in *that* moment, a poem can mean what you need it to mean.

Please stay connected with me so you can see what's coming next. Just because this incredible series has come to its epic conclusion, doesn't mean I don't have more planned. And who knows, maybe one day a character or two from this series may pop up in another series or standalone book I publish.

Many thanks again, you awesome-sauce readers!
Hearts & Smiles,

Kara Liane

# About the Author

Kara Liane is a lover of all things romance. She holds several degrees, including a master's in management from Wayland Baptist University. Her husband since 2002 proudly serves in the military. The family, which includes twin elementary-age sons and two adult dogs, resides in New Jersey.

Stay connected with Kara Liane by visiting her web site: www.karaliane.com

www.ingramcontent.com/pod-product-compliance
Lightning Source LLC
Chambersburg PA
CBHW022111170626
46808CB00002B/685